The moment she realized Buck was shooting

under the cars to hit her, the tire she hid behind blew. She squeezed her eyes shut as she tried to make herself smaller by pressing her body into the SUV. The Morse code of bullets hitting metal started up again. She could've sworn she felt the SUV shaking with the continuous beat of bullets slamming into it, except the shaking was below her feet. It started gentle but as soon as she noticed, it became violent.

Earthquake!

She fell backward and struggled to get back up. Her body bounced up and down and rolled from side to side simultaneously. A light came crashing down from the ceiling and slammed into the concrete floor with such power it exploded into a trillion stars. Glass shot out in all directions like the Big Bang. Beth screamed and covered her face with her hands as tiny pieces of glass bit the skin on her arms.

She fought onto her hands and knees and hugged the tire to keep from falling over again. The intensity of the tremors grew. The concrete below her feet didn't feel solid anymore. It felt alive, as if two gigantic gophers burrowed through the earth. The truck behind her slid with the vicious shock waves and bumped into her, pushing her roughly into the tire. She let out a cry of panic.

Praise for Chrys Fey

"From the remnants of a Florida hurricane to a San Francisco earthquake, Fey puts you in the middle of the devastation as Donovan and Beth forge the bonds of new love while tracking a killer across the country in this nail-biting romantic suspense."

~Lilly Gayle, author of Slightly Noble

Seismic Crimes

by

Chrys Fey

Disaster Crimes Series

Seismic Crimes

Cover Art by *Kim Mendoza*

The Wild Rose Press, Inc.
PO Box 708
Adams Basin, NY 14410-0708
Visit us at www.thewildrosepress.com

Publishing History
First Crimson Rose Edition, 2016
Print ISBN 978-1-5092-0725-1
Digital ISBN 978-1-5092-0726-8

Disaster Crimes Series
Published in the United States of America

Dedications

This book would not exist if it weren't for three people:
Bradley Poage,
who wanted to know what took place
before *Hurricane Crimes*;
Anna Coy,
who asked for a novel-length story;
and my mom
who helped me realize the story wasn't finished yet.
~*~
Just as I had help in starting this story, I had loads of
help perfecting it. A big thank you to C. Lee McKenzie
for her insight about San Francisco, Tammy Theriault
for being the first person to read this story and offer her
witty and sarcastic advice, as well as Lilly Gayle for her
medical knowledge and eye for perfection.
You three ROCK!
~*~
I also wouldn't be here without all of my blogger
buddies, including the countless individuals I've "met"
through the Insecure Writer's Support Group.
Your support is amazing!
~*~
A special shout out to Sherry Snider Fundin for
winning the contest to name the antagonist in this story.
Jackson Storm really is a great name.
~*~
Finally, a big hug to my editor, Lori Graham; my cover
artist, Kim Mendoza; and everyone else part of The
Wild Rose Press team that made this book possible.

Chapter One

Beth didn't die.

The anxious weatherman forecasting Hurricane Sabrina's arrival was wrong. She didn't even die at the big, slightly calloused hands of Donovan Goldwyn, as she had thought she would. Accused of killing his brother, Donovan had shown all the signs of being a murderer, but she later realized he wasn't a killer despite his suspicious mannerisms. Together, they had taken down one of the police officers responsible for killing Donovan's brother, but one of the killers got away.

Now they were paddling her canoe through the floodwaters leftover from Hurricane Sabrina. Seeing the devastation all around broke Beth's heart. A tree had fallen onto a house they passed, severing the house in half. She wished they could stop there to see if anyone needed help, but they had to get to the Orlando Police Department as soon as possible.

With great regret and a silent prayer the owners had evacuated, she looked away to see even more destruction. Some houses appeared untouched by Sabrina's wrath, but many hadn't been so lucky. Roofs had been ripped off; lawn decorations and furniture, that hadn't been moved inside, had been thrown everywhere, as if Sabrina had thrown a tantrum. Even a children's swing set had been knocked over.

Beth looked away from the heartbreaking scene and forced her gaze to stay glued ahead as she paddled with their only oar. In front of her, Donovan used a shovel. As the canoe cut through the water, time blurred.

Her arms and neck were burning with fatigue by the time they reached the police department. Donovan pulled the canoe up the steps and held out his hand to her. Her knees shook as she stood and stepped onto solid ground. Standing in front of Donovan, her hand in his, she looked up at him. She couldn't imagine the turmoil he was going through inside, but she could see signs of it. His brows were drawn; his eyes streaked with red lightning bolts. She reached up with her free hand and laid it against his cheek.

He put his hand over hers and then pulled her in for a soft kiss. When he inched back, he whispered in her ear, "This may sound crazy, but I love you."

Beth gazed into his eyes, saw it was true. Her heart twirled in relief.

"I love you, too." She glanced at the police department. "Are you ready for this?"

His jaw tensed. "Doesn't matter if I am or not. This needs to be done."

Hand in hand, they walked inside. Five officers stood near the entrance, guzzling water from bottles and listening to the reports coming in on their radios. A woman manned the front desk. She answered the phone that never stopped ringing. Beth couldn't imagine how many calls were coming in on the emergency lines. Hundreds of people were probably calling for help, but the police wouldn't be able to respond to every call, not in their squad cars with this flood. During past hurricanes, the State Emergency Rescue Team went out in trucks and boats to rescue stranded people, and they would have to again.

A few civilians, who had to ride out the storm in the department, milled about anxiously. The mingled scents of stale coffee and sweat teased Beth's nostrils. Large ovals of perspiration spread beneath the officers' arms and trickled down their backs. They looked as though they were about to dissolve into puddles. Although the generators were working, the A/C was weak, and the air inside the station was more humid than outside.

The officers' heads swiveled to Donovan and Beth when they stepped through the doors. Their heat-exhausted faces registered surprise.

"Holy shit," one of them said. "That's Donovan Goldwyn!"

In the next instant, the five officers rushed toward him, with their guns drawn. Donovan put up his hands. Two officers grabbed his arms, wrenching them behind his back to restrain him. "Donovan Goldwyn, you're under arrest for the murder of Ryan Goldwyn."

Beth's eyes widened. "Wait a minute! He didn't do it."

The moment she spoke, every pair of eyes turned to her. "Arrest her, too," a deep voice snapped. She didn't even have time to blink before an officer slapped a cuff onto her left wrist. It bit into her skin with cold, metallic teeth.

"No." Donovan whipped around, causing the two officers holding him to stumble. "She had nothing to do with this. She gave me shelter, not knowing I was wanted for a crime, and helped me to get here. That's all."

Beth looked at him. *Is that really all?* She wanted to smack him. *I shot a man to save his life for goodness sakes.*

"Please," Donovan continued. "She has my brother's journal and the footage from the hidden security cameras inside and outside his house. Both will reveal my brother's killers and prove my innocence." He glanced at her. "Beth." He nodded, assuring her it was okay to give the officers the evidence.

Beth wished she had his confidence as she relinquished the leather journal and the memory card from the hidden camera in Ryan's living room, which they had risked their lives to retrieve, to the officer in front of her. He ripped them from her fingers like a father yanking a toy from a naughty child.

As soon as her hand was empty, the officer behind her stole her wrist, yanked her arm behind her back, and clicked the second cuff into place.

Shit.

"We'll look these over, but you're not free, Goldwyn," an officer said, with his lips pulled back in a snarl.

"I didn't think I would be," Donovan replied.

Beth studied Donovan. Two officers restrained his handcuffed arms, but he looked unperturbed. *How can he be so calm? He's being arrested, accused of murdering his own brother.*

"Ma'am, you're coming with us, too."

She swallowed, revealing her nerves with the slight movement. No doubt, the officers made a note of it, marking it as a sign of guilt. *Damn, I'm going to go down with him.*

One officer stayed behind the front desk, probably to keep an eye out for more wanted criminals who might waltz into the station to surrender. Two officers held Donovan's arms, one grasped her arm, and the last officer brought up the rear.

Apparently, they weren't taking any chance of them escaping.

When they reached a metal door, the officer gripping Beth's arm led her to a line of chairs against the wall and pushed her down onto the first one. Donovan peered over his shoulder as three officers ushered him into an interrogation room.

"It's okay," he told her.

The door closed, blocking his reassuring gaze.

Beth stared at the door and whispered, "How do you know?" He said it would be okay, but she had a feeling they were a long way from anything being okay.

She glanced at the officer blocking the end of the hall and her way out. Sighing, she leaned her head against the wall, giving up to whatever would happen next.

Five minutes later, the door to the interrogation room opened. An officer with graying sideburns stepped into the hall and dangled a key in front of her. "I'm going to uncuff you." She shifted in the chair as he unlocked the cuffs with a scrape of metal against metal.

"Thank you," she said as she settled her hands in her lap. He nodded and went back into the room where they had Donovan.

That has to be a good sign. Right? They wouldn't remove my cuffs if they thought I was a threat.

The lights above Beth flickered with the hum of a generator. She settled into the stiff plastic chair, but her mind raced with the events from the last twenty-four hours—saving Donovan after he crashed his car in front of her house, riding out the storm, making love to Donovan, killing a corrupt police officer, and telling Donovan she loved him.

She shook her head at that last one. Falling in love in one day, with a man she thought was a murderer half the time, was one thing but telling him was another thing all together. *But he told me first, and people fall in love at first sight all the time, so what's the big deal?*

The big deal is you don't even know him.

I knew him well enough to have sex with him.

Ha!

Beth's mind was in a war with itself.

She thought about Donovan and his gentle touch when he cleaned her wounds. His sexy smile, the way he made love to her as if he had known her for years, and his violet eyes. Donovan was an amazing man; there was no doubt about that. And she couldn't ignore her feelings, either. When she realized she would do anything for him, even kill to protect him, she knew she was in love. Yes, in love with a man she barely knew, but in love nonetheless.

The clock hanging on the wall was wrong, but the minute hand continued to move. Each tick frayed Beth's nerves. Donovan had been in the interrogation room for thirty minutes. *What is happening? What are they putting him through?*

Her hair hung in damp ropes to her shoulders, and her clothes were wet, offering a bit of coolness to her heated skin. She stretched out on the chairs, letting exhaustion take over her body, and drifted off to sleep.

Chapter Two

Donovan sat with his back straight against the metal chair and his cuffed hands clasped on top of the table. An officer sat in front of him. The other two flanked his chair.

"Just watch the footage," he told them, aggravation growing inside him like acid reflux. "You'll see I didn't kill my brother."

"Well, that's something we're all curious about," the officer sitting at the table said. "How did your brother's murder just happen to be recorded?"

"It didn't just *happen* to be recorded," Donovan seethed. "My brother was a cop. He was in the Internal Affairs unit." He spoke slowly as if he were drilling the words into the officers' heads. "He had a security system to protect his home. It wasn't a piece of shit system, but an elaborate one. He had two separate systems of hidden cameras outside and inside his house."

An officer beside him snorted. "If your brother had such an elaborate security system, how did they break into his house?"

"Once again, they were cops. And they were fucking dirty no matter what you say. I don't know everything about alarm systems, but I'm sure they do and easily could've disconnected it by cutting wires, using a jammer, or some shit like that." Frustration was all but spilling out of his ears. "Maybe the alarm did go off when they got in and tipped off Ryan. I don't know all of that. You'd have to watch the footage.

"The point is there would be no way for them to know about the hidden cameras. They've been installed for years and are not part of the alarm system, and they record twenty-four-seven. They would've recorded everything up until the moment when the power went out. In other words, in case you're having a hard time keeping up, they recorded Chewy and Buck murdering my brother. So, watch the damn footage."

"Don't be a fucking smart ass," one of the officers snapped. "We *will* watch it, but you're still facing a lot of charges."

"I told you why I ran. What I find ironic is that you can't locate the other officer. Buck."

"Buckland."

"Whatever. My point is...I don't know if I can trust you." He glared at the officers surrounding him. "Not when two of your fellow officers murdered my brother."

The officers looked at one another.

The officer in front of him raised his hands off the table. "Let's all try to calm down and be civil here." He looked at Donovan. "I'm Officer Burnett, and I'm just trying to get the facts. Two of our men called in a murder of an Internal Affairs investigator and cited you as the suspect they saw at the murder scene. Then you fled from them. Now you're here, and you're telling us you and the woman out there killed one of our men in self-defense. You're lucky we didn't stun you on sight. Why don't you tell us everything from the beginning? You said your brother called you. Why don't you start from there?"

Donovan took a deep breath. He rolled his shoulders as he transplanted his mind into the past.

"I got a call from Ryan two nights ago. He told me to meet him outside. The line went dead before I could ask him what was going on. He was parked several spaces away from my apartment and had the lights to his car turned off. When I got into the passenger's seat and looked at him, I was shocked. Stubble covered his face, and he hadn't cut his hair in a long time. It was longer than he would normally let it grow. Immediately, I sensed something was wrong. Ryan wouldn't show up late at night looking like he hadn't slept or bathed in days for no reason."

Donovan shook his head at the memory. He felt guilty for not being in contact with his brother during the weeks leading up to that night. *Could I have done something to prevent the events that took place?*

"What happened after you got into the car?" Officer Burnett prompted.

"I asked him what was wrong, but he told me not to say a word and drove onto the main road."

"Did he seem agitated, jumpy, anxious? Tell us about his demeanor."

In his mind's eye, Donovan could clearly see his brother, as if he were in the car again, going for a secret ride in the middle of the night. "His hands were tight on the steering wheel, knuckles white. Whenever a car came up behind us, he'd flinch and look into the rearview mirror."

Burnett finished scribbling notes and looked up at Donovan. "Where did he take you?"

"To Cocoa Beach. He parked the car down a street

with beach access, cut the engine, and got out. I followed him down a dock to the shoreline. When we got there, he told me that his house, my apartment, and even our cars weren't safe. He said he brought me all the way out there to tell me *everything*."

"And what did he tell you?"

"Several months ago, he was given a case that involved missing drugs from a few departments throughout Orange County. He had been looking into many officers, specifically two in his department—Viktor Chuman and David Buckland." He said their names as if they left a bile taste in his mouth. "Ryan noticed that whenever they were involved in drug busts, the drugs, or at least most of them, would go missing. They also spent a lot of time in the evidence locker where the narcotics used in sting operations are locked up.

"He said he had seen Buck with a few big-time drug dealers but could never catch him exchanging money with them. Recently, he questioned one of the officers in charge of the evidence locker. This man admitted Chewy and Buck paid him off to keep his mouth shut about their dirty dealings, that they had been pilfering drugs for a year and selling them to drug dealers. Ryan got him to sign a statement but promised he wouldn't use it until he had more evidence. Last week, his one witness turned up dead."

Burnett exchanged glances with the other officers in the room before speaking. "We know about Dan Morgan's murder. It really shook this department. He was beaten to death." He paused. "There aren't any persons of interest in that case."

Donovan glared at him. "Of course, there isn't. The

persons of interest are cops."

Burnett took a deep breath. "What else did Ryan tell you?"

Switching his train of thought back to the night before Hurricane Sabrina hit, Donovan visualized Ryan standing with his back to the waves, looking up and down the beach as if he expected someone to pop out of the surf. "He gave me a leather journal full of information about Chewy and Buck, including the signed statement from the evidence officer, a log of all the threats he had received, and a list of other suspicious officers he believed were working with them. He wanted me to hide it, to keep it safe."

I trust you with my life, Don, so you're the only one I trust with this. Promise me you'll hide it until I ask you for it again. Ryan's plea came back to him, knotting his stomach with dread; he had trusted Donovan with his life, and yet, he was dead.

"What happened next?"

Donovan peered at Burnett. He didn't trust him, didn't trust any of them, but he had to clear his name and get justice for Ryan. The only way to do both was to tell them everything. "Ryan dropped me back off at my apartment, and I hid the journal in the bottom of my oven's drawer. But yesterday morning, I got a text message from Ryan."

"What did the text read?"

Donovan recited the text from memory. "It said, *'They're following me. Stay sharp.'* When I got that text, I grabbed my keys, the journal in case I needed it to back up Ryan's claims, and hopped into my car. Before driving away, I locked the journal in the glove compartment, which is where it had nearly been destroyed by the storm.

"At my brother's house, I spotted a police car parked several houses down, at the opposite end of the street. Using my spare key, I opened the front door and…" He stopped. When he had pushed open the front door, he had frozen on the doormat like a fucking ice sculpture, because in the living room two police officers were bringing their batons down upon his brother's body.

"Ryan lay in the middle of the floor with his arms raised to shield his face, but he wasn't moving. Blood streamed from his nose and mouth. It looked as though the batons had smashed every inch of his skull. There was so much blood."

The hollow thumping sound of the batons hitting Ryan's body came back to him. He squeezed his eyes shut and swallowed the bile rising in his throat.

"Do you need a moment?" The sympathy in Burnett's voice had Donovan second-guessing his initial reaction to hate the man.

"No, I want to get this over with." He thought back on the moment when he realized his brother was dead. After the last blow had been delivered, the taller of the two officers had faced the other, turning toward the doorway. Beneath loose strands of dark hair, blood-thirsty brown eyes glared at Donovan.

Ice laced his spine again just as it had during that moment.

"I ran," he said. "I got in my car and drove to the highway, with the cop car on my ass the whole time. After passing a couple of exits, I swerved onto an off-ramp and into a small city. I was driving past a church when a pine tree leaned over the road. At first, I didn't realize it was falling until it was nearly on top of me. My car slipped under the tree's trunk with seconds to spare, but the cop car couldn't get through. I got away."

He skimmed over the details of running into a tree and taking shelter in Beth's house. He definitely didn't want to detail their lovemaking.

"A few hours ago, Beth and I traveled by canoe to Ryan's house to get the security footage to prove my innocence. I entered alone because I didn't want Beth to see Ryan's body, except Ryan wasn't there anymore. I was walking through the flooded living room when Chewy came out from behind a wall. I asked him what he did with Ryan. He said he threw Ryan out like trash. When I heard that, I attacked him."

The feel of his fists cracking into Chewy's face one at a time, and the snap of Chewy's nose beneath his knuckles, had felt good. If he could, he would do it all over again. And then again and again.

"Chewy tackled me into the wide-screen television and pummeled my ribs. And then he brought out a gun. I hit his arm with a lamp, causing the gun to fall into the water. We dove for it and wrestled each other to get to it first, but Chewy hit me on the side of the head and pinned me beneath the water. The next thing I knew, Chewy wasn't on top of me anymore. I sat up to see Beth with a shovel in her hands. She had hit Chewy with it."

Seeing Beth like that would forever be burned in his memory, just as the image of his brother beaten to death on the living room floor would be.

When Donovan finished, he met Burnett's intense stare. Anger radiated through him, and he crossed his arms. "If you don't believe me, why don't you watch the footage?"

Burnett sighed. He nodded at the officer closest to the door. "Okay, let's watch it."

The officer left and returned with a laptop. He inserted the memory card and found the footage for the previous morning. They watched Chewy and Buck break into Ryan's house and quickly disappear down the hallway. A heartbeat later, Ryan came running into the living room, aiming for the front door, his one way of escape, but the two men were right behind him. Chewy struck out and hit him in the back of the head with a baton.

Donovan turned his head away from the laptop, not wanting to see the beating a second time.

The footage was fast-forwarded to an hour after the two men chased after Donovan. The door opened again. This time, the officers were returning. Chewy grabbed Ryan's arms, and Buck grabbed his feet. Instead of taking him out the door to dump his body somewhere, they carried him down the hallway. They reappeared in the living room and had a short conversation before Buck left. Chewy didn't follow him out the door, though. He sat on the couch to ride out the storm in the house of the man he had killed.

"That explains why Chewy was there when you went back this morning," Officer Burnett said. "I think he was waiting for you. Probably thought you'd come back."

"And now I know my brother's body is in the back of the house," Donovan added. He couldn't believe his brother had been in the bedroom the whole time they were there.

Chewy had said they removed him, and Donovan

didn't think he had lied.

"Look, Donovan, I'm sorry for everything that happened."

Donovan looked at Burnett sharply, finding it hard not to hate all police officers at that moment. "I don't want your apology. I want you to help me get Buck."

Chapter Three

A hand cupped Beth's arm and gently shook her awake. She peeled her eyelids open to see Donovan crouching in front of her; an officer stood at his side with his arms crossed. Donovan's wide shoulders and defined chest were no longer bare, as they had been when he entered the department. He now wore a black T-shirt, and handcuffs no longer restrained him. She studied his face with tired eyes. A five o'clock shadow was creeping along his angular jaw and up his cheeks.

He smiled at her.

"They want you to confirm what I told them," he said, his voice deep and gentle.

Beth's gaze flicked to the clock on the wall, which told her she had been asleep for over two hours. *They questioned him for that long?* She pulled herself into a sitting position. With a hand on her elbow, Donovan helped her stand.

The officer took her arm, but she paused next to Donovan before stepping into the interrogation room. "Are they arresting you?"

"Not yet." He gave her a devilish grin.

She shook her head. "This is not funny."

"I know. It's not." He ran his hand down her arm. "Don't worry. Just tell them everything that happened. You'll be fine."

How could she say she wasn't worried about

herself? She was worried about him. *Okay, so I am worried I'll be charged as an accomplice, but that won't even be as bad as what'll happen to him.*

Sitting across from the four officers, one of them passed Beth a paper cup of water.

She drank it greedily, loving the feel of the liquid on her parched lips and dry throat.

"Thanks."

"Ms. Kennedy, tell us what happened from the beginning."

Taking a deep breath, Beth told them everything she knew from the moment Donovan's car crashed into her neighbor's tree. "The tree won," she joked. The cops smirked at that, and she continued her story, skipping over what happened in the bathtub but detailing what happened when they made it to Ryan's house.

"Chewy, one of the cops..." She stopped suddenly; her face burning as she looked at the four officers in front of her. *What if one of them is in league with Chewy? What if they all are? They could kill me and then kill Donovan.*

"It's okay, Ms. Kennedy," Officer Burnett said. "Please go on." His gentle smile and sincere, brown eyes calmed her, and she found the courage to tell the truth.

"Chewy was in the house when Donovan went in to retrieve the footage. I heard a gunshot, and I got out of the canoe to help him."

"And all you had was a shovel?"

"That's right." Beth explained how she saw Chewy hit Donovan and hold him under the water in Ryan's living room. "I hit Chewy in the back with the shovel so he'd release Donovan. He fired a shot at me and told me to drop the shovel. I did, and that was when I stepped on another gun under the water. It's in the canoe outside. I'm sure if you checked it you'd find it's registered to Chewy."

"We'll check," Burnett reassured her.

"I told Chewy I had Ryan's journal in the canoe because I knew he wouldn't want any evidence out there for someone to use against him. Chewy held the gun to Donovan's head and told me to back out of the house. I dragged the gun under my shoe down the driveway to the canoe and slowly reached inside. I brought out a journal, but it wasn't Ryan's. It was mine. When I saw Ryan's journal was identical to the one I wrote poetry in, I thought we could replace Ryan's with it. Before Chewy could take my journal, though, I threw it. He went after it, and I went for the gun. When I came back up out of the water, Chewy had his gun pointed at me. I fired before I could even think. The bullet hit him in the head."

Beth finished her story with their arrival at the police department.

"Am I in trouble?" She wrung her hands in her lap. "For…killing a cop?"

"No, Ms. Kennedy. It's clear you did it in self-defense."

"What about Donovan? Are you going to arrest him?" She glared at Officer Burnett. "Because if you are, that is seriously messed up. He ran to protect himself. If he hadn't, he'd be dead, too. Then he risked his life to get you the evidence, right after a hurricane might I add, and came here in a canoe to personally hand-deliver it. Considering what he's gone through, and what he's done to prove his innocence, he deserves a break."

"I couldn't agree with you more."

Beth was about to snap back when she realized what he'd said. "Really?"

Burnett smiled at her. "Really. Thank you for your cooperation."

"No problem."

Burnett held the door open for her. Donovan stood, and she went to him, needing contact with him. He hooked his arms around her and pulled her into his body. She closed her eyes, thinking about how close he had come to being charged with murder.

They may not know each other well, but already she couldn't imagine her life without him.

After a moment, a throat cleared. "Seems like the two of you are pretty close."

Beth peeked up at Donovan's grin. "Natural disasters can bring people together," he told Burnett.

"They sure can."

Beth shifted in Donovan's arms, but he kept her at his side. "What's going to happen now?" she asked Burnett.

"We'll take shields away from the cops on Ryan's list, Internal Affairs will investigate the department, and there will be a full-scale manhunt for David Buckland, as soon as the water goes down."

"By then he could be anywhere," Donovan pointed out.

Burnett lifted his hands. "We're going to do everything we can, but we're limited right now, thanks to the storm."

Beth felt Donovan's body tense against hers. Their

best wasn't good enough. She tightened her arm around him, hoping to reassure him with her simple gesture. He had reassured her, now she wished to do the same for him.

"Technically, the two of you are free to go," Burnett said. "But with the flood, I'm not sure if there is anywhere you can go."

Beth thought about it. They did have a canoe, but her home wasn't exactly habitable.

Burnett continued, "We have cots, plenty of canned goods, and the inmates were evacuated."

Beth smiled. "Are you offering us a temporary home?"

Burnett gave an uneasy shrug. "Until the water recedes."

"In that case, where's the ladies' room?"

"Make a right at the end of the hall. You'll find it."

Beth left Donovan and Burnett to talk. The lights in the women's restroom buzzed to life, illuminating the stretch of sinks and stalls. Pausing in front of a mirror, her reflection confronted her.

"Oh, Beth, you look terrible."

Her brunette hair was kinky and dull from the dirty floodwater. The strips of blood-dotted gauze, that covered the tree branch scratches, on her arms and chest were dingy. The rock Hurricane Sabrina had chucked at her shoulder had turned her skin into a canvas of bruises. Yellow, like the color of urine, crept toward her collarbone, and the purple in the heart of the bruise was darker than the skin of an eggplant.

She turned on the faucet, thankful for running water, and splashed a handful on her face. The coolness felt refreshing against her warm cheeks. Droplets slithered down her neck, tickling her, and soaked into the gauze covering the long scratch on her chest. With a grimace, she peeled off the layers of gauze and used a stack of brown paper towels to clean her many cuts. Once the dried blood was gone, she combed her fingers through her hair in a vain attempt to improve her appearance. *Honey, you look like Hurricane Sabrina chewed you up and spat you out. A blow dryer won't help at this point.*

Resigned to her battered looks, she finished washing her hands and rejoined Donovan in the front of the department. She lowered herself into the chair beside him, and her muscles sighed when the cushions molded to her aching back. She angled her body toward him. "Aside from not being able to do anything about Buck at the moment, what do we do now?"

"We?" Donovan tilted his head at her. "You don't need to be a part of this anymore, Beth. You're off the hook...if you want to be."

She looked at him, not believing he could dismiss her so easily, especially after their intimacy. If she were a logical woman, his words would relieve her. She'd cut all ties and forget about everything that happened, but she couldn't do that. She was changed forever by Hurricane Sabrina. Her life was changed forever by the man in front of her. "Donovan, this isn't over yet. Not by a long shot. I'm in it to the end."

Donovan took her hand, rubbed her knuckles with the pad of his thumb. "Thank you."

A happy warmth spread through her at the sweet contact. "So, what do we do now?"

"Now we wait until we can get out of here."

"That could take days."

"With you here to keep me company, I don't mind so much."

Beth grinned at him. "I hope you know I'm going to use this opportunity to ask you questions."

Donovan's brow lifted. "I hope they're not felony questions."

She scooted to the edge of her seat and lowered her voice. "Do you have any felonies?"

His teeth flashed. "What are your questions?"

She already knew about his deadbeat dad who got himself killed when Donovan was a boy, and she even knew of his dislike of spiders. In return, he knew about her cheating ex-fiancé and her fear of snakes. Yet, there was so much she didn't know about the mysterious Donovan Goldwyn, and so much she wanted to learn.

"How did you get into monster truck driving?"

Donovan leaned back, as if relieved she had asked an easy question. He still held her hand captive; his fingers skimmed over her skin, following the lines in her palm.

"I was big into basketball in high school. I also did wrestling and track when I could, but b-ball was my thing. Senior year, a few scouts were looking at me when I had an incident on the court during a big game. I was going up for a slam-dunk when someone from the opposing team jumped at the same time. We collided. I hit the floor first, and he came down after me. His full weight landed on my knee, breaking it. I was out for the season, and my doctor said I shouldn't play basketball anymore. I got my degree in computer science and then threw myself recklessly into monster truck driving." He grinned at her.

"It seems like you throw yourself recklessly into

many dangerous situations."

"I can't help myself." He reached out and trailed a finger down her arm. "And you? How did you become a self-defense instructor?"

"When I was in high school, a girl I knew was raped and murdered. My friends and I were scared, so we enrolled in self-defense classes. I liked how strong and confident I became because of that class. I continued to go long after my friends stopped. When I graduated high school, I became an assistant to the teacher who taught me. During the day, I assisted classes. At night, I did psychology courses online. Then I started to teach my own classes. My parents helped me start my business by buying my studio and the equipment I needed. Many of the people in the classes I taught followed me to my studio, and they still go today." She smiled with pride.

"I've said it before, and I'll say it again...you're amazing." He lifted her hand to his lips and kissed it.

"Thanks." She let her fingers twine with his. "You mentioned you grew up in Michigan. How did you get down here to the Sunshine State?"

"After I graduated college, I wanted a fresh start. I still didn't know what to do with my life, so I came down here to live with Ryan. I partied a lot." He winked at her. "But Ryan sat me down and gave me a talk, like any good father would. The next day, we went to a monster truck show, and the rest is history."

Beth recalled Donovan telling her how Ryan played double-duty as a brother and father while he was growing up. *And now he's gone.* Sympathy rushed through her.

Donovan turned to the window behind them and

pointed at the red canoe. "You saved us with your canoe and poetry. Do you have any other hobbies I should know about? In case we ever have to utilize them to survive?"

Beth laughed. "I'm afraid not. Your hobbies are going to have to save us next time."

The two of them talked for hours, sharing every detail, asking every question that popped into their heads. Beth found out Donovan's favorite color was red and he had an obsession with horror movies. *Not surprising.* And she revealed she always wanted to move out of Florida, an idea that was sounding better with each passing moment.

Peanut butter sandwiches were passed out to everyone for dinner. Beth took her sandwich and bottle of water to a table in the small break room. She was removing the plastic wrap from her sandwich when Donovan stepped up to the chair across from her.

"I know this isn't typical, but I think we know each other pretty well by now," he said. The look he gave her suggested he wasn't just talking about their marathon chat but their shared intimacy. "I was hoping we could call this our first date."

Beth's heart skipped a beat at the simple romanticism of Donovan asking for a date. "I wouldn't mind that."

It only took them a few minutes to polish off their sandwiches, and before long, Beth was laughing. She felt at ease with Donovan, as if she had known him longer than a mere twenty-four hours. She could have stayed up all night talking to him, but after a few hours, she struggled to keep her eyes open.

Burnett handed Donovan a key. "This will unlock

cell number nine. We've been using the inmate's cots to sleep on, but they're clean."

"Thanks." Donovan took the key and Beth's hand. She followed him into the cell, and the moment she saw the bed, she dissolved onto it.

Donovan knelt beside the cot and stroked her hair. "You've been through hell, Beth."

She gave him a fatigued smile while fighting back a yawn. "Hell had to put up with me," she corrected.

He grinned. "It certainly did." He kissed her forehead. "Now go to sleep."

"Where do you get off ordering me around?" Even as she said it, her eyelids sealed, but the sound of the door banging shut had her opening her eyes again. She lifted her head to see Donovan on the other side of the bars. He smirked at her as he removed the key from the lock and tucked it into his pocket.

He locked me in. The bastard actually locked me in the cell!

"What are you doing?" Even to her ears her voice sounded deep with exhaustion and suspicion.

"There are five male officers stuck here. I'm protecting what's mine."

"Yours?" She squinted her eyes at him. Part of her wanted to say she wasn't a possession he could own, but the other part of her liked how he said it.

Donovan nodded once. "Mine."

Beth swallowed. Her heart skipped an excited beat. "Goodnight, Donovan."

"I'll be joining you soon." He winked at her and left.

If he thinks I'm going to have sex with him in a jail cell, he's sadly mistaken.

With a yawn, she settled back onto the cot and fell asleep as smoothly as light slipping through a wormhole. She woke once when Donovan eased onto the cot and took her into his arms.

Chapter Four

Donovan didn't mind being stuck in the police department. He had been there countless times with Ryan, so he felt comfortable. And he hadn't lied when he said Beth's company made it better. He liked being near her, seeing her out of the corner of his eye, and especially feeling her in his arms.

When he woke on the cot that morning, Beth's shapely legs and long arms were knotted with his. He trailed his fingers down the silky skin of her arm. She shivered against him, causing an immediate reaction within. He shifted to prop himself above her. Her eyelashes lay against the curve of her cheek. Her bowtie-lips were lush with sleep. He laid a finger against her mouth, feeling the velvety softness of her skin. He traced her cheekbones and slid the tip of his finger down the bridge of her delicate nose. Every bit of her, he found beautiful. He bent his head and kissed her forehead, the tip of her nose, and her cheeks. Then he took her sleeping mouth. Beneath him, he felt Beth awaken. Her lips twitched to life and accepted him. He leisurely explored the inside of her mouth.

Beth's fingers curled in the thickness of his hair, and her hands drew him closer. He slipped a hand between their bodies, sought the heat of her skin. When his palm flattened against her belly, Beth's body reared up and bumped into his. A gasp flew from her mouth.

She untangled her fingers from his hair and pushed him back. Her head turned to the cell next to them.

Donovan looked, too, and saw an officer stretched out on the cot. He glanced at the other cells to see them all occupied. He resisted the urge to groan. Leaning his head to Beth's forehead, he schooled his breathing back to normal and waited until his body calmed before drawing away from her warmth. She sat up and dropped her chin onto his shoulder. Her arms came around his sore chest.

He turned his head to press his lips to her forehead. "The moment we're alone, I'm going to indulge in you," he whispered. His voice faded with the promises of what he wanted to do to her, with her.

Beth unlocked her arms from his middle and shifted back. Her brown eyes seemed to study him, to see if his promise was real. She must've found what she was looking for because she nodded and laid her lips against his in a soft kiss.

Donovan rose from the cot, took a cold shower in the men's locker room, and put on a pair of gray cotton pants usually given to inmates. Then he asked Officer Burnett for a phone. "I want to call my mom. I want to be the one to tell her about Ryan."

Burnett nodded and led him to an office in the back of the department. "You can use this phone."

Donovan was glad for the privacy as he shut the door and dropped into the chair behind the desk. He picked up the phone, relieved to hear a dial tone, and dialed the number. As the phone rang, he tried to think of what he'd say. He never thought he'd be in this situation.

The ringing stopped, and his mother's voice came

on the line. "Hi, Mom. It's me, Donovan."

"Donovan! Oh, my boy, I've been worried sick. Are you okay? I've been hearing terrible reports of the conditions in Florida."

Dread pierced his heart like a double-edged dagger. "I'm okay. There's extensive flooding, and the power is out everywhere."

"What about your cell phone? I've been calling you and Ryan every hour since Sabrina hit."

Donovan swallowed. Ryan wouldn't be answering his phone anymore.

"I'm sorry, Mom. My cell phone got damaged." It was in his totaled car.

"Well, I'm glad to be talking to you now. Have you heard from your brother?"

The breath fled from his lungs. "Mom, there's something I have to tell you." He paused, bracing for the aftermath of his words and decided getting it over with quickly would be the best option for both of them. "Ryan was murdered working on a case."

A moment of silence stretched on the other side of the phone, much like the calm before a storm. Then his mom emitted a cry. Her grief vibrated the phone in Donovan's hand. He pulled it away, turned his head, and closed his eyes. Her cry continued for several heart-wrenching seconds. When there was a pause, he brought the phone back to his ear.

"Mom?" he said it softly, cautiously, as if approaching an injured animal.

Another wail broke free, then another, and another. Donovan dropped his head, heavy with her sorrow. He tightly clutched the phone, with the earpiece pressed to his forehead as he listened to her sob from a shattered heart. Tears quietly slipped from his eyes.

Other than his grandmother, he and Ryan were the only ones left in his mom's life. Now she was down one son.

He remained on the line while she cried. He might not be there to comfort her, but he could stay on the phone until her tears stopped flowing. It took a long time. He didn't quite know how long. When grief was involved, minutes could feel like an eternity. But when her crying quieted, and she was able to catch her breath again, she said his name.

"I'm still here," he told her and realized the truth of that statement. Ryan was gone, but he was still there. "I'm going to find the man who killed Ryan. I'll make sure he's punished. I promise you that."

A sigh touched his ear. "You always were the reckless one as a child, but I don't want to lose my last son. Swear to me you'll be careful."

"I swear."

"Good. I love you."

"I love you, too. I'm going to buy you and Grandma tickets as soon as I can find a flight into Orlando. Don't worry about anything. I'll take care of it all."

Donovan hung up after saying goodbye, hating those words because Ryan didn't get a chance to say goodbye. He sat behind the desk for several minutes with his mom's cries echoing in his ears. Rubbing his face with his hands, he swiped away the tears on his cheeks and went to look for Beth, needing her comfort. He found her in the front of the department, gazing out the windows at the devastated world. He went to her, wanting to embrace her, but not sure if he should.

Stopping behind her, he caught the smell of soap on her skin.

"If we were dating, I'd wrap my arms around you and hold you while we looked out that window together, but I don't know if you want to date me or not."

Beth turned to him. When she caught sight of his face, she put a hand on his chest. "What is it?"

"I just got off the phone with my mom." He swallowed back a cork of tears. "I told her about Ryan."

"Oh, Donovan, I'm so sorry." She wrapped her arms around him.

He closed his eyes, letting her embrace heal him. She didn't let go until he pulled back. Even then, she kept her hands on his shoulders. "I care about you. I care enough to have killed someone for you. And I have the desire to be with you beyond today, beyond this disaster. It's safe to say we're dating." She turned her back to him. "Put your arms around me."

Smiling, Donovan wrapped his arms around her waist, pulling her to him. They stood like that while watching the sunlight reflect off the floodwaters.

"It doesn't look like it's gone down any," she said.

"It looks that way, but it's probably gone down a few inches. Tomorrow, you'll be able to see the difference."

Beth groaned and knocked her head back onto his shoulder. "I'm not a patient person."

He nuzzled her neck. "I can see that."

She rotated in his arms, and he locked his hands behind her. "And what's your flaw?"

"If I told you that, you wouldn't want to date me anymore."

She nudged his shoulder with her fist. "I'm serious."

Donovan thought a moment. He had his hot-headed moments and liked things his way. He also tended to get into a lot of sticky situations. "I guess my flaw would be my recklessness."

"Ah. I should've known." Her gaze lowered, and her fingers tugged the string on his pants. "These are nice." The look on her face and the way she batted her lashes told him she was teasing him. "You came close to wearing these for the rest of your life."

"Would you have visited me?"

"Hm." She bit her bottom lip as she considered his question. "I don't know. I think things would've been different if they had hauled you away."

He nodded, knowing she was right.

A throat cleared behind them. Burnett stood, hands on hips with a smugness tugging at his mouth. "Try to keep the PDA down or I'll arrest you two."

Beth pulled free from Donovan's hold. "Sorry, Officer."

Donovan lifted his hands in the air. "I'll do my best."

Throughout the day, Donovan's desire to touch Beth, taste her, sink into her as he did during the hurricane, swelled inside him. While sitting side by side, he rubbed his thumb along her thigh. She shifted her leg out of his reach with a shake of her head. Later, when she talked to the woman at the front desk, his gaze feasted on her as she folded her arms on the top of the counter and bent forward in conversation. Her legs went on forever from the small jean shorts she wore. Her curves called out to him, tempting him to fondle them. His hands twitched. She glanced at him. Could she sense his gaze on her? Electricity passed between them. If they were alone, he'd stalk over to her and crush her mouth with his.

To keep his thoughts off Beth, Donovan did what he could to assist the officers who would be working his brother's case. Although Burnett had used a tape recorder when he questioned Donovan, a recording couldn't capture Donovan's thoughts and senses. He took a legal pad and pen to the break room and documented what he could remember about the moments leading up to Ryan's murder and following it. Forcing himself to recall every detail was difficult, but he did it for his brother. He did it in the hopes of finding Buck.

When he finished, he had pages of information, things he never wanted to think about again. Things he knew would forever haunt him. He wasn't sure if any of it would be useful, but he felt better after getting it all down on paper.

Beth silently entered the room as he read through the report, double-checking that he hadn't forgotten anything. She sat down across from him but didn't say a word until he lowered the legal pad and dropped the pen to the table.

"I wish there was something more I could do," she said.

"That's exactly what I was thinking," he admitted. "I'm trapped in a police department. I have to admit I find that irony pretty funny. But we're powerless while Buck is out there running. Every minute that goes by is another minute taking him farther away."

Beth leaned across the table and took his hand.

33

"The cops will get him."

He looked into her calming brown eyes. "How do you know?"

She squeezed his hand. "Because I have faith."

Chapter Five

Beth and Donovan were stuck in the police department for three days until the water went down enough for vehicles to pass. Beth personally couldn't wait to leave. The body odor of the five police officers, as well as herself, stained her nose hairs. She was sure she'd smell BO for weeks afterward.

During the last day of their stay, Beth's sanity frayed with boredom. She thought about making pillow people under all the blankets in the cells to freak out the inmates when they returned, but she didn't have the energy. All she could do was set up dominos in spirals and send them tumbling with the flick of a finger.

When Burnett declared he could drive them home, she felt like kissing him. They piled into the back of Burnett's squad car, and he peered at them from the driver's seat. "Where to?"

She felt Donovan's eyes on her and thought about her home. "There's a hole in my roof, and last time I was there, about six inches of water was on the floor. I don't think I can go home. Wildlife could be taking up residency in my bedroom." She thought about the snake Donovan had killed and got chills.

"Is there anywhere else you can go?"

She started to shake her head; she didn't have any family left.

Donovan recited an address from beside her. She

shifted to him. "What's there?"

Donovan met her questioning gaze. "My place."

Oh!

He turned in the seat, and his leg brushed hers. "You said yourself you don't have anywhere to go." He dipped his head, and his stare penetrated her. "Live with me."

Her eyes widened. She shook her head. "You don't have to put up with me just because I'm homeless and don't have a working car. My studio is okay. I can use the backroom until I have money for an apartment. It would have to be cheaper than dirt, but I'll manage. You don't have to worry about me."

Donovan captured her chin with his fingers. "Are you done?"

She nodded.

"Good." He took her face in his hands. "I want you at my place. I like having you close, and I don't want you to leave."

She slowly nodded. "Okay, but I'm going to pay half the bills."

Donovan smiled. "I think I can deal with that."

Burnett drove them to a sturdy apartment complex, untouched by Hurricane Sabrina. Beth climbed out of the backseat and stared up at the three-story building. Metal shutters covered all the windows.

"When will someone be going to Ryan's house?"

Beth turned when she heard Donovan's question. He was bent over, talking to Burnett through the passenger window.

"A car is going there right now to put crime scene tape around the house. Today, we're more concerned with rescuing people trapped in their houses." Burnett sighed. "And we may find more dead." He looked at Donovan with drawn, heavy eyes. "Search and rescue is more important right now, but I'll try my hardest to get a team to your brother's house tomorrow morning."

Donovan nodded. Without another word, he moved toward the building. Beth hurried after him, wishing she knew what to say but not finding the right words. They quietly climbed the stairs to the top floor.

Donovan took a key out of the light fixture and opened the door to his apartment. Darkness greeted them. He reached out and flipped the switch just inside the door. Light flashed on.

"There's electricity." He smiled over his shoulder.

"That's good." She followed him into the living room as he turned on more lights. She took in the tan walls, brown suede couch, flat screen TV, and pool table. Typical bachelor pad.

"Your place is nice."

He turned to her and touched a strand of hair that had fallen loose from her ponytail. "And it's just gotten better."

His claim caused her stomach to coil. Knowing she was inside his apartment, alone with him, sent lust rushing through her body like a geyser. "Do you mind if I take over your bathroom for, oh, an hour? I've wanted to take a boiling shower for days."

"Why would I mind you being naked in my bathroom?"

Beth blinked at his straightforward response. "I guess you wouldn't."

Donovan's smirk widened. "I'll get one of my shirts for you to wear. I'm sure one of my sweats will cover you, too. We'll have to go back to your house to get your things and save whatever isn't damaged."

"Your car is wedged into the side of a tree," she reminded him.

"I have a truck in the parking lot."

She nodded while considering that. "Maybe you should've driven your truck and not your car. You might've had better luck."

He took a step to her. "But my bad luck brought me to you."

Beth fought against a surge of desire. "Bathroom?"

"That way." He pointed to the hall to her right.

"Thanks." She walked to the bathroom and closed herself in. A black curtain hid the shower. Next to the sink was a blue toothbrush and a green bottle of cologne. She picked up the cologne and sniffed the nozzle. The fresh wintery-green scent made her stomach erupt with flutters.

She stripped out of her grimy clothes and stepped into the shower. Water beat down on her, washing away the sweat and grit that clung to her skin and hair. Her scratches cried against the burn of the hot water, but her muscles sighed. She massaged shampoo into her scalp and rinsed the suds down the drain. The sound of the bathroom door clicking shut had her pausing in the act of lathering a bar of soap between her hands. Tilting her head beneath the spray, she peered at the tall figure on the other side of the shower curtain. The curtain swished aside. Donovan stood there stark and handsome. Beth's chest tightened. Her knees weakened.

He stepped into the shower and stood a breath away from her body.

"I wanted to thank you."

She swallowed. The bar of soap forgotten between

her hands. "You already did. Outside the police department."

His gaze bore into her. "Not like this." He dipped his head and took her lips. His touch electrified her, creating a whirlpool in the pit of her stomach. She parted her lips for him, and he immediately filled the space to explore her mouth.

The first time they kissed, Beth had tasted the danger inside Donovan. It was toxic and delicious. She was able to shackle her desires then, but he persuaded her to unleash them. She sank into his passion faster than quicksand. She had almost regretted the act and thought it had poisoned her judgment, putting her in greater risk. Now that she knew he was good, and after what they had been through together, she could no longer deny her clawing needs.

Donovan eased back. She looked at him, hungry and aching. He took the bar of soap from her and slicked his hands with suds. With a soft touch, he ran his hands over the healing gash on her chest. The contact both stung and aroused her. She closed her eyes as his hands left a sheet of bubbles up her neck, down her arms, and across her abdomen. His body pressed against hers, his arms looped around her waist, and his hands stroked her back. The feel of his slippery palms sliding up and down her back enticed a moan out of her. When the hot water rinsed off the suds, leaving her skin clean and wet, Donovan pressed his lips to her shoulder. Then his soapy fingers slipped between her legs. A gasp fluttered from her lips. Her hands grasped his sides, and she dropped her head onto his shoulder.

Just as her body hummed with pleasure, Donovan withdrew his hand. Her eyelids cracked open. Steam rose around Donovan. Drops of water slithered down his chest and beaded on his shoulders. His eyes were pools of amethyst passion and they were pulling her down into their sensuous depths. She took the bar of soap, filled her hands with sweet-smelling foam, and rubbed her palms over his body. Touching him thrilled her. He had sexy cuts in his torso, defined abs, and toned muscles. When she touched his length, he stiffened. His jaw tensed. A few strokes and Donovan grabbed her wrist. He shifted their positions, letting water course down him. Once all of the soap was gone, he shut off the water and picked her up. She let out a surprised yelp as he carried her to the bedroom, leaving a trail of wet footprints. He approached the bed, and she squirmed in protest.

"We're dripping."

Donovan ignored her statement and lay her in the middle of his bed, atop a black comforter. He hovered over her and slowly, achingly lowered himself onto her. "I don't care."

The weight of his body and the feel of his hot, wet skin excited her. She hooked her arms around his neck as he kissed her. Her tongue glided next to his, her fingers plunged deeply into the soft locks of his brown hair. A moan curled up from her throat, mingling with their tangled tongues.

While they kissed, their tongues urgent, Donovan's hand massaged her breast. Volts of electricity speared through her. She grasped him as desire melted the cartilage in her body. His fingers teased her relentlessly, working her nipple to a point of excruciating pleasure. Her hips began to grind against his, begging him for more.

Donovan released a groan and dragged his mouth away. "I promised I would make up to you everything you've done for me. And I promised that the moment we were alone I was going to have you. And that's exactly what I intend to do." His fingers moved up her thigh. "Say yes," he whispered into her mouth.

"Yes," she breathed.

Pulse thrumming, she hooked her legs around his hips and drew him between her thighs. Their mouths found each other while their hands explored. She stroked his abs and felt his muscles squirm with lust. Her legs tightened around him, tugging him closer until she felt his arousal.

Donovan's lips left hers and fluttered down her throat. She tipped her head back, granting him access. He dipped his tongue into the groove at the base of her throat and planted kisses along the fragile lines of her collarbones. When he reached the red, irritated gash on her chest, he paused. His gaze swept over the injury, eyed the still nasty looking bruise on her shoulder, and drifted down the scabbed cuts on her arms.

"I can't enjoy you as I want to," he said. His gaze met hers. She lifted her hands to his face and grazed her fingertips down the stubble growing on his cheeks. "When all your wounds are healed, I'm going to kiss every inch of your body. And that's more than a promise. Until then, I'm going to do what I can." Donovan's fingers skimmed the inside of her thighs and touched her. Her hips jerked. His fingers stroked her so exquisitely she had to bite her lip against the pleasure.

"One day, one day soon, I'm going to have you memorized by touch," he told her.

What he was doing to her pushed her to the brink.

Her hands curled in the comforter as she called out her ecstasy. She wanted, needed, had to have more. "Donovan."

Hearing his name catching on her voice must've been his undoing because he quickly thrust inside her, submerging himself in her flesh. Then, perfectly still, he cupped her face in his hands and stared into her eyes. She stared back while panting. The look etched on his handsome face replicated the look he wore when he told her he loved her.

Beth leaned forward and pressed her lips to his mouth, punctuating her feelings with a kiss. And with their gazes locked, Donovan began to move, slowly at first and then with energy. Beth's legs flexed around his hips, encouraging him to go faster, harder. Her sighs grew louder and became more frequent until she imploded. He dove into her three more times before growing rigid.

Chapter Six

After sleeping for as long as possible, Donovan woke to find Beth curled next to him. Her face was soft with sleep, and her hair was mussed around her head. Donovan eased out of bed so he wouldn't wake her. He went into the kitchen to start the coffee and took a mug to the dining room table. As he drank he thought about what he needed to do next. He was on his second cup when Beth emerged from the bedroom.

"There's coffee," he said.

She smiled sleepily and went into the kitchen. A moment later, she joined him at the dining room table. She took a sip and moaned. "This is good. The stuff they call coffee in the police department could burn stomach lining." She took another long sip. "Do you want breakfast? I could create something with whatever you have."

Donovan sighed. "No, thanks. I'm going to my brother's house. I have to make sure he's really there."

She shook her head. "Donovan, I saw my parents after they died, and for the longest time, that's how I saw them when I thought about them. Your brother has been dead for days and he's been in water." She put her hand over his. "You don't want to see him like that."

He looked at her. "I need to see for myself."

She closed her eyes. "Okay, but I'll go with you."

"No. It's a crime scene. You could get into

trouble."

"So could you."

He sighed. "Beth, I have to do this. Alone."

She stared at him a long moment. Her eyes were drawn, and her eyebrows were low with sympathy, but all she said was, "Okay."

****

Donovan drove his truck to Ryan's house, ducked under the crime scene tape, and used the spare key to gain access. He stepped over the threshold. The wood flooring beneath his feet felt weak, soggy, as if it could give under his weight. A dark stain claimed the area where his brother had lain. Not even the rainwater that flooded the living room could wash away a mark of murder.

He walked through the living room to the exact point where he'd stood when Chewy walked out into the open with a gun. He paused there a moment before moving to the hallway. Chewy wasn't there now, of course. No one was.

The stench of decay already touched his nasal passages. He went into the kitchen, picked up a dishtowel, and held it over his mouth and nose as he walked down the hall. He didn't know in which room Buck and Chewy had put his brother's body, so he checked each one. He opened the bathroom door with his hand protected by his shirt and peeked inside. His brother's green toothbrush lay next to the sink. He never thought a toothbrush could cause his throat to tighten, but it did. For as long as he could remember, his brother had a green toothbrush and he had blue.

He opened two walk-in closets to find empty suitcases and boxes labeled "Michigan Clothes" and

44

"Camping Crap." The guest bedroom was also empty except for a neatly-made bed and a bedside table with a lamp. Donovan had crashed there after nights out with his friends and an abundance of alcohol. It was also where he stayed when he first moved to Florida to start his own life.

Outside the master bedroom, Ryan's room, Donovan took several slow breaths beneath the hand towel, bracing for what he'd see on the other side, but he knew he would never be able to completely prepare himself for the sight waiting within.

When he opened the door and moved around the king-sized bed, he froze in horror. Ryan's skin was splotchy with a thick layer of yellow, waxy coating. Black and purple veins crisscrossed along his neck and arms. His face was so swollen from the floodwater and beating that it was unrecognizable. Maggots crawled along his face, seeking the holes of his nose and mouth. His body was bloated to the point that his shirt—a Wolverines football T-shirt—was stretched out of proportion, revealing putrid, mottled skin. Seeing his brother like that made Donovan sick. He hurried out of the house, put his hands on his knees, and dropped his head as he fought the urge not to vomit. The coffee he drank earlier resembled acid.

Although he shut his eyes against the sickening image, he could still see his brother's milky eyes staring lifelessly up at the ceiling fan. Every time he blinked, he saw the blue lips, the marble skin. What lay on the floor in the bedroom was not his brother. Not the brown hair crusted with black blood and slick with slime. Not the face—smashed, bloated, and deformed. Nothing.

Donovan couldn't hold it down any longer; he

vomited into a bush. Even with his stomach empty of food, the coffee now gone, he continued to hack. He could still smell decay as if it stained his skin, filled every pore, clung to him, swam in a cloud around his head. Tears ran down his cheeks as he heaved. When his stomach stopped rocking, he dragged his feet—his knees shaking—away from the vomit and sat down on the driveway, with his back against the garage door. He took shallow breaths in through his mouth and out through his nose. Several minutes went by as his stomach muscles unclenched and his shaking eased.

A police car pulled up to the house. A cop was not a welcome sight at the moment, but it was Burnett who stepped out and walked up the driveway.

"Goldwyn, what are you doing here?" He stopped in front of Donovan, with hands on his hips. His eyes fell to angry slits as he studied Donovan's state, no doubt noticing the beads of sweat along his forehead. "You did not just break into a crime scene."

"I had a key," Donovan said and wiped his face with the kitchen towel. He drew it away immediately and dropped it beside him—the smell of decay clung to its fibers.

"Damn it, Goldwyn," Burnett roared. "You could've destroyed evidence by going in there, or whatever evidence that wasn't already ruined by the flood. Going in there before the scene was thoroughly investigated was a dumb thing to do. I should arrest you for this."

"Then arrest me," he spat. "I'm sorry, but I had to go in. I had to see…" He dropped his head into his hands. The fight in him fled as grief settled in. "I had to." His voice sounded weak and distant, even to himself.

Burnett sighed and shuffled his feet. "I'm not going to arrest you. You're lucky I came here to check on the place before the crime scene unit got here, which should be any minute. You need to leave."

Donovan shook his head. "I'm not going anywhere."

"Fine. Then go sit in your truck. You can watch everything from there."

Burnett held out his hand. Donovan accepted it and got to his feet. He looked at Burnett. "Thanks."

Burnett nodded. "Don't mention it. And I mean that. If anyone finds out you went in there just now and I let it slide, my ass will be in a sling."

"But I was already in there. With Beth."

"I know. We still have to take precautions."

Accepting that, Donovan went to his truck. He picked up a bottle of water, which had probably been in his car for a week, and used the warm water to rinse out his mouth. Then he sat in the front seat, the windows rolled down, while he waited for everyone to arrive.

The coroner's van came first, soon followed by the crime scene unit. They went inside in full protective gear, including masks. Minutes went by as Donovan imagined them taking pictures of his brother's body, of the bedroom, and of the bloodstain on the living room floor. Twenty minutes later, the workers from the coroner's office wheeled a black body bag out of the house and loaded it into the back of the van, like an object that never held life, never carried a soul, and was nothing more than empty waste. The van pulled away, taking the last part of his brother—as unrecognizable as it was—that remained in this world.

He continued to sit and watch as investigators went in and out of the house carrying bags of evidence and cases of equipment. When they finished, nearly two hours later, Burnett walked up to his truck.

"They're done. They'll be performing an autopsy on Ryan. After the reports are finished, they'll release him." He paused, as if he didn't know what to say next. "You'll let me know when and where the funeral will be held?"

Donovan faced Burnett. "Yeah. And you'll let me know if you find anything out about Buck? And I mean anything."

"You have my word that I'll tell you the moment we hear something about Buck."

"Thanks."

****

Donovan drove with the windows down and rock music blaring to keep his thoughts from running back to what he saw in his brother's house. He ran up the stairs to his apartment and went in. The door banged shut behind him. Beth stood up from the couch where she was watching the news and took a step toward him.

He put up his hand, stopping her. "Don't…I need to take a shower."

He rushed to the bathroom where he stripped off his clothes and stuffed it all, even his boxers, into the trashcan. Hoping to dispel the odor of death, he blew his nose. In the shower, with the water as hot as he could stand it, he scrubbed his body with soap until his skin was pink and washed his hair.

At the sink, with a towel tied around his waist, he took the time to shave, brush his teeth, and rinse his mouth with mouthwash to get rid of the taste of raw vomit. He sprayed cologne, inhaling deeply. When he was dry and dressed in fresh clothes, he felt cleaner. But he wasn't done yet. He picked up the trashcan, carried it into the kitchen, and dumped his clothes into a large trash bag that he knotted twice. He didn't want the clothes in his apartment, not even in a trash bag, so he walked barefoot to the Dumpster behind the complex and tossed the bag inside.

Back in his apartment, he leaned against the door, suddenly exhausted. Beth stood a few paces back. He could tell she wanted to approach, but she didn't know if he wanted her to or not. Her concern and desire not to intrude speared him in the middle of his chest. He gestured with a nod of his head. "Come here."

She immediately went to him, wrapping her arms around him. Lowering his head, he took in the scent of her hair. Although it smelled like his own shampoo, he liked it. And yet the horrible memory of the smell of his brother's body came back to him. He buried his nose into her neck, seeking her soapy fragrance.

Beth's hands stroked his arms a moment before she leaned back in his embrace and stared up into his face. His gaze traced the arch of her brows, the almond-shape of her brown eyes, and the curve of her wide lips.

"I'm going to lie down," he said.

"Do you want anything?"

He gently kissed her. "Just that." In his bedroom, he stretched out on the bed and closed his eyes. Forcing himself to imagine Beth's face, he sank into a fitful sleep haunted by his brother's voice. *I trust you with my life, Don.*

He woke to the aroma of tomato, basil, and garlic, and found Beth in the kitchen wearing one of his black shirts with a belt around her hips. The shirt fell to the tops of her thighs. Despite what he had gone through today, a smile manifested on his face.

"What are you cooking?"

Beth twirled on her bare feet. "Lasagna. I walked across the street to the grocery store to get the ingredients I needed and used the money you left for pizza. There's also garlic bread." She paused. "I wanted to do something nice for you. After everything we've been through, and all the peanut butter sandwiches we consumed at the police department, I figured we deserved a good, home-cooked meal."

He smiled. To some, a meal might be a small thing, but to him, it was a big gesture. "It smells great." He peered down at her body. "And I can see you raided my closet."

"I don't have any clothes here, so I created a makeshift dress out of your shirt and belt. Do you like it?"

Donovan pulled her to him and devoured her lips. Beth reacted instantly, grabbing his shoulders and moaning. He hadn't meant to get carried away, but feeling her reaction to him exploded whatever control he possessed. Needs clawed at his chest, cravings becoming unbearable. He cupped the back of her head, and his fingers tangled with her maple locks as he deepened the kiss. He doubted the lasagna, as great as it smelled, would taste better than the flavors in her mouth—sweet and strong, hot and addicting.

Donovan pulled back a fraction. "That's how much I like it," he said between her parted lips.

Beth stared up at him. Her eyes glistened.

He took her mouth again in a heavy kiss that was

all tongue and moans. His hands grabbed her butt and lifted her so she was on tiptoe. Their bodies banged together. The contact electrifying.

Beth suddenly pushed him back a step. His hands released her, and she dropped back onto her heels. "All right, all right, all right," she said and closed her eyes. "Pheromones are high right now. I would love nothing more than to indulge in you, but the lasagna won't be good if it cools."

"Then it's a good thing I'm starving."

"Sit at the table. I'm going into the kitchen to compose myself. I'll bring out the food in a minute." Beth hurried away as if she wanted to escape the pull of his desire.

Smirking, he sat at the table she had set with paper napkins and the emergency candles he had in his hurricane supplies.

She came back with two plates heaped with steaming squares of lasagna. She put one in front of him and pushed the garlic bread toward him.

"I haven't had a dinner like this since my mom's last visit."

"Well it won't happen all the time, so don't get used to it. The next dinner I make for you might be soup from a can." Beth picked up her wine glass. "How about a toast?"

Donovan picked up his glass and examined the bright, red liquid swimming inside it. "Is this wine?"

"No, I didn't have enough for wine. I made do with cherry Kool-Aid."

He grinned. "What are we toasting?"

"How about to disasters that bring people together?"

Donovan's grin widened. "To disasters," he repeated.

Their glasses clinked.

Chapter Seven

Donovan's mom and grandma arrived the morning of Ryan's funeral. They wore their black dresses and pantyhose on the flight. Their eyes were red and puffy when Beth and Donovan found them at baggage claim. The second Donovan's mom spotted him, she ran to him and wrapped her arms around his middle. She was a petite woman with her head coming to rest against his chest. She buried her face in his shirt as she cried fresh tears. His grandmother shuffled toward them; a hanky pressed to her chest as tears streamed down her cheeks.

From a couple of steps back, Beth could hear Donovan whispering to his mom. "It's okay, it's okay. He'd hate to know you're crying. He never liked to see you sad."

"I'm not supposed to bury one of my sons. You're supposed to bury me," she sobbed.

"Hush, now." Donovan drew her away and framed her face with his hands. "We're going to get through this together. And we're going to live safely and happily, because that's what Ryan would want us to do." He pulled his grandmother into a hug.

"Ryan's with your grandfather now," the older woman said with a tearful voice. "Your grandfather will take care of him."

Donovan's mom nodded in agreement, sniffed, and wiped her nose with a tissue. Her gaze drifted to Beth then. "Oh, is this—"

Donovan shifted and held out his hand to Beth while keeping his other arm around his mom's delicate waist. Beth joined him. Meeting a boyfriend's mother was always hard. She wanted to impress and was constantly afraid she'd fail. "Beth, this is my mom Meredith and my grandma Lily. Mom, this is Beth Kennedy, the woman who saved my life…twice."

Beth hit him playfully in the side. She was about to say she did no such thing when Meredith launched herself forward. Beth had to grab her and return the embrace or she would've ended up flat on her back.

"I could be burying two sons if it weren't for you!"

Beth looked at Donovan over Meredith's head as she rubbed the woman's back. She didn't know what to say. All she could offer Meredith was the comfort of human touch.

The four of them went back to the apartment so Donovan and Beth could change. Beth slipped into a simple black skirt and blouse and came out of the bathroom to find Donovan fooling with a purple tie. She put her hand on his arm, took the tie, and began to work it into a knot. His eyes were more prominent with the tie accentuating their color. She gazed into them and brushed a lock of brown hair off his forehead with her fingers. "Are you okay?"

Donovan nodded and then surprised Beth by picking up her hand and planting a kiss in the center of her palm. Linking his fingers with hers, as if he didn't want his kiss to fly away, he led her out of the room. They held hands during the entire drive to the church and sat beside each other in the front pew with Meredith and Lily on the other side of him.

The service was honorable and simple. Flowers didn't clog every nook. Bows didn't choke every pew. At the front of the church, with a backdrop of stunning stained glass windows, was a platinum casket. A large photo of Ryan in his dress uniform stood on the raised platform next to a wreath of white lilies and a few white candles.

When it was time for people to pay their respects, Meredith stood and walked to Ryan's casket. The church fell silent, as if angels cupped everyone's mouths. No one sniffled, no one coughed, so when Meredith collapsed onto her knees and let out a wail loud enough to reach the heavens, it shook the very air.

Tears clogged Beth's eyes and throat. Her hand flexed on Donovan's a fraction of a second before she released it. He stood. Everyone watched as he went to his mom, scooped her into his arms, and carried her outside, into the healing sunlight. Beth's heart bled for them.

At the end of the service, she took Lily's arm and walked with her behind the pallbearers. Questioning stares warmed her back. Many women whispered to each other behind their hands, with their eyes on her. As she passed two of them, she heard, "Who do you think she is?"

"I think she's with Donovan."

"No way! I wonder how she made that happen."

Beth kept her chin up and pretended not to hear them, but inside, she felt a mixture of pride, for being Donovan's woman, and disgust at the rumors that would no doubt circulate from the mouths of the women. *At a funeral, no less.*

The sun was bright at the graveyard. A beam of

light kept ricocheting off the metal casket and landing in Beth's eyes, but she was able to see Donovan, Meredith, and Lily each toss in a handful of dirt. The sound of the Honor Guard firing gunshots rang in her ears, making her jump. Even when the firing stopped, the bangs echoed solemnly in her head, reminding her of Donovan's loss.

They went to dinner afterward. Beth tried to eat, but seeing the grief of the other two women tightened her throat so she couldn't swallow a bite. The next morning, Meredith and Lily left to return to Michigan. Beth was sorry they didn't have longer to get to know each other beyond the introductions at the airport, the tears at Ryan's funeral, and the silence during dinner. But something she didn't expect happened when they said their goodbyes. Meredith embraced her and whispered in her ear, "I can see the difference you've had on my son. I'm happy he's found you."

Meredith's words stunned her. All she could do was nod. Donovan didn't seem different from when they'd met a few short weeks ago, which made Beth wonder what he had been like to make his mom think she'd made a difference.

****

In Donovan's apartment, in his soft bed, Beth lay in the crook of his body with the morning sun warming her skin. For the past several minutes, she had been debating how to approach the subject of going to her house to cleanup and inspect the damage. With the flood waters down and Ryan laid to rest, she felt it was the best time to get this task done. She took a slow breath, let it out, and ended the peaceful quiet with her question, "Can you drive me to my house today?"

When Donovan didn't answer right away, she continued, "I should try to save what little isn't ruined and I think it's time I get some clothes. I can't keep wearing your shirts."

"I like you in my shirts."

She smiled. "I bet you do."

"We can get a moving truck for whatever furniture isn't damaged, and we can box up everything else."

"That'll help a lot. Thank you."

Donovan enlisted a couple of his monster truck buddies for some extra muscle. He bribed them with a six pack of beer—each. Beth contributed with the promise of pizza when the job was done. His friends readily agreed.

At Beth's house, Donovan pulled his pick-up truck behind two other equally large trucks.

Their apparent love for big vehicles made her smile. She hopped out of Donovan's truck to meet two tough-looking men. One had sleeve tattoos on both of his arms and hair shaved into a short Mohawk. The other had a bald head and a thick beard.

"Hey, I'm Smith." The man with the tattoos held out his hand.

The gentlemanly gesture touched Beth. She clasped his hand, returned the shake.

"I'm Beth."

"I know, and Donovan is one lucky son-of-a-bitch." Smith turned to the other man. "Can you believe he crashed in front of her house?"

"Bastard couldn't be luckier." He smiled beneath his beard. "I'm Gordon."

Beth chuckled, liking them already. "Thank you both for coming out to do this on your Sunday."

"We'll do anything for beer and food," Smith said with a big smile.

While Donovan, Smith, and Gordon took out their equipment, Beth studied her house. The last time she saw it, it had been on its own island with rainwater lapping precariously close to the front door. After the ground had a chance to suck down the water, and the sun's rays beat down on it, evaporating the wet particles, the level dissipated, revealing a lawn of dead grass.

Across the street, Donovan's car was crammed into her neighbor's tree. *I guess no one called to have it removed.* She walked toward the car and trailed her hand along the trunk. At the rear door, she peeked through the empty square to see the brick she'd used to smash the window resting on the far seat. Her raincoat was still spread over the seat where she'd left it; a piece of glass poked through the yellow plastic. Thankfully, it hadn't cut her. A cut like that would've made survival next to impossible on top of everything else she'd had to deal with at the time.

Mosquitoes swarmed inside the car, attracted to the foot of murky water at the bottom. The hum of their music beat against her eardrums.

She moved to the driver's door and bent down to peer through the window. For a moment, she saw Donovan sitting there, with his body hunched over the steering wheel. She nearly lifted her hands to bang on the window as she had done before, but she heard his voice behind her and knew the vision wasn't real. When she blinked, her eyelids swiped the vision away like windshield wipers. Movement caught her attention. Cupping her hands against the glass, she saw ripples dance along the water's surface. She squinted to see better and vaulted backward when something leapt out of the water, somersaulted in the air, and landed with a splash. A catfish had made Donovan's car into a swimming pool. She couldn't stop the laughter from bubbling out of her mouth.

Donovan came up beside her. "What's so funny?"

Beth pointed. "You have a catfish in your car."

Donovan bent down to have a look for himself. "So I do."

"How do you think he got in there? The water didn't get high enough for it to go through the back window."

"The wind was strong. He could've slid inside with a small wave."

"I suppose. Do you have a bucket? We could get him out and transport him to a pond or something."

"Smith," he shouted. "Get the bucket out of the back of my truck."

Donovan stood ready with the bucket when Beth opened the driver's door. The water rushed out, and the catfish slid over the doorjamb and into the bucket. She peered inside and smiled. "There you go, fella."

Donovan snapped the lid into place and smiled at her. "I never thought I'd find a woman with compassion for catfish." He kissed her on the forehead. "You're one-of-a-kind, Beth Kennedy."

Beth smiled back. "So are you." She glanced at his car. "I think we should call a tow truck."

"Oh, I still might be able to drive it."

"Sure, into another tree."

"Careful, or I'll spank you in front of my friends."

She arched a brow. "I'd like to see you try."

Turning to her house, Beth's smile faded. Hurricane Sabrina had destroyed the home where she had grown up, the house her parents had left her in their will. The fence she had helped her father build—and by build, she helped hammer nails into place—lay on its side, flattened by the deadly winds of a super storm. The garage door was like a wad of crumpled paper. A fallen pine tree stretched across the lawn, blocking the front door.

She trudged around the back. The patio—where she and her mom would sit in the evening to talk and watch the sunset—was plastered into the side of the neighbor's house. The sliding glass door was shattered. She stepped over the glass shards and into her home. Except it no longer resembled any home she knew. A giant hole stretched from the dining room to the living room. Musty leaves covered the dining room table and floor. Roof shingles that had fallen through the hole in the roof now resided in the kitchen. Insulation stuck to the tops of furniture like pink mold, and mildew covered the couch. The cards they had been playing poker with were stuck to the floor, faded and withered. The jellybeans they'd used to place bets were melted globs.

Beth felt Donovan behind her. She spoke without turning. "At this table, I would carve pumpkins, decorate Christmas cookies, and dye Easter eggs with my parents."

"The table looks to be in decent shape." Donovan knocked on the wood with his knuckle. "It just needs to be sanded and varnished."

She faced him with despair weighing her down. "That's not what I meant." She lifted her hands with her palms pointed to the ceiling. "A year after my studio opened, my mom passed away and..." Her voice caught. "And then my dad. They left me the house and the bit of money they had. I grew up here and now the place I always called home will never be my home again. There's too much damage with the walls, the ceiling, the floor. Too much that can't be repaired. I'd have to start from scratch, and I can't do that." Her shoulders dropped.

With a sigh, she brushed past him and went into her bedroom to pack. What she found waiting for her made her yelp. Hundreds of hungry ants crawled over the poisonous snake Donovan had killed. A long line of them extended away from the snake, up the wall, and to the corner of the window. They carried away scales and chunks of snake meat. Beth spun away with her hand over her mouth as she gagged.

After seeing the problem, Donovan left and came back with a bath towel. "Can I?"

"Please!"

Donovan moved around her. A second later, he told her it was okay to look.

She did so cautiously. Donovan had draped the floor with the towel, hiding the revolting sight of the ants picking apart the rotting snake, but she could still see the wavy shape of it. If she looked close enough, she could still see the ants moving.

Stepping cautiously around the towel, she examined her belongings. Half of it she tossed into a garbage can. The clothes and shoes that were salvageable went into black bags to wash later. Books that weren't warped and all the knick-knacks that had survived Hurricane Sabrina's ransacking went into boxes. With each item she tossed out, with each box she taped, her heart grew heavier. While she was busy going through her bedroom and bathroom, Donovan and his friends removed the dining room table, dresser, and the full boxes. After walking through the house—an empty shell of what used to be her home—Beth removed the large painting of the beach from her bedroom wall.

"This is the last of it," she told Donovan.

He took the painting from her and studied it. "Who's Rachel Reagan?"

"My mom. Reagan was her maiden name."

"She painted?"

"She did. I would watch her paint on the patio every Sunday morning. It was like our church. When she finished, we would have a fabulous brunch with fresh fruit, scones, and chocolate."

"Your mom and my mom would've gotten along real well."

Once outside, Beth gazed upon her home. She tried not to feel as if she had lost her parents all over again, but that's exactly what it felt like. Losing her home was a funeral in itself. And the thought of never coming back brought tears to her eyes. Life went on. Not many people were lucky enough to live on the same street their whole life, but that street was where she'd learned to ride a bicycle and where her bus stop was all throughout school. She liked to think her life could've played out completely on that street, in that house, but her dream had been shredded by Hurricane Sabrina.

Chapter Eight

Donovan drove down the interstate in his truck. One month after Hurricane Sabrina wailed on Florida with her giant fists of wind, the Sunshine State was close to being back to normal. When the deep floods of her vengeful tears reduced to puddles, Floridians began cleaning the debris she'd left behind as a parting gift. Filth covered the streets, city workers had to dissect fallen trees, and the governor brought in sand by the truckload to repair the deteriorating coastline.

Several beach homes had fallen into the turbulent waves. A few clung to their stilts, leaning precariously over the edge of crumbling dunes. Blue tarps covered many roofs in need of repair, and several buildings with substantial damage still had storm shutters hiding their windows. Many establishments had sheets of plywood blocking their front doors with spray-painted messages stating they were closed.

From the interstate, the only visible damage from Hurricane Sabrina was to the billboards. She had torn them apart, but there was no time to fix the signs because homes, banks, schools, and football stadiums needed repairs first. Worse than any physical damage was knowing Buck was still at large.

Donovan pulled his truck into a plaza with a grocery store, sandwich shop, and nail salon sitting side by side. He parked in front of Beth's studio, The

Fighting Chance, where she taught self-defense classes. Since her car still needed a radiator transplant, Donovan had been driving her to and from work. He didn't mind, though, because he got to see her after classes, when she was hot and sweaty.

The sun was submerging into the horizon, leaking oranges and pinks across the sky. Seeing such a beautiful sunset brought back the memory of the bruised skies from Hurricane Sabrina's hulking mass.

Amazing how nature can reward us with beautiful things one moment then punish us on a whim.

He entered the studio to the sound of sneakers pounding the blue mat and gloved hands punching protective gear. Corissa, Beth's front desk receptionist, a young woman with 24-karat gold hair and diamond eyes—a pale gray bordering on translucence—beamed at him as she put down her psychology book.

"Hey, Donovan. They're almost done."

He glanced at the blue mat where Beth coached seven people on how to get out of a bear hug by lifting their elbows and rotating from side to side as fast as they could. Some connected with the head of their attacker and others didn't, but the objective was to loosen the hold around their middle so they could spin out of the hug, grab their attacker, and finish with a knee to the groin.

Donovan had been amazed when he saw Beth's studio the first time. She had done a great job creating her business and studio. White walls with purple words—Strength, Rise, Strive, Live—encouraged her students as they learned to protect themselves. At the far end of the room, Beth had turned the wall into a slate of signatures. Everyone who had ever set foot on the blue mat had signed his or her name. Quite a lot of names were already scribbled in permanent marker.

Donovan leaned against the desk and tapped Corissa's psychology book. "How's your class?"

"Interesting. I'm learning a lot." She smiled suddenly, revealing a tiny gap between her front teeth. "Beth told me if I read anything that sounds like you to let her know."

Donovan smirked. *Does Beth still think I'm a closeted killer?*

"She said that, did she?"

"Oh, she was just kidding."

"I bet."

He was amused and pissed off at the same time. *If Beth thinks there might be the slightest possibility I could be a psycho, then why in the hell is she with me?*

"Looks like they're finishing up," Corissa said.

Donovan turned to see Beth standing in front of the seven sweaty individuals.

"You were all spectacular," she told them. "Seeing how much you have grown since your first lesson has made me proud. Next week, I'll be teaching you how to do this." She nodded at the man beside her who was equipped with padding and a helmet. She turned her back to him, and he wrapped his arm around her neck, pressing a plastic knife to her throat. Her arms shot up, and she gripped his wrist with her hands, one on either side of his arm. Then her head shot back, butting the helmet. When her attacker stumbled, her hand fell, striking him in the groin. As he doubled over, her elbow rammed him in the ribs, and the back of her fist jabbed his face. Free from his hold, she spun away from him, while wrenching his arm, and slammed him into the ground.

Excited chatter and applause followed Beth's maneuver. She faced her students with a grin on her face. "Until then, be safe."

She exchanged hugs with a few of her students and clapped her pretend attacker on the arm. "Thanks for being such a good sport."

"Always for you," he told her with a wink.

Donovan glared at him. *If he touches or flirts with her one more time in my presence, he's a dead man.*

Beth glanced his way as if she could hear his thoughts. He lifted his brow at her then narrowed his gaze on the man at her side. She said something to her assistant that had him leaving. As he passed Donovan, he smiled meekly.

Keep smiling, asshole, you just averted disaster.

"Corissa, you can leave. We'll lock up," Beth shouted from the mat.

Donovan turned to Corissa. "See you tomorrow."

She picked up her psychology book and purse.

"Oh, and if you read anything that sounds like me…" He glanced at Beth and leaned in, lowering his voice. "Let *me* know first."

Corissa laughed. "You've got it."

Donovan escorted Corissa to the door, keeping an eye on her until she made it to her car. He went to Beth as she wiped down the equipment with sanitizing wipes. She wore a pink tank top and black workout pants. Her hair was in a high ponytail that swung back and forth every time she moved her head. Sweat glistened on her chest. The deep cut that had been there was a faint pink line above the collar of her tank top. Donovan's insides clenched, and his mouth watered. He wanted to run the tip of his tongue along that scar, wanted to taste the saltiness of her skin.

He put his hands in his pockets. "You're full of surprises, Beth Kennedy."

She grinned. Her eyes were alight with life, as they always were at the end of her classes. "We've known each other for a month. You have a lot more surprises coming your way."

"Bring 'em on." He winked at her and enjoyed seeing her flushed cheeks brighten. He glanced at the blue mat. "No man would have a chance against you."

"I was up against you, and you apparently had a chance," she said with a bite to her words.

His lips spread. "I'm a different kind of man."

"You certainly are," she mumbled. She picked up a can of disinfectant to spray down the mat but paused in her chores with a hand on her hip. "How exactly did you stop my attempts to hit you?"

"I knew what you were going to do a second before you did."

She glowered. "Don't let anyone know that or I'd be out of a job."

"Any other man, baby, and you definitely would've crushed his nuts and beaten the crap out of him with that candlestick holder."

"You pinned me on the floor."

Donovan thought back. After he yanked her into her house, seconds before a tree crashed onto the welcome mat, he had rolled her beneath him to stop her struggles. He nodded once. "I did."

Her maple eyes darkened. "I know how to get out of that hold. I *teach* people how to get out of that hold."

"Beth." He took her shoulders in his hands. "I was

67

prepared for you to fight me. I pushed my body weight onto your hips so you wouldn't be able to pivot me off you. My brother did martial arts for years and taught me everything he knew. I knew what I was doing. Don't think just because you couldn't get away from me, or hit me, makes you an inadequate self-defense instructor. We both know that's not true."

Beth looked up at him. "I appreciate that." She pulled away from him and headed to the other end of the blue mat. "And if it wasn't a little windy, you definitely wouldn't have hit that tree."

Donovan rotated, watched her uncap the disinfectant. "What did you say?"

She peered over her shoulder. "You heard me."

He eyed her. *Is she seriously challenging me?* She bent over to spray the mat, aiming her butt at him. A smirk stole across his lips. *I'm going to teach her a lesson.*

The sun was down, and the sky was darkening when they left Beth's studio. Donovan reversed out of the parking space and turned in the opposite direction of his apartment.

Beth zipped up her athletic jacket to fight the chilly November night and turned to him. "Where are we going?"

Donovan kept his eyes on the road. "I'm taking you somewhere."

"Donovan, I'm tired and sweaty. I just want to go home, shower, and lounge on the couch with you."

He smiled. "We can still do that. *After.*"

"After what?"

"We have a little fun."

She shook her head, but he could see a small smile

on her lips as she settled back into her seat. Thirty minutes later, on a deserted road, he put the truck in park and got out to unlock the gate blocking their path. Then he continued down the dirt road to a clearing of land with a single cement building. When he cut the engine, Beth turned to look at him. "What is this place?"

"You'll see." He got out of the truck, stole Beth's hand, and led her to the building where he crouched in front of the white garage door to unlock it. He stood up. "Beth, I'd like to introduce you to—" He lifted the door, revealing a neon-green monster truck "My truck, *Venom*."

"Holy crap." She stepped into the garage. Her hand stroked a black cobra poising to strike along the side of the truck. Donovan watched her hand, his stomach tightening. He wanted her hands on his back, chest, everywhere.

He cleared his throat. "Do you wanna go for a ride?"

Beth grinned at him. "Of course, I do."

Donovan opened the passenger door. "Hop in." She swung herself into the seat, strapped on the helmet he handed her, and swiftly buckled herself in with the safety harness. He couldn't stop from chuckling.

"Shouldn't we be wearing fire suits or something," she asked.

He looked at her and admired how sexy she looked wearing a helmet. "I'm not going to do anything that we would require fire suits to protect us. I wouldn't risk you getting hurt, Beth. Trust me, okay? You're in good hands." He turned the key, igniting the engine and savoring the roar of the five hundred and seventy-five cubic foot engine coming to life.

Beth examined the console with the curiosity of a six-year-old. "Why do you call your truck *Venom*?"

Their gazes locked.

"Because venom is fast and lethal." He revved the engine, sending vibrations up their legs and spines. "Don't worry," he repeated. "There are three kill switches."

When Beth blinked at him, he stepped on the gas pedal. The monster truck shot out of the garage. He maneuvered it around the building toward the course he had built to practice stunts. Earlier in the month, he had to rebuild the ramps that had gone flat and muddy from the flooding.

Driving along the edge of the field, he forced the truck to go as fast as its engine would allow. Adrenaline coursed eagerly through his veins, like the methanol flushing through the engine.

Venom.

Deadly, but addicting.

Grinning, he whipped the steering wheel to the left, lifting the truck off the two outer tires.

Beth's body slid in her seat, tipping her toward Donovan. Out of the corner of his eye, he saw her groping for the harness keeping her in her seat. With a jerk back on the wheel, he leveled the truck onto all fours and zeroed in on an obstacle ahead—a series of small mounds. The truck rolled over them, applying its nitrogen-charged shock absorbers. Despite the twenty-eight-inch suspension travel, they jostled in their seats. Donovan heard Beth curse. As the truck hopped off the last mound, he put the throttle to the floor, knocking the truck back onto its hind wheels so the nose pointed skyward.

Beth let out a small scream. Chuckling, Donovan risked a glance in her direction to see her hands over her eyes. Amusement fluttered through him. She could take on a killer cop, but the thrill of a fast truck made her want to hide.

"Open your eyes," he insisted. "Look at the stars."

She lowered her hands and Donovan heard her intake of breath as she looked at the ebony sky and the blurring streaks of starlight. "Wow."

Smiling when he heard her breathy praise, he said, "Hold on." He let up on the throttle, dropping the truck forward, and immediately accelerated again. With his foot never flinching off the gas pedal, he turned the wheel while releasing the clutch, causing the truck to spin in a tight circle. And it didn't stop.

Beth's laughter rang in his ears, reminding him that donuts were always his favorite stunt. He broke out in a grin as he continued to hold the steering wheel in place. The truck had no other choice but to rotate wildly. The tingles in his hands and feet from the engine heightened his own excitement. He threw back his head and let out a whoop. A few more rotations and he eased his foot off the throttle.

Even when the truck stopped, Beth didn't quit laughing. Her hand was pressed to her chest, and her head was bowed. *She's not laughing. She's giggling.*

She looked at him with glimmering eyes and flushed cheeks. "That was fun."

Donovan's lips split wide. Seeing her delight was contagious, but he wasn't done yet. "Wait."

Her eyebrows shot up, but exhilaration hid behind the gesture. "More?"

He grinned in answer and lined the truck up with the biggest ramp on the field. The truck zoomed up it.

"Oh shit," she gasped.

Donovan felt the shock absorbers compress while they built up pressure. They sprang back with such force the truck boosted into the air like a frog leaping off a lily pad. Beth raised her hands, as if she were riding on a roller coaster, and let out a cheer.

Gravity wrapped its transparent hands around the truck and yanked it down. They bounced in their seats when they hit the ground. Donovan stopped the truck to get a good look at Beth. She faced him with the biggest smile he had ever seen.

"Can we do that again?"

Her enthusiasm elevated him. He had the desire to show her every stunt in the book. "Not tonight," he said. "I have to refuel and fill the tires with more air."

He backed the truck into the garage and climbed down. Beth met him on the driver's side. "That was amazing!"

She launched herself at him, taking him by surprise, but he managed to catch her in his arms as her mouth stamped his. He could taste her adrenaline on the tip of his tongue.

She pulled back and looked up at him, panting. "You're one hell of a driver, Donovan."

"Thank you."

Her eyes strayed to the hood of the monster truck. "Have you ever had sex on your truck?"

Her question threw him off balance. His eyes strayed to the hood and then back to Beth. At first, he didn't think she could possibly mean what he thought she did, but her chest was rising with shallow breaths and she was looking at him with hungry eyes. His mouth peeled open as he drew in a slow breath. If it wasn't obvious before, it was clear at that moment Beth was the girl for him.

"No, I can't say I have."

"Would you like to?"

Her words alone caused his stomach to tighten. His pulse quickened at the promise of a release. After driving his truck, he was full of energy, energy he wanted to use on Beth. He felt movement in his pants with the mere thought of her lying naked on the hood of his truck. He reached out to touch the place where he imagined her. "It's warm."

"So?"

She clambered up the tire, using the deep trenches in the rubber to make her way up. Her feet slipped a few times, but she managed to get to the top where she scooted over the hood so her feet rested on the bumper.

She peered over her shoulder at him. "What do you say?" she said, tempting him.

And he took the bait.

He moved around the giant tire and stood in front of her. "Take off your jacket and sit on it so you don't get burned." Wordlessly, she followed his instructions. When she sat on her jacket, he removed her shoes. They dropped to the concrete floor. Then he took the band of her workout pants with his fingers.

"Lift."

With her hands on the hood, she lifted her hips. Donovan tugged the cotton down her legs, depositing it with her shoes. With his gaze on her, he pinched the fabric of her boy shorts. She pushed her hips off the hood again, and he peeled away her underwear.

Donovan caressed her bare legs with his hands and eased her thighs apart, exposing her center, which was level with his eyes. Since she was open in front of him, he took the opportunity to commit her flesh to memory. His gaze flipped up to hers. For several seconds, they exchanged intimacy with a stare.

He stepped up the tire and shifted onto the bumper. With his hands on Beth's hips, he moved her higher. When she was in the middle of the hood, he climbed onto it, planted his knees in-between her legs, and hooked his hands above her head.

He gazed into her eyes. With the heat of lust swirling between her lashes, they reminded him of warm whiskey. "Comfortable?"

"Very."

"Good." He unzipped his pants slowly, unleashing his manhood. "Hold on to me." Beth bit her bottom lip as she hooked her legs around his hips and secured her arms around his neck. Seeing her lips caught between her teeth sent a rush of liquid fire through his body. He couldn't contain himself anymore. He drove into Beth and rode her more vigorously than he had driven his truck. He didn't care if they dented the hood. It would be well worth it.

Beth's cries and his groans filled the small garage. Every noise she made urged him to go faster, harder. Being inside her felt exquisite; he couldn't get enough of her. Nor would he ever.

He felt himself on the verge of release, but he wouldn't allow himself to leave Beth behind.

Stiffening his body, clenching his teeth, he plunged harder, hitting her deeper.

The instant she climaxed, he let go.

Chapter Nine

The next day, Beth got a call from her insurance company and received a rude awakening. Her homeowner's insurance didn't cover everything she needed it to, such as flood damage and mold. What they were giving her wasn't enough to rebuild. Her only option was to demolish the house and put the land up for sale. With the money from the land, she would have enough to relocate as soon as the market stabilized.

With a heavy heart, she looked up a realtor to help her with the details, and Donovan accompanied her to the realtor's office. While she talked to the front desk receptionist, he studied the brochures on the wall.

"Hi, I need a realtor," she said.

"Is there a specific realtor you want?" The receptionist was an older woman with glasses and gray roots. She smelled like stale cigarettes and dead roses. And she didn't seem happy to see Beth.

"Not really, just someone who deals with land. Hurricane Sabrina damaged my house, so it's set to be demolished, and I'll be putting the land up for sale."

Beneath her red-rimmed glasses, the woman's gaze lifted and settled over Beth's shoulder.

Beth frowned but continued to talk. "It's a decent sized lot that can support a large house, a swimming pool, and still have enough room for children to play in the backyard."

The woman's eyes widened. "Oh my God!"

Her sudden exclamation startled Beth. "What?"

"It's the Hurricane Killer," she whispered.

Beth blinked. "Who?"

"He's behind you," she hissed.

Beth turned but the only other person in the office was Donovan. Then it hit her. *The news bulletin!* Apparently, she wasn't the only one who'd seen it. She whirled back around. "No, no, no, you don't understand. He's not a killer." She peered back at him in panic.

Donovan was staring at her now, with his eyebrows raised. He took a step toward her, which prompted the woman to scream. She reached under her desk and brought out a pink handgun.

"What are you doing? Are you crazy?" Beth shifted into the line of fire. "He's not a killer."

"Get out of the way, Beth." Donovan grabbed her arm to move her, but she stood firm.

"Don't come any closer!" The woman waved her gun in the air. "I'm calling the cops."

Beth put up her hands, hoping to calm the woman before she could put a hole in the wall, or in her head. "That's not necessary. He's not dangerous."

"Beth, shut up." Donovan's voice was a growl of irritation. "Let her call the cops."

Beth turned and watched Donovan set a chair in the center of the small lounge and sit down. Her mouth fell open. "What are you doing?"

Donovan stretched out his legs and crossed his arms. "Waiting."

Beth couldn't stop the woman from calling the cops no matter what she said, so she gave up and leaned against the counter, keeping the gun and Donovan in her line of sight at all times.

Ten minutes later, Officer Burnett sauntered into the building. He grinned at them. "I hear there's a killer in here."

Donovan stood. "That would be me."

The two men shook hands, and the woman balked in disgust. Beth only smiled.

"Ma'am." Burnett went to the woman behind the counter. "There's been a mistake. The report you saw a month ago was false. Donovan Goldwyn here is a model citizen, not a killer."

His gaze lowered, and he pointed to her weapon, which she still pointed at Donovan. "Do you have a permit for that?"

The woman's face fell. She sputtered. "Uh...well...um...no."

"I'll be taking that, ma'am." Burnett held out his hand.

Mumbling a few curses, the woman gave him her gun.

"Thank you." Burnett turned to Beth and Donovan. "I'll contact people I know at the local news stations and ask them to put out a retraction on the report they aired about Donovan being a murder suspect."

"That would be nice," Donovan said.

"And, Goldwyn," Burnett added under his breath, "don't scare any more old ladies."

Stifling a laugh, Beth faced the flabbergasted woman. "Now about that realtor."

****

Beth sat on the couch with Donovan as they watched the evening news. Donovan's picture stared back at them from the screen. A male reporter explained that authorities had uncovered evidence clearing Donovan of his brother's murder and he was no longer a person of interest. It lasted a minute, but it was enough.

"Well, you're no longer a killer," Beth said.

She felt Donovan laugh silently beside her.

"That's always good to know," he said.

Beth grinned. "I agree." She leaned into his chest as relief filled her. Being named a suspect in his brother's murder had been hard on Donovan. Now that he was free of all suspicion, he could heal.

Chapter Ten

Thanksgiving morning, Donovan woke to the smell of coffee and French toast; the aroma of vanilla and cinnamon was having a love affair with the fragrance of Colombian coffee beans. Beth made breakfast in his high school basketball jersey with the Thanksgiving Day parade on in the background.

Since neither of them had to slave over a feast, Donovan watched the football game with Beth, and he was pleased to learn she was fluent in the ways of football. She knew what first down meant, understood a referee's call, and knew the main players by name.

"I had no idea you were a fan," he said during halftime.

"Yup," she said and took a swig of soda. "I had to find some way to bond with my dad, being an only child and all. I wasn't interested in fixing up cars, which in hindsight would've saved me a lot of money on my piece of crap car. So, I started to watch football with him when I was eight. I fell in love with the game." She shrugged as if it didn't matter, but Donovan thought it was amazing.

When it was time to eat, they put together a simple meal and sat down to eat. In the middle of the table were two Cornish hens, a box of turkey dressing, a can of cranberry sauce, and instant potatoes with a glob of garlic butter to make up for the bland taste. It might've been simple, but it was better than what Donovan did last year when he ordered Chinese takeout.

"I know it's a bit of a cliché," Beth said. "And that this isn't exactly a time to be celebrating considering everything that's happened, but are you thankful for anything?"

Donovan looked into her eyes from across the small table. "Actually, I *am* thankful for something...you."

She blinked at him. "What?" Her voice was soft.

"Beth, I would either be dead or in jail right now if it weren't for you. You're what I'm thankful for."

Her cheeks turned a pretty shade of pink. "Oh."

"Your turn. What are you thankful for?"

"Well..." She tilted her head in contemplation. A slow smile captured her face. "Good sex!"

Donovan barked with laughter. "I think we both can be thankful for that."

"All humor aside," she continued, "I'm thankful that fate had you driving through my neighborhood. I'm even thankful for Hurricane Sabrina. She shoved your car into that tree because she knew we needed each other."

Donovan picked up her hand, kissed her knuckles. "Amen."

They finished the night with a game of poker. Donovan wanted another chance to beat Beth since Hurricane Sabrina interrupted their last game by ripping off the roof to Beth's house. This time Starburst candy was at stake. An hour later, Beth folded after losing three-fourths of her candy. "It's not fair! You have the best poker face in the world."

"I can make it up to you."

She dropped her chin in her hand and batted her lashes. "Oh, yeah? How?"

Donovan scooped her out of her chair and carried her into his bedroom.

****

For Christmas, they bought two tickets to Grand Rapids, Michigan. Their trip would begin a week before Christmas, and they'd leave two days after. The morning of their departure flight from Orlando, Donovan stood at the apartment door next to his luggage. When Beth came toward him with her suitcase in hand, he frowned.

Beth stopped short. "What? What's wrong?"

"Nothing." His gaze lowered to her suitcase. "It's just...are you sure about spending Christmas with my mom and grandma?"

Her face fell. "Do you not want me to go?"

"No. I mean, yes, I do." He sighed and raked his hands through his hair. "I just don't want you to feel pressured to go for my sake. You don't have to go. You're not obligated."

"No, I'm not obligated, but since my parents passed away, my Christmases have been pathetic. Last year, I didn't even have a Christmas tree. I went to one holiday party and then watched all *The Godfather* movies by myself. I'm happy to go. Your mom and grandma are wonderful women, and I want to spend more time with them." Her smile doubled. "Besides, I've never seen snow before."

Relieved, Donovan drove to the Orlando International Airport, which was close to bursting at the seams. Toddlers throwing inopportune tantrums, children sneaking away from their frazzled parents, and groups of Asian tourists planning to hit the amusement parks reminded Donovan why he hated airports. Holiday travelers going home for Christmas elbowed each other and hurried to catch their flights with their luggage rolling behind them. Security personnel watched everyone, and airport employees helped frustrated people who couldn't find their luggage or their departure gate.

At the security checkpoint, they removed their shoes, had their carryon bags scanned, and stepped through metal detectors. With a firm grip on Beth's hand and the other on his duffel bag, Donovan navigated through the flood of bodies to the gate where the other passengers for the flight to Michigan were already accumulating. He dropped into a chair with a grunt. Beth sat next to him. They were thirty minutes early. Thankfully, the small talk Beth created helped the time pass quicker than if he were there alone, glaring at the noisy occupants around him and willing the second hand to tick faster.

On the plane, Beth huddled next to the window, and Donovan stretched out near the aisle. After the flight attendant gave all the redundant in-flight instructions, the plane taxied onto the airstrip and picked up speed, pushing everyone into their seats. The plane lifted off the asphalt, tipping them back. Donovan turned his head to the window where Beth stared eagerly, watching the highways, cars, and houses shrink, becoming toy-like as the land below turned into puzzle pieces. The plane soon burst through the clouds and glided above white formations that reminded Donovan of cotton balls. Higher up, the clouds stretched into wispy sheets.

Beth faced him with a smile. Her eyes shone with wonderment. "I love takeoffs."

Donovan couldn't stop his own smile from forming. "I can tell." He put on his headphones and settled back with Beth to watch a Christmas movie.

Their flight bumped to the ground a few hours after takeoff. They were walking toward the front of the airport when Beth pulled him to a stop.

Donovan frowned at her, noting how she chewed on her bottom lip. "What's wrong?"

"I'm nervous."

"Why?"

"Because I'm afraid your mom's not going to like me."

"Beth, she already met you. When I bought our tickets and told her you were coming, she squealed into the phone."

"Squealed?"

"Yeah, you know the sound women make when they're excited? It nearly burst my eardrum."

Beth laughed, but her smile turned into a frown. "Then why did you tell me I didn't have to come?"

He brushed his finger along her jaw. "Because I wanted it to be your choice."

Leaning into him, she touched her lips to his. "I wouldn't want to be anywhere else." She took his hand. "I feel better now. Let's go."

Beth took a step, but Donovan didn't move. Out of the corner of his eye, he thought he saw a familiar figure. His head whipped around to the large hallway leading travelers away from baggage claim and deeper into the airport. A shadow disappeared behind the wall.

"Stay here," he said. "Don't move!" He dropped

his duffel bag and jogged toward the hall. Flying around the corner, he came face to face with nothing. The hall was empty. He ran to the other end and searched the expansive area where people poured in from all directions. His gaze jumped from person to person, but he couldn't see anyone retreating with the build of David Buckland. He could've sworn he had seen Buck lurking behind the wall, staring at him and Beth. With a shake of his head, he berated his imagination.

Beth waited for him exactly where he'd left her. She hadn't moved an inch. When he grew closer, he recognized concern in her eyes. Her eyebrows were low and pinched together. She hadn't seen Buck, didn't understand his reaction, or his order for her to stay put. But she did what he asked her because she trusted him. "What's wrong?"

He took his duffle bag from her. "I thought I saw someone."

"Whom?"

He let out a breath to release the pent-up tension that had knotted his stomach into coils. The tension remained. "Buck."

Her eyebrows shot up her forehead. "Why would Buck be here? If he *were* in Michigan, he sure wouldn't be in an airport unless he had one hell of a good disguise. Maybe you thought you saw him because he's on your mind all the time." She took his free hand. "Forget about him, okay? Burnett and Chief Cormac are doing everything they can to find him, and they aren't going to stop because you're out of the state."

She was right, but he couldn't dampen his urge to call Burnett and demand updates, despite the fact he'd called before boarding the plane and they weren't any closer to finding Buck.

"Let's go," Beth said, gently tugging his hand. "Your mom and grandma are waiting for us."

Finding his mom and grandma wasn't hard. Grandma was the only one wearing a big red sweater with a Christmas tree in the center, a matching skirt, and black tights. Christmas was her favorite time of the year and she liked everyone to know it.

His mom stood beside her. "Donovan!"

He lifted her feet off the floor in a hug, and then he bent down to embrace his grandma and kiss her cheek. Seeing them again, and in different circumstances, filled him with happiness. Instead of tears, their eyes gleamed with the joy of the season. Their bodies weren't shuddering with silent grief but were light with cheer. Warmth spread through him as he watched Beth exchange hugs with them.

"Oh, Beth, we're so happy you came," his mom said. "I brought cookies. They're in the car."

"I can never pass up cookies," Beth said.

In the backseat of his mom's van, she cracked open a red and gold tin canister. The aroma of the snowball cookies Donovan grew up eating wafted out and touched his nose. Beth selected a cookie on top, bit into it, and let out a content moan. "These cookies are delicious."

"I'll have to give you the recipe. They're easy to make," his mom said.

"That would be great. Thank you."

Grandma turned in her seat and held out a thermos. "Don't forget the hot chocolate. It's the real stuff, too, none of that instant crap from a package."

Donovan took the thermos, unscrewed the cap, and gave it to Beth. She took a sip. "Wow. Can I take the two of you home with me?"

Laughter filled the van.

Seeing Beth getting along so well with the two other women he loved brought up a surge of emotions he couldn't tamp down. Didn't want to tamp down. As it consumed him, he had the urge to show her how much she meant to him. And he didn't care who saw it either.

Beth took another bite of a snowball cookie. Before she could lick away the dusting of powdered sugar on her lips, he caught her chin with his fingers and molded his mouth to hers. The powdered sugar melted and the sweetness touched his tongue. He deepened the kiss, drawing out the flavors of her mouth and the lingering flavors of the cookie. When the last of the soft, white powder was gone, he ended the kiss with a gentle nibble of her bottom lip.

"What was that for?" she hissed, her cheeks red with mortification.

He brought his mouth to her ear. "That was for you."

She had dropped her cookie into the canister on her lap. Her hand was still poised in the air, with her thumb and index finger spaced an inch apart and a layer of powdered sugar on the pads of her fingers. Donovan lifted her hand and tenderly sucked off the coating from her fingers. A soft sound escaped from a crack between her lips.

She put her hand on the side of his face and pressed herself into his chest so her mouth was next to his ear. "Stop," she breathed, practically begging him.

Pulling back, her gaze met his. Heat swirled in her eyes, and he knew he had undone her. In his mom's van. With his mom and grandma sitting in the front seats.

"Here." She picked up a snowball. "Have a cookie."

****

Christmas lights sparkled along the gutter of Donovan's childhood home. A wreath hung on the front door, and red velvet bows decorated the trimmed bushes in front of the windows. Stepping through the front door, the fragrance of cinnamon and nutmeg circled him, bringing the spirit of the season. The inside hadn't changed much since he left for college except for an occasional new picture on the wall or knick-knack on a shelf. A bowl of assorted nuts sat on the coffee table, a ceramic village complete with fake snow, toy cars, and plastic people occupied the length of a cabinet, and a row of nutcrackers lined the fireplace mantel.

"Your home is so cozy," Beth said as she took in her surroundings.

"Thank you. I've always believed a home should be well-lived in." His mom turned to him with a happy smile. "Why don't you show Beth your old room?"

"Right this way." He led Beth upstairs. At the top, he paused next to the first door.

"This was Ryan's room." A pang of grief stole his breath. Part of him wanted to open the door, to let the memories of his brother flood him, but he knew it wasn't the time. He opened the door across the hall. "And this one was mine."

Walking into the room felt like passing through a

time warp. A faded blue and yellow Michigan State rug covered part of the floor in front of his twin-sized bed. Trophies from basketball, track, and wrestling cluttered the top of a dresser positioned against the wall. The fact they were dust-free told him his mom had come in to clean. On the other side of the room was a desk with a Batman action figure propped against a small lamp.

"So, this is where the mysterious Donovan Goldwyn grew up." Beth studied the monster truck posters and the stack of crime novels on his desk. She lowered onto the plaid comforter on the bed. "Are there dirty magazines hiding under your mattress?" She patted his bed.

"I would never leave anything like that behind for my mom to find."

Her hand trailed along the blue comforter. "So…how many girls did you bring up to your room to fool around with in this bed?"

"One. My first real girlfriend when I was sixteen," he answered honestly.

She blinked at him. "Really?"

"You sound surprised."

"I am. I figured you would've had a slew of girls in your room."

"Oh, I had a slew of girls, but I knew better than to bring them home when I wanted to get into their pants. I did that all over the city."

Beth elbowed him. "Real nice."

When she started to leave, he caught her hand. "If it makes you feel any better, you're the first girl who has met my mom since I moved to Florida." He could see her consider that. "Since I graduated from college," he added, so she'd know how long of a time period he was talking about. "A woman like you is impossible to find, Beth, but I found you. I plan on keeping you."

She kissed him. "That's better."

After a dinner of meatloaf, baked potatoes, and asparagus, Donovan took Beth on a walk around his old neighborhood. A few blocks from the house, they arrived at an elementary school. A fence circled the playground where a slide, jungle gym, and swing set occupied a bed of mulch and snow.

"This is where I had my first fist fight," he said.

Beth looked toward the playground. "What grade were you in?"

"Third. I started young."

Grinning, he took her arm and led her to the parking lot where he pointed to a large oak tree standing tall at the edge of the schoolyard. "You see that tree? That's where I had my first kiss."

"On school property? You were a true bad boy, Goldwyn."

"I was eight."

"Was this before or after your first fist fight?"

"The same day."

Beth laughed.

"I think the girl I kissed still lives around here somewhere. I should drop in on her. I mean, that was one memorable kiss. As first kisses go."

Beth stopped laughing. Taking his hand, she tugged him across the lot and shoved him against the trunk of the tree. She branded his mouth with hers, creating a lightning storm in his body, and clearly staking her claim. He got the message all right. She kissed him with an intensity that warned him never to mention another woman's kiss, not even a girl's kiss.

Her kiss was nothing like his first. That kiss had been a boy's kiss—awkward and a little too wet. This kiss was all heat and passion. When Beth's tongue glided into his mouth, warm and silky, he was ready to sell all his memories of previous girlfriends so he would only have memories of Beth. Her hands slid down his chest, and her fingers grabbed the buckle of his belt.

Using her hold on the buckle, she pulled him closer to her body.

Donovan took her shoulders and switched their positions. While cupping her face, his body crushing hers in a way that allowed him to feel her quiver with excitement, he took control of the kiss. Driving his tongue into her mouth, extracting moans from her body, he pushed his arousal into her, letting her feel the reaction her kiss caused. When he unlocked his lips from hers, small clouds escaped their mouths and collided.

"I hope that made you forget *what's-her-face*," Beth panted.

Donovan nodded. "Mission accomplished."

****

When all the women were asleep that night, Donovan snuck downstairs with his cell phone. In the study, with the light down low, he called an unlisted number for a hacker he'd become acquainted with through Ryan.

"Who is this?" a man snapped on the other end.

"Greg, it's Donovan Goldwyn."

"Oh, Donovan, I didn't recognize the number." There was a pause. "I heard about your brother. I'm sorry."

"Me, too. Listen, I know who killed him, and I plan to catch the asshole. I could use your help, though."

Greg's response came immediately. "How may I be of service?"

Donovan figured it wouldn't take much persuading on his part for Greg to agree to help. When a corrupt cop tried to pin Greg as the one who stole sensitive police information, Ryan proved Greg innocent and nailed the cop as the hacker. Ever since, Greg had been a loyal friend.

"Search your impressive database for David Buckland. I want to know everything about him...where his family lives, the names of his acquaintances, where he went to school, his favorite vacation spots, as well as hospital and DMV records. I also want to know if he has any ties to Michigan...if there's a chance he could be in Michigan right now."

"I'll work on it tonight and email you what I find."

"Thanks."

Donovan disconnected and trudged upstairs to get some rest, although he suspected sleep wouldn't likely come for hours.

Chapter Eleven

Beth stretched in the bed as sleep paralysis gradually faded from her limbs. She cracked open her eyes to see rays of wintry sunlight streaming like liquid through the blinds. She turned over, wanting to cuddle into the side of Donovan, and found the bed next to her empty. The glowing numbers on the clock told her it was after six, a time usually too early for Donovan, even if a gallon of coffee was involved. She kicked back the thick comforter, instantly regretting the action when the cold pinched her bed-warmed skin, giving her chills.

Her sweater hung over the back of the chair at Donovan's desk, a desk she figured wasn't put to use during Donovan's youth. She imagined him to be a rowdy boy climbing the walls, not sitting quietly at a desk. Slipping the gray cotton over her head, she eased open the door. The house was quiet. With each step she took, wood groaned, and she was positive she was waking up the whole city.

She checked the living room, dining room, and kitchen, then poked her head into the study. All four rooms were devoid of human life. The house was spotless. She suspected a single sugar ant didn't dare march into Meredith's territory.

She peeked through the front window, searching for Donovan on the stoop. The world outside was calm, sleeping beneath a blanket of snow. Donovan wasn't out there. He wasn't anywhere.

Heading back upstairs, her palms began to sweat. *Where could he be?* The bathroom door was wide open and empty. She checked his bedroom again and even went as far as to open the closet, thinking he might be changing. He wasn't there, not even naked.

He can't just disappear. She was tiptoeing down the hall when she noticed the door to Ryan's old bedroom stood ajar. The implication of what that meant made her breath catch and her body turn to stone. She stood there, transfixed by the crack between the door and the frame and the bit of light squeezing through it.

Taking a deep breath, she touched the door with her fingertips and gently pushed it open. The walls were a peaceful blue. The bed sat in the corner, freshly made as if waiting for someone to crawl beneath the blankets, but all that was in the bed was the folded American flag from Ryan's funeral. It lay propped against a pile of pillows. A shelf of action figures hovered above the bed. A giant boom box took up space on top of a dresser next to a framed photo of Ryan in a cap and gown. A blue and yellow tassel dangled from the corner of the silver frame.

At first, Beth didn't see Donovan until she turned to leave, and she saw him wedged in the corner next to the closet. His arms were crossed on his knees, and his head was down.

Sympathy tore Beth's heart. Her chest tightened as she crossed to him and knelt between his legs. "Donovan." She spoke softly, not wanting to stir the ghost in the room, and laid her hand on his arm. "Donovan?"

He raised his head. His eyes were red and swollen; his cheeks wet. He had been crying, and knowing that made tears bite the back of her eyes like needles.

"I couldn't help it," he said, his voice wavering. "This is the first Christmas without him. I couldn't help it."

"I know." She pressed her palm to his cheek. "I know," she whispered.

The first Christmas after her parents passed on was excruciating. Every Christmas song she heard, every holiday movie she watched, every sweet scent she smelled reminded her of Christmases past with her mom and dad, and she'd burst into tears like a popped water balloon. Living in her childhood home didn't help, where every inch contained a memory of them. It took a long time for her to remake the house so she could live there without sadness weighing her down.

"When I came in here," Donovan continued. "I was bombarded with him. I didn't think it would be that powerful. It's as though he never left."

Beth framed his face with her hands. "It's okay to miss him. It's okay to be angry. And it's okay to cry. If you let it out, you'll heal faster. Trust me. Let it out and let it go." She scooted closer. "I'm here. It's okay."

Donovan stared at her; the dam of water covering his eyes grew thicker. After a moment of startling silence, his arms snaked around her. She cradled his head in her hands as he unleashed his grief. Seconds bled slowly into minutes, and minutes crawled as if with two broken knee caps. His tears soon ceased, but he continued to hold her as if to keep afloat in the wake of his breakdown.

When Beth felt enough time had passed, and that

Donovan's mom and grandma could be waking up at any moment, she eased out of his hold. "We should leave and close the door. We don't want your mom to see you like this."

Donovan nodded in agreement and slowly rose to his feet. His shoulders were hunched forward, his head low. He took small steps as if bruised by his tears.

Beth shut the door behind them and gazed into his raw eyes.

His Adam's apple bobbed a moment before he spoke. "I'm going to take a shower."

"Okay." She turned to go, but he put his hands on either side of her face and brought his lips to her forehead.

"Thank you."

She squeezed his wrist in understanding. "I'm going to start the coffee. When you're ready, you can find me in the kitchen."

She descended the stairs and entered the homey, apple-red kitchen. Hunting through the cabinets, she found the coffee and scooped in two generous heaps for a full pot. She sat at the table while the water dripped and the scent of coffee swam through the house.

"Good morning, Beth." Meredith swept into the kitchen wearing a pink robe. The bottoms of red flannel pajama bottoms peeked out from beneath the hem. "I would've had the coffee ready for you if I had known you were an early riser."

"Oh no, I'm usually a late riser, but I'm excited. I couldn't sleep."

"That's understandable." She opened the refrigerator and took out a small tube. "How do sticky buns sound?"

"Divine. Can I help?" Beth started to get up, but Meredith shooed her away.

"Sit back and relax, sweetie. This will just take a few minutes."

Beth was enjoying her first sticky bun with Meredith and Lily when Donovan joined them. "Good morning, ladies." He gave Meredith and Lily each a kiss on the cheek.

Beth took a sip of coffee flavored with a dash of cinnamon and studied him. He appeared fresh with no sign of the sadness that had weighed him down so heavily earlier, but was he really better or was she seeing what a good, hot shower could do for someone emotionally beaten? She took a generous bite from her sticky bun as Donovan lowered into the chair beside her. He swiped a bit of vanilla icing from her lip and sucked it off the tip of his finger. His eyes twinkled.

Her heart skipped a beat with the desire he ignited in her. *Oh, yeah, he's back to normal. For now.*

****

Throughout the day, Donovan entertained Beth's snow fantasies by building a snowman with her that looked as if it had breasts thanks to Donovan's sculpting skills. When the snow started to fall heavily, they ventured back into the house for lunch and played a heated game of Uno. Beth enjoyed herself and fell more in love with Meredith and Lily the longer she was around them.

She lingered over pecan pie after dinner while talking to Meredith and Lily and found out Meredith had been a nurse for thirty years before retiring.

"I got a lot of practice with this one for a son," she said with a teasing smile aimed at Donovan. "He always needed bandaging up."

"I learned a lot, though," he said.

"You sure did. I couldn't let you run wild in the world, getting into God-knows-what kind of trouble, without me there to patch you up." She turned to Beth. "I taught him and Ryan a few basic survival skills, like how to make a splint out of whatever items he has on hand. He's really good, too. When he couldn't play sports anymore, I had hoped he'd go into the medical field, but he chose another dangerous profession." She shook her head at Donovan as if disapproving, but Beth could see the love behind the gesture.

Meredith asked Beth about her life in Florida, so Beth told her all about her job, her love of canoeing, and her few girlfriends from school and the studio. Donovan stuck around until the conversation turned to stories of his childhood. Even when the dessert plates were scraped clean with their forks, the three women continued to chat, share, and laugh. Beth enjoyed every second of it.

"Dear, I know you haven't known Donovan long," Lily said, "but the two of us are curious about your feelings toward him."

Beth felt her cheeks sear red. She glanced at the women who waited for her reply while she carefully weighed her answer. "I care about him a lot. He's an amazing man."

"Have you slept with him?" Lily blurted.

Beth's jaw dropped.

"Mom!" Meredith shook her head disapprovingly. "What she meant to ask is if you're in love."

Beth felt as though a cloud of butterflies were set loose inside her body. Her heart rate fluttered frantically at the mention of the L word. "It's a little early for that." She looked from Meredith to Lily. "Isn't it?"

Meredith shrugged. "You tell us."

Beth swallowed. "I…uh…" She knew she was in love with Donovan, but she hadn't admitted it aloud since she'd told him outside the police department. "I think I am. Yes."

The two women beamed at her, seemingly pleased with her response.

Beth took a sip of coffee, finding it cold and bitter. The look in Meredith's and Lily's eyes dashed the joy she felt a moment ago. The look said they hoped for marriage and babies. Lots and lots of babies. But Beth wasn't ready for diapers and formula yet. The thought of being a mother for the rest of her life terrified her. How could she raise a child to be a good person? What if she screwed up? Although she had excellent parents, she wasn't sure if she had the mothering gene.

"I'm going to go check on Donovan. I'm sure he's probably bored up there by himself." She took the stairs slowly, hoping the flush along her neck and face would dissipate by the time she reached the top landing. Now was not the time to tell Donovan his mom and grandma were already planning their wedding. Flowers and all.

The conversation she had with Meredith and Lily ran over an hour, so Beth expected to find Donovan snoozing on his bed, with his arms folded behind his head. What she didn't expect was to find him sitting at his desk, his shoulders hunched over his laptop. When she walked into the room, she thought he'd turn around, but whatever was on the screen captured his attention— a map of the United States. Upon closer inspection, she noticed red blimps pinpointing several cities from coast to coast.

"What's that?"

Donovan jumped. He was about to snap the lid shut, but Beth put her hand on it to stop him. "I didn't hear you come in," he said.

"I didn't think anyone could sneak up on you. You must really be distracted." She leaned closer to the screen. "What are you doing? What are those pinpoints indicating?"

"They're places linked to Buck," he explained, though Beth sensed his reluctance.

She arched a brow. "Linked?"

"Friends, family members, and places he's been to throughout his life."

This is extreme. Even for Donovan. "Why'd you do this?"

"I needed to know if Buck could be in Michigan."

She leaned forward. "There isn't a blimp on Michigan."

"No, but he has ties to Ohio, Indiana, and Illinois. If he came to Michigan, he would be near several people he knows and can go to for help."

Beth shook her head. "There are blimps all over the map. You can't tell where he is based off this."

"It's a damn start." Donovan slammed down the lid and shoved to his feet.

She caught his arm when he tried to storm out of the room. "Please don't obsess about this," she begged. His reaction and the fact he was searching for clues on Buck's whereabouts scared her. "There's no proof Buck is anywhere near Michigan, and we're here for Christmas. Let's enjoy it."

"How can I enjoy myself when my brother's killer is roaming free?" His voice was an angry hiss.

Beth sighed as she thought back on what she'd done when she lost her parents. "You live in the moment."

Donovan sneered. "Live."

She could almost hear his thoughts. *My brother's not living because of that piece-of-shit.* She racked her brain for something to say. "If you wanted to obsess about Buck, then why did you bring me here for Christmas? We could've stayed in Florida and spent Christmas in the police department, formulating plans with Burnett and Chief Cormac."

"Ryan and I came home every year for Christmas. I didn't want my mom and grandma to be alone."

Beth nodded as she reached out to touch his arm, hoping the contact would soothe him. "So, honor your brother's memory by having a good time with them. That's what he'd want, isn't it?"

The tension in Donovan's body slowly unraveled before her eyes. His shoulders lowered, his furrowed brow smoothed upon his forehead. "You're right," he sighed. "Ryan wouldn't want me trying to track Buck right now. Not here." He shoved his hands through his hair. "I'm sorry."

He hooked his arms around her waist, and she accepted the kiss he gave her. "You're forgiven."

****

As the days went by, Beth watched Donovan grow tenser. He tried to hide it from her, but she could read him. When he took her shopping so she could find Christmas presents for Meredith and Lily, he would look twice at every man with a slight resemblance to

Buck. Every time they'd turn down a new aisle, his shoulders would raise a couple of inches, and his hands would bunch into fists, as if preparing for an attack.

His behavior started to make her jumpy. She ended up grabbing the closest items at hand and marching Donovan to the registers at the front of the store. On their way back to the house, she thought about the gifts she'd chosen, hoping Meredith would like the picture frame and Lily would have a sense of humor about the dancing frog statue.

With presents waiting to go under a tree, Donovan took Beth to the town's local lot to pick out a Christmas tree. She'd grown up using artificial trees, always wishing they were real, so she was excited for this new adventure. She bundled herself up in a pink scarf, hat, and mittens and was out the door ahead of Donovan.

The Christmas tree lot went on for blocks. Cars were parked bumper to bumper and lined both sides of the road. Families and couples milled about, searching for the perfect tree to put up in their homes. Beth and Donovan were among them. The mingling scents of Blue Spruce, Douglas Fir, and all the other Christmas tree variations swirled luxuriously in Beth's nostrils, bringing an instantaneous smile to her face. Her boots crunched in the snow, and her breath came out in puffs like car exhaust as she trudged down each row.

"This place is gorgeous." She reached out to touch soft green bristles on a branch.

Donovan smiled. "This is the same lot I came to as a kid. It's owned by a local family who work here every Christmas."

"That must be nice." Beth took a deep breath. The air was frigid and froze her lungs, but it was magical all the same.

She examined every tree she passed and eliminated each one from the running for being too short, too bare, or too sappy. Donovan followed her, not saying much or offering his opinion. She could tell he was mentally somewhere else. At one point, he shoved her to the side, stalked past her, and hurried to the next row where he stood at the entrance, with his feet spread apart.

Beth joined him and looked down the empty pathway. "What are you looking at?"

"Nothing," he clipped, but how he said it made it clear he thought something, or someone, had been there.

She studied him, nerves knotting her stomach. She hated seeing him this way. *Ryan's murder is haunting him. If we don't find Buck soon, he's going to snap.*

To be safe, she took his hand and led him past several rows, back toward the heart of the lot. Halfway there, she came to a halt and faced a Douglas Fir. The tree stood about six feet tall. It was full-bodied and lush. The highest bough was the perfect length for a star, and all the other branches were big and sturdy.

This is it. This is the tree.

Out of the corner of her eye, she saw a figure step around a tree then disappear. She was so busy picturing lights, tinsel, and ornaments on the tree in front of her that she didn't think anything of it. Not until she finished daydreaming and noticed Donovan no longer stood by her side.

She peered left and right. "Donovan?"

A scream pierced the wintry air, and Beth knew it wasn't because a tree had fallen on top of someone. She could sense it was because of Donovan. She ripped off her scarf, tossed it onto the tree's branches, and took off running. Her heart raced two steps ahead of her. With the way Donovan had been acting lately, on edge even at home, she couldn't fathom what kind of trouble he was causing. She followed the sounds of a forming crowd and burst into a small clearing to see Donovan pinning a man to the ground. He was punching him with a glove-less fist.

A little girl stepped forward. She wore fuzzy white earmuffs and red pigtails. "Daddy!"

Beth's eyes widened. *Oh shit!*

She sprang forward, grabbed Donovan's arms, and asked the surrounding men for help. Two of them successfully managed to haul Donovan to his feet. With the two men holding him still, Beth moved in front of Donovan and put her hands on his chest. He was fighting against the men restraining him, trying to get free to continue his beating.

"Donovan!"

His thrashing continued.

"Donovan, listen to my voice. He's not Buck! Look at him again. He's a father."

Beth watched him refocus and look at the man with the bleeding nose. She could see understanding register in Donovan's eyes, followed quickly by regret.

"I could've sworn it was him," he whispered.

"I know." She put her hand on his arm. She knew he felt bad for what he'd done to this innocent man, but everyone else was regarding him as though he was a menace. "Just take a step back, please."

When he retreated, Beth approached the man Donovan attacked. His daughter hugged his hips and his wife wiped the blood from his nose with a stained tissue. "Excuse me?" Beth took one more step then stopped. She needed to fix this somehow but was afraid it was beyond fixing.

"I'm really sorry about what happened." The man's wife looked at her with disgust while he just looked wary. "I know what I say won't excuse his actions, or make up for them, but I thought you should know the reason behind them. It had nothing to do with you. Any of you."

She paused to take a breath and spoke slower. "A couple of months ago, he witnessed his brother's murder. The man who did it is still out there, and you look a lot like him. When he saw you—" She shook her head. "—he couldn't control his grief or anger. And I'm so sorry for that. You and your family suffered because of it. I don't have any right to ask, but in the spirit of the season and with our deepest apologies, would you consider not pressing charges?" She held her breath, knowing it would take a Christmas miracle for the man to agree.

He looked to his wife, who shrugged beneath her puffy winter coat. He pulled the tissue from his nose with a sigh. "I won't press charges."

"Thank you." Beth glanced behind her to Donovan. She waved her hand at him to let him know it was okay. He stepped forward with his hand outstretched.

"I'm so sorry for what I did," he said the moment he was in front of the small family.

After a slight hesitation, the man shook his hand. "Your wife told us about what happened to your brother."

Beth did a double-take at the title the man had given her. Her mouth peeled open to fix the error, but she closed it again. Now was not the time to pick at details.

Donovan glanced at her with a weak smile. "I wish I had control over myself. If I did, I would've been able to see you're not the man who—" His words died. He cleared his throat as he gathered his thoughts. "I'm just terribly sorry. I hope you can forgive me."

The man's gaze slid to his wife again. "I do, and we're sorry for your loss."

"Thank you." Donovan's head lowered, and Beth followed his line of sight to the little girl. Silent tears continued to stream down her pink cheeks. "I'm sorry I ruined your day," he added. "Please, let me pay for your tree."

After they paid for two Christmas trees and returned to the house, Beth escaped upstairs to Donovan's room. She didn't even assist Donovan with hauling the tree into the house.

She sat down on Donovan's bed and dropped her head in her hands. Her body was tense with the events of the day and not even her cozy surroundings could lessen them. After what transpired at the Christmas tree lot, she wondered if Donovan could have post-traumatic stress disorder. His aggression pointed toward that theory.

Worry swam in her head like a cloud of carbon monoxide. *What have I gotten myself into? Did I really think I could ease his pain? Police officers killed his brother. He may never recover from that. I wouldn't.*

What do I do? How can I help him?

Her head was still in her hands when Donovan entered the room and knelt in front of her. "I'm sorry, Beth." He put his hands on her knees. "I know you looked forward to having a nice Christmas here and I'm ruining it for you."

She lifted her head. Her anxiety, which had grown heavier since they arrived in Michigan, was now the size of a boulder, threatening to break her back. "I want you to have a nice Christmas, too, Donovan." She dropped her hands in her lap and peered at him in exasperation. "Buck is not in Michigan. And even if he was, he wouldn't be at a Christmas tree lot or in the airport. For all we know, he could be in Alaska. You need to relax. Be *here* with me, and when we get back home, you can bug the shit out of Burnett if you want, but please let it go for now."

Donovan took her hands. "I'll do my best. I swear. But if I cross the line again—"

"I'll kick your ass back over it." She'd never want to break his heart, but she could sure as hell kick his ass if necessary.

****

For the rest of the trip, Donovan kept his promise and Beth's worries over him evaporated. Christmas morning, she presented Meredith and Lily with their gifts. Lily got a real kick out of the dancing frog, and Meredith urged Beth to pose with Donovan in front of the Christmas tree for a picture to go in the frame.

When it was her turn, Beth was surprised to open her gift from Meredith—a beautiful red journal with gold-tipped pages.

Meredith smiled. "Donovan told me your other journal suffered damage because of the storm."

Beth glanced at Donovan. From his nod, she knew he didn't tell his mom exactly what had happened to her journal, that one just like it played a role in his brother's death. She flattened her hand on the smooth cover. "I love it. Thank you."

Lily's gift to Beth was a gold fountain pen in a mahogany case. With her gifts in hand, Beth felt as if she had a family again, and that feeling made her heart lighter than previous Christmas mornings when it usually felt like lead.

"Time for you to open my gift." Donovan presented a box with the name of a well-known jeweler scrawled on the lid.

Beth swallowed hard. The last time she opened a jewelry box, it was an engagement ring. That engagement had burned up in flames when she found out her fiancé was keeping his manhood warm inside another woman. But that's not why she was suddenly light-headed. She was shocked Donovan had gone into a jewelry store, and she was nervous to see what he picked out and what it could mean.

She lifted the lid, and her nerves fizzled like stale soda. Lying on the inside, on top of a strip of thick cotton, lay a silver charm bracelet with a single charm, an odd spiral with two tails, one going to the left and the other going to the right.

Being a Floridian, she knew what it symbolized. "It's a hurricane."

Donovan nodded. "A hurricane is significant to us. It's how we met."

She beamed up at him, her heart swelling. "It's perfect."

Taking the bracelet from her, he hooked it around her wrist and then kissed her hand.

"Now it's your turn." She picked up the present with snowflake wrapping paper from underneath the tree. The package had taken up so much space in her suitcase that she ended up having to evict a pair of boots so it would fit.

"I feel silly about my gift now," she admitted, shifting from side to side as he opened it, her fingers twiddling with the expensive charm dangling from her wrist.

Donovan pulled out a pair of black and neon green boxing gloves. "In case you ever want to go one on one with me," she said.

He slipped his hand into one of the gloves and winked at her. "You know I will."

Heat rushed through her, because she knew just how their one-on-one sessions would end. "I was hoping you would."

****

Dinner was a marvelous feast of roasted Christmas goose, green bean casserole with crisp onion curls on top, real mashed potatoes, fresh cranberry sauce, and chocolate fruit cake for dessert. With their bellies full, they listened to Christmas carols and played a game of Scrabble. The Goldwyns had their own rule that whoever put a word relating to Christmas on the board would earn double the amount of points. Donovan won by a landslide, and Beth was positive he cheated. She went to bed happy, happier than she had been on a Christmas night in many years.

She was sad to leave Michigan two days later, but Florida waited for their return.

Chapter Twelve

New Year's Day, Donovan woke with Beth in his bed next to him. He liked seeing her there with her hair mussed, her lips plump with sleep, her face without makeup, and her body curled beneath the gray comforter. He wouldn't tell her, wouldn't risk it, but he wanted to always wake up to her gentle breathing.

He was going to watch her sleep for a few minutes before sneaking out of bed to start the coffee when his landline shrilled, shattering the morning quiet. Beth's eyelids popped open, and she let out an unhappy groan.

"Stay in bed." He kissed her shoulder. "I'll get it."

He hurried into the kitchen and snatched up the phone on the third ring. "Goldwyn."

"Hey, Goldwyn, it's Burnett. Welcome home."

"Thanks. What can I do for you?" He switched on the coffee maker.

"I need you and Beth to come to the station."

Donovan's spine snapped straight. "Why? What's happening?"

Burnett sighed on the other end. "It's better to talk about this in person. When can you be here?"

"One hour."

"See you then."

Donovan cut the connection and set the phone down. "Shit." Whatever Burnett wanted to talk about either had to do with the Internal Affairs investigation into the department or with their search to find Buck. The fact Burnett wouldn't say over the phone wasn't good.

"Who was it?"

Donovan followed Beth's voice to the entrance of the living room. Wearing nothing more than boy shorts and a spaghetti strap shirt, she was breathtaking. "Burnett. He wants us to come into the station."

She frowned. "What for?"

"No idea." He turned to the coffee maker and watched the dark liquid drip into the pot. Bracing his hands on the countertop, he dropped his head. Not being in control of every detail, not knowing all the information the second something happened, and not being able to make the decisions had made the past two months unbearable. At times, he felt like lighting a fire under everyone's asses to get them to work faster, to produce the results he desired. Helplessness weighed heavily on him. He found himself dreaming of avenging his brother during the dark of the night and in the silence of morning.

Beth walked up behind him and wrapped her arms around his middle. Her strength seeped from her pores and into his body. Her breath warmed his back. "It's going to be okay."

Donovan shook his head. "How do you know?"

"That was the same thing I thought when I was sitting by myself in the police department after you told me everything would be okay, and you were taken into the interrogation room. I trusted you, and it was okay." Donovan faced her. "So now you have to trust me."

****

At the police department, Burnett ushered them

into a room with two other men. One was a detective named Thorn, who ran sting operations, and the other was Chief Cormac. Donovan knew them both.

"What is this?" Donovan demanded.

"Have a seat," Burnett instructed.

"I'll stand." Burnett glanced at the other two men, trying Donovan's patience. "Will you get on with it," he snapped.

Chief Cormac crossed his arms. "As you know, IA has been investigating the department, hoping to weed out any officers who might be involved in Officer Viktor Chuman's and Officer David Buckland's narcotics operation."

"Yeah. And?" Donovan was not in the mood for guessing games.

"And I've fired five of my men. IA uncovered a rumor that their operation spread to other houses. We've found seven other officers who worked with them."

Beth gasped. "Seven?"

"They were also working with known drug dealers." This came from Detective Thorn.

"We've been keeping close tabs on them, staking out their places, following them, and we think one of them is in contact with David Buckland. The problem is we can't put a cop undercover to get any information out of him because he'll be able to smell a cop through his door."

"I'll do it," Donovan offered without a thought.

Detective Thorn shook his head. "We can't use you, either. He might know all about you, and we can't risk that." He paused. "We need a civilian. Someone he won't expect to be working with us." His gaze strayed to Donovan's left. Donovan looked at Beth. It took a nanosecond for him to understand Thorn's intentions.

His head spun around, pinning Thorn with an angry glare. "No!"

"Donovan, it's the only way to find out where Buckland is hiding."

"Then find another civilian."

"We can't take a chance with another civilian who doesn't understand the situation, and we don't want to tell anyone beyond this room about the investigation. So far, we've kept this under wraps, but if we bring in a civilian or investigator who's not involved, we could lose the advantages we have as well as any hope of finding Buckland."

Donovan clenched his hands into fists. He couldn't let Buck get away, but he wouldn't allow Beth to be used as bait.

"You're sure there's no other way to find Buck?" This came from Beth.

"Positive," Thorn said and addressed Donovan again. "I've kept my ear to the ground, and this is the first time I've gotten a lead on Buckland since he disappeared. If we don't do this now, you could kiss your justice goodbye.

"Beth will have a wire," he continued. "We'll hear everything that goes on and know if something happens. She won't be alone. We'll be right down the street, seconds away from her."

"Donovan." Beth drew his attention. "Let me do this for you," she begged. "Remember when we were trapped in the department, and I said I wish I could do more? Well, this is my more. Please let me do what I can."

"You're asking to go undercover, Beth. Undercover is another word for danger."

"I know that. I've been in a lot of danger before and made it out just fine. I'm strong, I'm smart, and I teach self-defense. I want Buck caught, too, and if that means I have to do something to help, then I'll do my part."

Donovan turned away as he considered what she was asking to do. He'd been a murder suspect when she helped him retrieve evidence to prove his innocence. But how could he let her walk into a dangerous situation on her own? He gazed back at her and saw the fierce determination in her eyes.

I don't have a choice.

"Fine," he hissed.

Beth let out an audible breath. With her shoulders squared, she faced the three other men in the room. "What do I have to do?"

Chapter Thirteen

Beth sat in the back seat of an unmarked police car. Detective Thorn sat in the driver's seat, with his body turned as he addressed her, and Donovan sat beside her; his body as tense as a granite statue. She had spent a considerable amount of time on her appearance; she was supposed to look like a crack addict going through withdrawal. So, she smeared a bit of red lipstick around her eyes and dusted brown eye shadow over her eyelids. Her lips were pale, too, thanks to the concealer she dabbed over them. She wore jeans with holes at the knees, dirty sneakers, and a ripped hoodie.

"Now remember, Beth," Thorn said. "The objective is to find out where Buckland is hiding. Don't worry about getting him to sell to you."

She nodded. "Piece of cake."

"We need a safe word. Can you think of one you'll be comfortable with?"

She mulled it over a moment. "How about green? They wouldn't suspect it as a safe word because money and weed are referred to as green."

Thorn nodded. "That's good. When you get out of the car, go that way." He pointed behind her. "Head around the corner onto Manson Street. The house you want to go to is the third one on your right with the pimped-out Cadillac out front. And the man you want to talk to is black, six-foot-two, shaved head, beard, with a snake head tattooed on his forearm. He goes by the name Viper."

She nodded once. "Got it."

"Whenever you're ready."

Beth unbuckled her seat belt, bent over so her hair fell to the floor of the car, and shook her fingers through the roots. She flipped her hair back and was satisfied it looked knotty enough for someone who may not own a comb. From Donovan's hand, she stole his bottle of water, unscrewed the cap, and poured a small stream into her cupped fingers. She patted the water across her forehead.

"How do I look?" she asked Thorn.

"Like a sweaty crack whore."

"Whore isn't what I was going for, but I'll take it."

Donovan had been silent the whole time. His eyes probed hers. "Are you sure about this?"

"She's as ready as she's ever going to be," Thorn said from the front seat.

Donovan's jaw tightened. "I wasn't talking to you."

Beth took his hand. "I'm going to be fine."

He picked up her hand and pressed his lips to her knuckles. "Be careful."

"I will." Deep down, Beth knew she could be as cautious as a mouse tiptoeing through a house crawling with cats, and it wouldn't matter, because it was still dangerous. She had no control over the drug dealers who would be in that house. Nor did she have any idea what they would or wouldn't do to her once she stepped over the threshold into their territory.

She pulled her shoulders back, preparing herself. "I'll get in and out as fast as I can."

Thorn nodded, but in the glow of the overhead light, concern shimmered briefly over his cucumber-green eyes. "You've got this."

She smiled and then snatched the can of Mountain Dew he had cracked open and set in the center consol. "Thanks!" She hopped out of the car and began to walk down the sidewalk. The scrape of the bottom of her sneakers against the concrete filled the air. No other noise met her ears—no barking dogs, no playing children, no cars—nothing but her breathing and the beat of her shoes. She passed beneath a flickering streetlamp. The halo of light it created didn't help to lessen the darkness of the night; it punctuated the gloom.

As she moved farther from the car, she could feel their eyes on her, like Superman's laser gaze on her back. "Stop staring at me," she hissed with her chin dipped toward the wire hidden under her hoodie. "You're both making me nervous."

She was thankful when she had to turn the corner, but the moment she did, her feet skidded to a stop. Rolled out before her was a street without a single streetlight. It looked as though the Grim Reaper had cast his cloak over it, shrouding the entire street and every house in pitch-blackness.

Wheeling in her courage, she continued on her way. To play the part of a withdrawing junkie, she dragged her feet and slumped her shoulders. She was relieved when she came upon the third house on the right, but moving up the driveway—packed bumper-to-bumper with cars—brought a new anxiety. In a matter of seconds, she'd be in front a criminal known as Viper. She pulled open the screen door and stepped inside the dark porch. The screen door banged shut behind her, trapping her.

Swallowing hard, she slapped at the door, trying to sound desperate. The light above her head snapped on, and the door swung open, releasing a cloud of marijuana smoke that punched her in the face. She blinked through the haze. A man with nutmeg skin and eyes the color of vanilla beans scrutinized her with a sneer as moths looped around her head.

"Whatcha want?"

Beth lifted her free hand to the top of her head and half scratched, half pulled her tangled hair. "I'm here to see Viper."

The man peered over his shoulder. "Hey, Viper. There's a tweaked-out white girl here to see you."

"Let her in," came a voice from deep inside the house.

He held the door open for her, and she stepped through. The stench of burning marijuana assaulted her, plugging her nostrils. A thick cloud of it hung overhead. She chewed on her lip while her left arm jerked at her side, and her fingers fiddled so fast the muscles in her forearm ached. Bodies jammed the living room. Far more than she had expected to see, and they were all men. Several of them were crammed on the couch playing a video game and shouting at each other. A few of them laughed when they saw her, but she didn't care. She had to portray a druggie; she didn't give a damn if she looked pathetic as long as she was convincing.

On a chestnut coffee table, with marijuana crumbles sprinkling the surface, were two bongs, about a dozen beer bottles, and three opened bags of chips. A scale occupied one corner with a baggie of green sitting on top. Adding more to the bag was a man wearing a black wife beater and diamond studs in his ears the size of Skittles.

Viper.

His stare swept over her. "I've never seen you before."

Beth gave a jittery shrug. "That's 'cuz I bought what I wanted through Buck."

Viper eyed her. "And how do you know me?"

She pursed her lips and gave him a don't-be-fucking-stupid look. "Everyone in this city who does any kind of drug knows ya."

Viper cracked a smile, showing a row of blinding white teeth. One of his canines gleamed gold. "And how'd you know where to find me?"

Beth lifted the heel of her right foot and let her leg dance in place. "Buck told me." Viper cocked his head at her. She shrugged and continued her story. "Before Sabrina hit, Buck gave me enough crack to last the storm, but now I need more. He always said if I couldn't get a hold of him to come to you."

Viper nodded slowly, appearing to measure her. "Take a seat." He indicated the leather chair across from him.

Her heart shuddered with fear. *Oh shit. I didn't think I'd be sitting with him chatting about drugs over tea and cookies.*

She moved to the chair, stepping clumsily over the outstretched legs of Viper's high friends, and dropped into the chair. *Hard.* Viper leaned back, uncovering a dollar sign belt buckle speckled with diamonds, and that was how she noticed the silver gun resting in his lap. Ice laced her spine. Her gaze scanned the other men in the room while she scratched her neck, hiding her nerves with the jittery movements of an addict in desperate need of a hit.

Her heart paused for several beats when she realized they were all carrying. They either had a gun in their lap or lying next to them. She gripped the can in her hand and hoped she adequately hid her fear. After all, a drug addict would be used to this scene, but she was terrified. Criminals surrounded her and they were all armed.

Viper smirked, sending chills down Beth's spine. "So, what can I do for you?"

She took a swig from the Mountain Dew, letting her hand shake. "I haven't been able to get a hold of Buck, and I ran out a long time ago. I need a fix."

"I don't sell crack."

She glared at him. "I know that! I ain't stupid. I need fucking something to take the edge off, and I have twenty bucks."

Viper threw back his head and laughed. His gaze hardened like streams of bullets. "If all you've got is a twenty, get your ass outta here."

Panic rose inside her like bile. *I can't leave yet! I need to get answers, and I won't have another chance. I have to make this sale to get him to trust me. Otherwise, I'm screwed.* She thought about the gun but kept her gaze from it. *And I won't be walking out of here.*

She gave him a ballsy glare. Both of her legs bounced a mile a minute. "Twenty dollas is better than no twenty dollas. And if I can't get in contact with Buck, I'll be back with larger bills. Or if you can get me some crack, you'll get more money from me than any of your—" She glanced at the men lounging on the leather couch beside her and rolled her eyes. "Buddies. Trust me." She pulled out a crinkled twenty-dollar bill from her pocket. "What do ya say? Come on."

With a shake of his head, Viper took her money, reached to the side table next to his chair, and pulled open a drawer. Inside she glimpsed bundles of packaged marijuana and boxes of ammunition.

She flinched when Viper threw two tiny bags at her. She greedily snatched them up. "Thanks." She shoved to her feet, adding a sway for affect.

"What's your hurry?" Viper's stare narrowed on her. "You can smoke that here."

Her palms went damp with fear. *Does he know I'm lying? Did I do something to blow my cover?*

"This is going to have to last me until I can come back."

"Then take a drag on one of my bongs."

Her chest constricted. *He knows!* She thought she would throw up, spewing Mountain Dew and Doritos all over herself.

"If I start on that…" She pointed at a bong resembling Darth Vader's head. "I'm not going to stop until I pass out. No offense, but this ain't the kinda place I'd wanna be unconscious." She pointedly flicked her eyes at his friends.

Viper's lips spread into a wicked sneer, causing her stomach to roll. She had the sickening feeling he wasn't above taking advantage of a woman passed out in his crib. "Anyway, do ya know where Buck is?"

Viper stood slowly, taking his gun in his hand. Her breath caught painfully in her chest. *This is it. He's going to pop a bullet in my head.*

Separated by the coffee table, he pinned Beth in place with his dark glare. "Why the hell you wanna know?"

"Because he's my dealer. Dealers are more important than blood."

Viper eyed her a moment before replying. "Last I heard he was in San Fran."

Beth made a sound of annoyance. "Course he'd go there. Cali is full of celebs looking for drugs." She held up the bags. "Well, thanks for this." She turned to leave but came to a stop when Viper's hand clamped her forearm. He whipped her around, and she stopped breathing when he came within inches of her face.

"What's your name?" His question was innocent enough, but his tone made it sound like, "Who the hell are you, bitch?"

"Felicia. If you talk to Buck, tell him to call me."

Viper mulled over her answer, and he must've felt she told the truth because he released her arm. She turned her back on him with a stiff spine as she braced for a bullet to plunge between her vertebrae. She made it to the door and escaped out into the night. Once she was moving down the driveway, she inhaled the fresh air and expelled the smoke-tinged air from her lungs. She wasn't aware someone had snuck out after her until she heard him speak.

"Hey, girl, I can give you the money back you spent on those two dime bags if you show me a good time."

"Thanks, but no thanks," she said without slowing or even glancing over her shoulder. Passing the last car, she made it to the foot of the driveway when the man stalking her suddenly jumped in front of her. She recognized him as the man who'd opened the door.

"That's too bad. I guess I'll just take what I want." His hand lashed out and his fingers clutched her between her legs.

She dropped the can of Mountain Dew, grabbed his wrist, and twisted his arm until he doubled over in front of her. Then she lifted her foot and rammed her knee into his face with as much force as she could muster. She heard a sickening crunch of bone before he fell backward onto the driveway. A fraction of a second before she took off running, she saw blood gushing from his nose. Her battered sneakers pounded the concrete even as her knee ached from the contact. Her hands were in white-knuckled fists, her jaw tight.

"You broke my nose, you fucking bitch!"

Beth could hear his pissed-off voice shouting after her as she pushed herself to go faster, running in a weaving pattern along the sidewalk in case he had a gun. Her gaze locked onto the dim stop sign in the distance.

"Green, green, green," she chanted, hoping Thorn could hear her through her ragged breathing and the beat of her sneakers. "Where are you, guys? Hurry up. Come get me!"

Squealing tires pierced the air, and the black car skidded to a stop at the corner of the street. Beth didn't slow when the back door opened but leapt inside and slammed the door shut behind her. Thorn punched the gas pedal, and the car shot down the street. Leaning her head against the seat, she focused on slowing her heart rate. She vaguely heard Donovan's worried voice.

"Are you okay? Beth, are you okay? Damn it, Beth, talk to me!"

"I'm fine." She kept her eyes closed. After she managed to catch her breath, she realized she clutched something in her left hand. She uncurled her fingers to find the bags. She sat forward and held out her hand to Thorn. "Here." He took the dime bags and tossed them onto the passenger seat.

"You were brilliant, Beth. You did as good as a trained detective. Better even."

She nodded and mumbled thanks, but she didn't say anything else during the drive to Donovan's apartment.

In the parking lot, Thorn faced them. "Come into the station tomorrow so we can talk about what's going to happen next."

"Sure," Donovan said. "We'll be there."

Beth got out of the car without a goodbye and hurried up the stairs to Donovan's apartment. She let herself in and went straight into the bathroom. In the fluorescent light, miles from Viper's house, she let herself unravel. Her body shook as she plunged from her adrenaline rush.

"Beth?" Donovan knocked softly, and since she hadn't bothered to lock it, he let himself in. "Talk to me, baby."

"I was in a house full of criminals." She lifted her arms and shook them as if she were a child who thought cooties covered her. "And they all had guns. They had guns out in the open, in their laps, next to them, on every side table. Viper was standing practically nose to nose with me with his gun in his fucking hand. I expected him to shoot out my brains." Tears sprouted in her eyes, distorting Donovan's face.

"I was terrified. I thought...I thought I was..." She

123

was about to say she had thought she was dead when Donovan yanked her to his body and muted her shaking with his arms. She clung to him, buried her face in his shoulder, and surrendered to the emotions pouring from her body. It was exactly what she needed.

****

Beth woke not having opened her eyes once during the night, much to her amazement, especially with what she had gone through. After a quick shower, downing a cup of coffee and half a bagel smothered with peanut butter, she accompanied Donovan to the station to meet Thorn, Burnett, and Chief Cormac. The five of them crowded into a back room for privacy.

Thorn was the first to speak. "Thanks to Beth, we know Buckland is in California." He exchanged glances with Burnett and Chief Cormac. "Unfortunately, there's nothing else we can do at this point."

Beth felt Donovan bristle. "You've got to be kidding me," he exploded.

She laid her hand on his arm and addressed Chief Cormac. "What *can* you do?"

"I can notify the authorities in California and ask them to put their officers on alert in San Francisco, but we can't go at this as aggressively as we would like to if he were still in Florida."

Donovan radiated waves of anger beside her, and Beth wished she could do more. She hated seeing him so defeated, because she knew how important it was for him to see Buck punished for murdering his brother. She feared Donovan wouldn't get that chance.

"He must've crossed over into Georgia after Hurricane Sabrina left and hopped onto the first flight to California," Beth said.

Thorn nodded. "We think so."

"What about Viper?" Beth asked. "He had pounds of marijuana ready for distribution, and let's not forget all the weapons that were in plain sight. You guys know where he lives, so why haven't you busted him yet?"

Thorn cracked a smile. "Right after I dropped the two of you off, I made a call. SWAT stormed Viper's house. Every single person who was inside is now behind bars. They'll probably get off with a slap on the wrist, but Viper won't. He'll get the book thrown at him. I can assure you of that."

"Well, that's something," she said with a glance to Donovan.

"Yeah. We got a drug dealer while a murderer is still walking free. Let's fucking celebrate." Donovan spun on his heel and left with a slam of the door.

Beth closed her eyes. How would Donovan deal with his anger? How would he deal with his disappointment if they never found Buck?

"It's okay, Beth." She opened her eyes to look at Burnett. This was the first time he had spoken since they'd entered the room. "He's going to be mad for a while. The best thing to do is let him stew."

"I know. And I'm happy I, at least, was able to help you bust Viper. I do count that as something good."

"It's more than good," Thorn acknowledged. "See you later."

"Sure. Bye, guys." She went after Donovan, wanting nothing more than to be there for him in whatever way he allowed.

For days, he was quiet, angry, withdrawn. She gave him space, knowing he needed to be alone to think. A week later, she padded out of the bedroom to find him sitting at the dining room table tapping away on his laptop.

This is different.

"What are you doing?"

He didn't even look up when he answered. "Booking a flight to San Francisco."

Her head whipped around. "Excuse me?" Donovan lifted a brow at her sharp tone. She didn't flinch. "Why are you booking a flight to San Fran?"

His gaze met hers, and his irises were so cold she felt frostbitten. "Because I know where Buck is."

"Meaning?"

He smiled sinisterly. "Meaning I know what hotel he sleeps in at night."

Beth blinked. "How the hell do you know that?"

"I have connections."

She sighed. "Fine. Buy me a ticket, too. I'll pay you back."

"What?"

She crossed her arms when she heard the surprise in his voice. *He can't really think I'd let him go alone.*

"I've said it from the beginning we're in this together. Why can't you get that through your head? Let me make it clear for you." She advanced toward him. "You're not boarding a plane unless I'm right there beside you." She eyed him, daring him to say no.

Smirking, Donovan dropped his fingers onto the laptop. Then he gazed up at her. His eyes shimmered mysteriously. "We have a flight to San Fran tomorrow morning at eight."

Beth nodded. "Good. I'm going to make pancakes."

Chapter Fourteen

At the Orlando International Airport, a security guard selected Beth from the line waiting to go through the metal detector for a random search. As she followed the guard to the side, she cast a glare at Donovan.

He smiled back and shrugged. When she returned, he said, "How was it?"

"Bite me."

He leaned in to whisper in her ear. "Later."

On the plane, Beth eventually laid her head on his shoulder and fell asleep during the over five-hour flight. He woke her up when the pilot announced they were approaching San Francisco International Airport. The landing was smooth despite the jerk from the initial touchdown. The airport—all glass and metal—wasn't as packed as the Orlando airport. Or it didn't appear to be to Donovan's eye. He led the way, thankful they didn't have to go to baggage claim.

"Where are we going?" Beth asked.

"To BART."

"Who's Bart?" Grinning, she poked him in the ribs with her finger. "Your accomplice?"

"No. And technically, that would be you."

"Damn." She snapped her fingers. "That's right. So, who is Bart? He sounds like an ex-military sniper."

That thought made him smile. He didn't tell her any differently because he wanted to see her reaction when she found out for herself. "You'll see."

They entered an area resembling a subway station where a white bullet train with four blue stripes waited. Donovan looked at her. "Beth, meet BART, Bay Area Rapid Transit."

Her stare scanned the long, sleek machine. She threw her head back in laughter. "BART is a train?" Then her eyes doubled. "I have to get on that thing?"

He snatched her hand and pulled her aboard. "You'll be fine," he insisted.

They found seats and BART shot forward. They got off at Union Square, the heart of San Francisco. Walking along the two-and-a-half-acre square, they saw all the popular department stores and posh hotels. Even though it was January, people sat in the streaming sunlight, bundled in jackets, and children chased flocks of pigeons and squealed in delight when the birds launched into the air. Their wings created a loud ruckus like feathered helicopter blades.

Many people strolled along, several of them teetering from side to side to balance the weight of the shopping bags they carried. A few stood in front of windows, admiring the displays. A couple walked hand in hand into Tiffany & Co. Probably to pick out wedding rings, Donovan mused. His gaze sank to Beth's left hand. He tried to picture a diamond ring sparkling on her finger and could envision it clearly—a small, round diamond with a simple silver band.

He shook his head. *You're thinking crazy, Goldwyn. It's too soon to even think about marriage.*

Taking Beth's elbow, he steered her around the sleeping form of a homeless person.

They paused in the center of the square to admire

the Victory Statue, a green-tinged woman thrusting her trident toward the sky.

"She looks so beautiful and fierce," Beth murmured in awe.

"Not as fierce as you taking on a hurricane."

Or a man suspected of murder. He shook his head to dispel that thought.

"Come on, we should check in." He led her to a hotel not far from the square.

"Here?" Beth said. "Buck is staying here? You've got to be kidding me! How can he afford this?"

Donovan answered with three words. "He sold narcotics."

"Ah. But why would he stay in a place as nice as this?"

"Because everyone would expect him to be hiding out in crappy motels and dirty squats with druggies. He's smart." His hands balled into fists. "And he's a killer."

"Smart enough to check-in under his name?"

"He didn't check-in under his real name."

Beth looked at him sharply. "Then how do you know he's here?" He smirked. She crossed her arms in response. "Level with me, Donovan, or are we not partners?"

He nodded once. "We are...my brother had found out a lot about Chewy and Buck, including the aliases they used when they sold narcotics. I had a hacker I know search for Buck's aliases in San Fran and *ding-ding-ding*." He waved a hand at the hotel in front of them. "We have a winner. He's supposed to be staying in room 5F."

"How do you know we're not going to bust down

some poor dude's door who is unfortunate enough to have the same name as one of Buck's aliases?"

"I don't. And, frankly, I don't give a damn."

The hotel's lobby had a small chandelier dripping like rain from the ceiling, and a fountain that shot a continuous string of water toward the strung glass. Tile—a shade of blue that royalty made famous—was waxed to a ridiculous gleam so Donovan could see his distorted reflection on the surface.

A doorman stood inside the entrance. He wore a tuxedo complete with white gloves and black top hat. At the front desk, which was bone-white, stood a spit-shined woman covered in pearls like Aphrodite. Beth pulled back her shoulders in her plain black T-shirt and jacket when they stopped in front of the label-clad, Chanel No.5 one-too-many-squirts, front desk manager.

He looked down at Beth, admiring her sleek brown hair, sun-kissed skin, and face made up with the smallest amount of cosmetics. *Baby, you look more gorgeous in your sweatpants.*

"Good morning." The woman flashed too-white teeth at them. "Are you checking in?"

"Yes, ma'am. Under the name Kennedy."

Her acrylic nails ticked on a white keyboard. "Wonderful, you have our Turquoise Room. How would you like to pay for that?" Donovan handed her a card. "Perfect." She tapped his information into their database. Her enthusiasm was too much for Donovan after a five-hour flight.

When she passed the card back to him, he expected to see residue on the plastic from the spray tan that was no doubt oozing from her pours. He slipped it back into his wallet. "We're here meeting our friend Jay

Ferguson. He's supposed to be here by now. Could you let us know if he's in?"

The woman blinked her mascara-stiffened lashes at him. "Sure." A few more taps on the keyboard. "Oh, yes. I remember Mr. Ferguson. He checked in two days ago, but I saw him leave an hour ago, and he hasn't returned."

Donovan read her name from the tag clipped to her designer jacket. "Thanks, Paula."

"Here's your key." She held it out to him. "Are you from out of state?"

"Yes, we are."

"Ah, you missed our quake this morning."

Beth shifted beside him. "Quake?"

Paula nodded. Her blonde hair didn't move an inch. "We had a three-point-six quake at daybreak. Hopefully, there won't be any aftershocks while you're here." She signaled to the waiting bellhop. "Enjoy your stay."

A short elevator ride took them to the floor with their hotel room, a decent-sized space with a large bed draped in turquoise. Yellow, gray, and turquoise striped wallpaper covered the walls, and sheer drapes framed the window. Separated from the bedroom was a kitchen complete with a sink, refrigerator, and a row of cabinets. A mahogany table was positioned to the side with a crystal vase of white lilies.

Beth sprang into the air and landed back-first in the middle of the bed. With a yawn she said, "I need a nap."

"Haven't you heard hotel beds are filthy? Bed bugs, semen, hair?"

She lifted her hand off the mattress and flipped him

off. Chuckling, he stretched out beside her. She snuggled against him and nestled her head in the crook of his shoulder. A few minutes later, her breathing was soft and deep.

He loved how she could fall asleep in his arms anywhere, even in a cramped bathtub during a hurricane with a body screaming from bruises and cuts. He followed Beth into dreamland—fully clothed, with shoes still on his feet.

They slept for two hours, refueled with coffee, and left the hotel to sightsee after they asked the front desk manager if their pal had come back. He hadn't. For a late lunch, they ordered fish tacos from a food truck and enjoyed their grub and the cold weather on a picnic table beneath a palm tree. Stomachs satisfied, taste buds dancing with the flavors of fresh fish, lime, and avocado, they hopped into a cab and braved the California freeways notorious for their dangerous speeds.

Beth had one hand on the seat in front of her and the other on the door as she shouted at the driver. "Whoa, are you crazy? What the hell is wrong with you? You're going to get us killed!"

"Lady, this is California," he told her.

"Yeah? And this is my life. Would you like me to introduce you to it?" She faced Donovan. "I felt safer in your monster truck."

While traveling the one-point-seven miles over the Golden Gate Bridge, Beth pointed out it wasn't so much golden as orange. When they arrived at Golden Gate Park, they strolled hand in hand through the Japanese Tea Garden. Among exquisitely groomed Bonsai trees, they climbed over a bridge and navigated from smooth stepping-stones in ponds populated with plump Koi fish.

While staring at a statue of Buddha, Beth leaned her head against Donovan's shoulder. "This place is amazing," she breathed. "Aside from the crazy cab drivers, so far, San Francisco is awesome. Would you ever want to move here?"

Donovan shifted so she had to lift her head. "Move?"

She shrugged. "It was a silly thought. I didn't mean anything by it." She turned away from Buddha and continued to walk.

Is she getting the same bizarre thoughts I am? He recalled imaging an engagement ring on her hand and how real it had seemed, as if he could've reached over and pulled it off her finger. *Please, God, just don't let her think about babies.* Despite the nutty vision of a ring, he was nowhere near picking out baby names. *Yet.*

They drank a cup of tea in the pavilion before heading back to the hotel for quick showers.

"Do you have something nice in your duffel bag?" Donovan asked Beth when she stepped out of the bathroom in a robe.

"Describe nice."

"Something you can wear out to dinner."

She lowered onto the bed. Beads of water skimmed down her satiny legs. "I wasn't aware I was supposed to pack elegant clothes. Most of the things I brought are for ass kicking. Of course, I did bring a couple of just-in-case-outfits."

Intrigued, Donovan tilted his head. "Just-in-case-outfits?"

She nodded slowly. "Yeah. You know..." She

paused, with her gaze on him. "A leather skirt. A string bikini. Sexy lingerie."

He inhaled sharply between his teeth and took a step toward her as his imagination worked double-time. "We can always skip dinner and go straight to the lingerie."

"Oh no." Beth popped to her feet and scrambled to the other side of the bed. The robe parted to reveal her bare legs, almost giving him a full view of her goodies. "You can't take back a nice dinner. The only thing that's going to bring out that lingerie now is romance."

"That's okay," he said. "I don't mind a little romance." He took out his wallet and held up his debit card. "Here. Get dressed and go to one of the department stores in the square while I take a shower." He gave her his code.

She held up her hands, not accepting the card. "Whoa. I can't take that."

"I'm letting you. I know you're not the type of person to steal my money."

"You know that already, do you?"

"I'm a good read of people." He pushed his card at her. "I trust you, and I want to buy you something beautiful."

She bit her bottom lip, hesitantly taking the card. Her inner debate reflected in her brown irises. "You're making me feel like Julia Roberts in *Pretty Woman*."

"Isn't that a good thing?"

"I don't know. She was a hooker."

Beth was gone for forty-five minutes. When she returned, she had two bags in her hand. She plopped into a chair with a satisfied sigh. Donovan smiled. "Enjoy yourself?"

"Definitely. I don't normally go gaga over shopping, but seeing all the clothes in those boutiques was amazing. Don't worry about the bill, though. I felt odd with your card, so I found a dress, coat, and pair of shoes on sale." She hugged her bags and tilted her gaze up to him. "I think you'll like the dress."

"Do you need my help putting it on?"

She shook her head. "With your help, I'd never get it on."

"Exactly." He wanted her naked. The sooner the better.

Beth got to her feet. "I'm putting my new dress on, and you're not going to take it off."

He cocked a brow. *Watch me.*

"Until after dinner," she added before escaping into the bathroom.

While Beth got ready, doing all those ritualistic things women do, Donovan put on smoke-gray dress pants, buttoned up a white shirt, and went back to pacing. He was about to knock on the bathroom door and ask what was taking her so long when the door opened. His lungs forgot how to draw in oxygen, his jaw went slack, and he felt stirring in his pants.

She stood there, framed by the doorway, wearing a dark purple dress that hugged her curves. An interesting diagonal hemline rose to mid-thigh on one side and fell below her knee on the other. One sleeve came to her elbow, but the other was missing entirely, revealing a bare shoulder. On her feet, she wore gray suede heels that accentuated the delicious length of her legs. Her brunette hair was in an artistic knot at the top of her head, and her lips were a deep raisin.

"Stunning." It was the only word he could dig out

of his awestruck brain, and it came out on a breath that left his lungs empty. He sucked in air through his teeth. Every cell in his body felt electrified.

"Do you like it?"

"If I liked it any more, you wouldn't be wearing it."

****

A short cab ride later, they arrived at a restaurant in the Financial District. Dressed in a crisp white shirt and black skirt, a young woman led them to their table that offered a panoramic view of San Francisco. Beth peeled away from Donovan's side and wandered over to the expanse of windows. He followed her, catching her audible sigh at the view laid out before her.

"This is amazing," she whispered with the toes of her shoes touching the glass.

Buildings rose up around them, magical and romantic in the night, with squares of light like stars spotting the tall structures. Directly in front of them stood the bluish, glowing spear of the Transamerica Pyramid, and in the distance stretched the Golden Gate Bridge, which sparkled with hundreds of lights from the cars journeying up and down its impressive length.

Beth turned to him. "All day you've been showing me these beautiful places, and not once did you seem lost." She angled her head to the side. Her eyes glinted with the glimmer of candlelight. "Have you been here before?"

"A few times for monster truck competitions, or for fun. I like to catch waves at Half Moon Bay during the summer, if I can manage a trip."

"You surf?" Her eyebrows shot up her forehead.

Ah! I've surprised her yet again. He enjoyed

surprising her.

"It's one of my many talents."

"I've been wondering about your secret talents. Seems like you have a lot."

"Secrets or talents?"

"Both."

Grinning, he lifted their joined hands and pressed his lips to the back of her hand.

"Let's look over the menu."

Chardonnay filled their wine goblets, and the pale yellow liquid danced with the flickers of candle flames. Beth twirled linguine noodles coated in a creamy pesto sauce with her fork. Jumbo shrimp and flakes of parmesan topped the green heap of pasta, and Donovan ate bites of tilapia swimming in a lemon and orange caper sauce.

They lingered over their wine, talking in hushed tones. "We came to find Buck and yet we're having an elegant dinner." Beth's fingers trailed along the stem of her wine goblet. "What am I missing?"

"Nothing. Buck wasn't home, so I took the opportunity to spend some time with my girlfriend."

"I don't get it," she said while studying him. "During Christmas, you were wound up and about to blow. Now you're so calm. What's changed?"

"I know where Buck is. That's what changed." His voice was hard, purposeful.

Beth nodded. "Well, I'm glad you're relaxed right now. Even if it's just temporary. I had a wonderful day."

Donovan reached across the white tablecloth and took her hand. "It's not over yet." After dinner, he took her to the St. Francis hotel. They snuck in through the back and crept to the glass tower of elevators. Before anyone could see them, they hopped onto an elevator. Once inside, Donovan pushed the button for the thirty-second floor. The elevator whisked them up and broke into the night sky, granting them a bird's eye view of the cityscape.

Beth gasped and stepped up to the glass. She pressed her hands to it and gaped at the scenery. The buildings were shrouded in darkness and shining with the glow of lights. No streets were visible, but stoplights and cars offered a Christmas-like effect.

At the top, the elevator hummed to a stop.

When it stilled, Donovan slipped his arms around her and pulled her close. He kissed her below her ear. She tilted her head, and he trailed his lips down her neck. Hearing her soft moan, like a kitten's happy purr, he backed her against the rear wall and kissed her feverishly, as if he hadn't kissed her in weeks.

Grabbing the back of her knee, he lifted her leg to his hip. His hand roamed up her silky thigh, beneath her dress. His fingers curled around the band of her underwear and inched it down.

Beth's head jerked back, yanking her lips free. "What are you doing?" Her voice was breathless.

"We ate. Now I'm going to make love to you."

She put a hand on his chest and pushed, but he didn't move an inch. "Not in a public elevator."

"We're alone."

"It's glass! Someone could see us."

"No one is looking at the Westin with binoculars. And even if they were, they'd need to be night-vision binoculars. We're alone, it's dark, and I'm blocking you. Look over my shoulder." Her gaze left his, and he moved his mouth to her ear. "I want you looking at that view when you cum."

Taking her mouth, his tongue rubbed against hers until she released a moan. Then his lips journeyed back down her neck, over her naked shoulder, and down to her wrist. Kneeling at her feet, he sampled the skin on her thigh. When her fingers knotted in his hair, he slipped the swath of silk down her legs and stuffed it into his pocket. In the next second, he hoisted her off her feet. Her legs instantly wrapped around his waist.

He was reaching for his zipper when the elevator rocked from side to side causing him to lose his balance. Beth's legs dropped, and she stumbled on the points of her five-inch heels. He caught her in his arms as he struggled to stay standing. His shoulder rammed into the back wall, but he managed to steady himself with one arm secured around Beth's waist and his free hand on the railing.

The frantic shaking of the elevator stopped seconds later.

Eyes wide, Beth clutched his arms. "What was that?"

"I think that's the elevator's way of telling us to go back down to the lobby." He didn't want to tell her it was an aftershock, didn't want to scare her.

"Good idea," she said and accepted the panties he gave her.

When they stepped outside, the alarms of a few parked cars touched his ears. He looked left and right, searching for signs of distraught after the shocks, but the people he saw were calm as if nothing had happened. San Franciscans were used to aftershocks. Although the elevator had rocked significantly, no one else seemed rattled by it, which relieved Donovan. He hadn't released Beth's hand since pushing the button on the elevator for the first floor, and he continued to hold her hand during the cab ride to Union Square.

In the lobby of their hotel, he told Beth he wanted to see if Buck was home.

"Okay," she said. "I'll knock on his door."

He tugged her to a halt. "You'll what?"

"I'll go to his room, knock, and see if he opens up."

"Like hell."

"Donovan, Buck knows what you look like, but he's never seen me before. Besides that, look at me. I'm a woman who almost had sex in an elevator. Would you be able to resist me if I was on *your* doorstep?"

He blinked. Her hair was mussed, her cheeks flushed, her lips plump; she looked like sex on heels. No man in his right mind would be able to resist her, but damned if he would admit it.

"And what if he answers? What will you do then?"

She shrugged. "Oops, sorry, wrong room. You wouldn't happen to know where Mike Dawson is, would you?"

He exhaled in mild annoyance because he knew her plan made sense. "Fine," he agreed. "But if he answers, you better get out of there immediately."

"Understood, sir."

And when you're out of the way, I'll break down his fucking door.

From behind a wall, Donovan watched Beth strut down the hall in her heels. The site of her gorgeous backside swaying from side to side didn't increase his libido, it filled him with anger.

Does she have to be so sexy while knocking on a killer's door?

She paused in front of Buck's door, fluffed up her hair, and knocked briskly.

Donovan's hands balled into fists partly because of Beth's mussed hair, but also in anticipation. Even though he knew he shouldn't, he wanted to pound his fist into Buck's face, break his nose, dislocate his jaw, give him matching black eyes, and send blood flowing.

The door didn't open.

Beth laid her palms flat against the wood, leaned her breasts toward the door, and kicked up her right foot. "Mike, are you in there?"

Donovan ground his teeth. *If Buck opens that door, you're going to fall right into him.*

As if she had heard his thoughts, she stepped back and turned away. When she rejoined him behind the protection of the wall, she lifted her bare shoulder in a small shrug. "What if he's no longer staying here?"

He shrugged back. "I'll deal with that when there's proof he's somewhere else. Until then, I'm staying."

She linked her arm with his. "*We* are staying," she corrected.

Back in their room, Beth sat on the edge of the bed and bent forward to slip out of her heels. With his hands in his pockets, Donovan enjoyed the view of her long legs. Beth in heels was a delicious site. Beth barefoot in a sexy dress with purple polish on her toes was mouthwatering.

A slow smile spread across his lips. Lust rushed through his veins like a saline flush.

He hadn't been able to sink into her in the elevator, so he had a lot of pent up tension to release. Taking her in the hotel bed, her dress pushed up to her hips, sounded just as good as his earlier fantasy.

Setting her shoes aside, she looked at him with curiosity stamped across her beautiful features. "I never asked before, and I realize I should have—"

Now he was curious. "Ask what?"

"What are you going to do when we find Buck?"

His lips spread into a tight smile. His lustful thoughts faded. "Make a citizen's arrest."

"How?"

Without a word, he picked up his carryon, unzipped it, and took out two objects, which he set on the bed beside her.

Her jaw tensed. She pointed at the stun gun and handcuffs. "Where did you get those?"

"I have my ways."

Chapter Fifteen

Handcuffs and a stun gun. Beth couldn't believe it. Donovan obviously didn't have them at the airport, or on the plane, because security would've been on him instantly. So how did he get them? She didn't like the secrecy, but she doubted he'd tell her even if she pried.

Maybe the less I know the better. In case I'm interrogated.

Questions and scenarios circulated in her head while she tried to fall asleep. Before she knew it, Donovan was waking her up.

"What do you want?" she groaned.

"To bring you to China Town." He gave her butt a light slap. "Up and at 'em."

She sat up with a jaw-cracking yawn. "What if Buck came back during the night?"

"He didn't."

"How do you know?" she asked crankily.

"I just do."

She lifted a brow. "What did you do? Fix his door with a trip wire?"

"Maybe." He shook his head with a grin. "I called the front desk."

"Oh. Next time, can you tell me before you do something like that?"

He picked up her hand and kissed her knuckles. "I promise I will."

Room service arrived with their breakfast as she stepped out of the shower. In her bathrobe, she curled her legs beneath herself, picked up her cup of coffee, and peered at the covered plates. "What did you order?"

In answer, Donovan lifted the silver covers with a flourish. English muffins sat in the center of their plates topped with thick slices of Canadian bacon, a soft-boiled egg, and a stream of creamy hollandaise sauce.

"Eggs Benedict?" She turned to him. "This is all so expensive." She lifted her hands, indicating not just the meal or the hotel room but their whole trip. "I don't mean to pry, and you don't have to tell me, but are you sure you have enough money for all this? I may not have the money to buy a replacement car, but I have enough to pay my part."

Donovan waved his hand in the air as if shooing her question away. "Don't even worry about it. I inherited money from my grandfather when he passed away a few years ago. I never knew what to do with it, so it has been sitting in my bank account collecting interest." He shrugged and took a bite of his breakfast.

Beth blinked, surprised at his nonchalance. She had never before met a man with money who didn't like to show it in the form of fancy cars and clothes. And she rather liked that Donovan wasn't like that.

She ate her Eggs Benedict and then dressed in jeans, a button-up shirt, and a jacket before leaving the hotel with Donovan. After a short walk, they hopped onto the closest cable car. The car was full, so they stood on the running board. When the car lurched forward, Beth teetered backward, knocking into Donovan. Clutching the pole, she tried to straighten herself, but Donovan wrapped an arm around her and held her to him.

"Stay," he whispered in her ear.

She relaxed against him. Never in her life had she relished in the feel of a man's arms around her as she did at that moment. And she realized it was probably because she hadn't found the right man until Donovan. The craziness surrounding how they'd met didn't escape her, but she no longer questioned how she felt—it would be like questioning how you could breathe even while asleep. Pointless.

While listening to the hum of the subterranean cable and the clang of the bells, Beth felt oddly zen-like. Not even the fog hanging thickly overhead dampened her mood.

At the China Town Gate, Beth linked her fingers with Donovan's. Her gaze lapped up every detail of the gate. Three jade-green awnings hovered over the street supported by a stone base. Along the top of the highest awning stretched two copper dragons. Their heads and the spikes poking out of their backs were dark green. Two plump fish latched onto either end of the roof with their mouths; their bodies curled up so their tails pointed to the sky.

Two magnificent stone lions flanked the gate. During their flight, Beth read in a pamphlet that the male on the left, with his massive right paw on top of a ball, guarded the structure, and the female on the right, with a cub playing under her left paw, protected everyone inside China Town. Engraved into the stone above the small entryway on the right was Chinese calligraphy for peace and trust, while the characters over the left entry meant respect and love.

"There's a belief that walking through the gate is

good luck," Donovan told her.

Her fingers flexed on his. "Let's walk through it together." Knowing what the characters on the left meant, she led him to that passage. Together, they walked up the three small steps and stepped forward. On the other side, she smiled at Donovan.

Right at that moment, the ground beneath her shook. Beth stumbled briefly before the shaking quit, and she found her footing. "Was that an aftershock?"

"It's nothing to worry about," he told her. "After a quake, it's normal to experience aftershocks."

"Sure." But she wasn't convinced.

Pushing aside her fear, she faced the town spread out before her, and immediately felt as though she were in a different world. Red lanterns ran from one side of the street to the other. Flags of all colors dangled from the building fronts. Even the streetlights enchanted her; two small dragons twined the tops, propping up the ornamented boxes that would light up the streets after dusk.

While walking the length of Grant Avenue, Beth listened to customers and shop owners bargaining prices in loud Cantonese. The smell of musky incense, cigarette smoke, fish, vanilla, and Asian spices scented the air. They passed noodle shops and teahouses, bakeries and open-air markets. She enjoyed browsing among the colored vendors packed with jade jewelry, trinkets, and clothing. Being around all that culture made her feel rich. Tourists and locals of all races cluttered the streets. Many of them jostled her, but she was having such a great time that it didn't bother her.

She soon found herself in Portsmouth Square. Scattered throughout the area were wooden benches.

Several men played cards with flattened cardboard boxes as makeshift tables. Every so often, they encountered two men in a heated game of Chinese checkers. Crowds of interested bystanders circled them, anticipating the next move.

Beth paused in front of the six-hundred pound bronze sculpture of the Goddess of Democracy, another beautiful lady erected with a purpose. This Goddess—with her hands clutching a burning torch, her arms raised high above her head, and her hair blowing in a breeze—stood for human rights. Beside her was a playground full of delighted children using up their energy in play.

At the Kong Chow Temple, a temple for the Chinese God of War used for prayers of business and love, the hostess instructed Beth through a ritual that included bowing three times before an elaborate altar and throwing a pair of halved wooden goose eggs while making a wish. She cupped the egg halves in her hands and thought about possible wishes, but decided to ask a question instead.

Will Donovan and I bring David Buckland into custody?

She tossed the two halves before the altar and watched them land with the halves facing up. The hostess interpreted the meaning. "Yes."

When they were outside, Donovan inquired about her wish. "I'm not going to tell, but trust me when I say it's good for you, too." She patted his shoulder.

For a late lunch, they ate Dim Sum—bite-sized portions of shrimp dumplings, steamed buns, rice noodle rolls, crispy fried squid—and drank jasmine tea.

They were on the way to the Golden Gate Fortune

Cookie Factory when Donovan's cell phone sounded. He pulled it from his pocket and answered with a terse, "Yes?" Beth watched him curiously. His face didn't register a drop of emotion. "We'll be there."

He stashed his phone and faced her. "Buck is back. We have to go."

Beth frowned. "Who told you he's back?"

"The doorman."

"Why would the doorman care, and why would he call you?"

"I spoke to him this morning after I called the front desk, and I can be very persuasive."

****

"He's at the bar," the doorman whispered to them as they entered the hotel's lobby.

After a quick stop at their room so Donovan could get the stun gun and handcuffs, he made a beeline to the restaurant inside the hotel.

Beth hurried after him. "You can't go in there."

"Watch me."

"I mean it." She grabbed his arm, pulling him to a stop. "He'll bolt the second he sees you. And as far as we know, he's armed. You don't want him to start firing in a room full of people. Let me go and lure him out. Please." She could tell he was about to object. "Being in a crowded bar with him will be nothing compared to Viper's house. If I could handle that, this will be a cake walk."

"Fine, but I'm still going to be in that bar, and there's nothing you can say to stop me."

"I wouldn't want you anywhere other than close to me." She removed her jacket and lifted the collar of her shirt to her nose. "Ugh. I smell like China Town." She

148

twisted her body toward the front desk. Today, the front desk manager glowed in a pink silk blouse and white slacks. Plastering a smile on her face, Beth crossed the tile to the white desk.

"Good afternoon, Ms. Kennedy." Paula beamed at her with her unnaturally white teeth. "What can I do for you?"

Beth tried to look embarrassed. "I have an important meeting in the restaurant, and I spent all day in China Town. I don't have time to change." She plucked at her shirt and scrunched up her nose.

Paula held up her hand. "Say no more." She produced her designer handbag from under the desk, slipped her manicured hand inside it, and took out a square bottle with liquid gold swishing inside.

"Thank you," Beth said. She pulled off the crystal cap and spritzed her neck with the fragrance. Smelling like a frumpier version of Paula, Beth walked back to Donovan. "I'm ready."

"Great."

Resisting the urge to roll her eyes, she grabbed his arm and led him into the restaurant. The moment she stepped onto the thin carpet, she shoved his shoulder, pushing him so he faced the bar. "The only way your presence won't be noticed is if you sit here on this stool and nurse a drink like the rest of them." She nodded her head at the few other men seated at the bar.

Donovan took a stool, and she scanned the room for the man in the photo she had memorized. She turned her back to the room. "I see him," she whispered. "Five o'clock."

Out of the corner of her eye, she saw Donovan turn his head. "He's seated at a table, and he's alone." She rested her hand on Donovan's forearm, hoping to calm him. "I'm going to go to his table, engage him in a little chitchat, and try to get him to go to the garage. I figure he has a car to keep him on the move if need be, and I think a takedown would be better there. Safer."

Donovan reached out and fingered a lock of her shoulder-length hair. "You're a smart one, Beth."

"And don't you forget it."

With that, she walked across the bar while gathering her courage and wit. She didn't stop at Buck's chair, though, she sat right across from him. "I normally wouldn't be so up front, but you look like you could use some company." She smiled from ear-to-ear as she studied him. He had a square jaw covered in a thick beard and tousled molasses hair that looked as if he hadn't washed it in a week.

He looked at her with hard, walnut-brown eyes. "I don't want company," he growled.

"You may not want it, but you *need* it."

Buck's eyes narrowed on her, and he tilted his head. "Are you soliciting sex?"

Beth bit back a laugh. She hadn't meant to be *that* suggestive, but since she was winging it, she decided to go with it anyway.

"I prefer the word…offering." She leaned forward. "When I saw you, I thought you looked like a man who has had it rough recently and could use some fun, or at least a good ride." Biting her bottom lip, she let her words sink into his brain and reach his glands.

"How much?"

She pretended to consider prices. "Well, since I like you so much, the pleasure would be mutual. Fifty dollars."

"I could get laid for half that."

"Yeah, but she wouldn't be me, or as good."

His greedy stare lowered to her breasts then rose back to her face. Inside she cringed, but outside, she forced herself to remain poised and to appear as though she wanted him. It wasn't easy.

From over Buck's shoulder, she could see Donovan watching her. All she wanted to do was go to him, lock herself in their room, and scrub her body free of Buck's lusting gaze.

"Fifty bucks it is," he said.

She grinned. *If I was undercover, I could get him for prostitution, too.*

"I'll be worth it," she promised him.

"I'm sure you will be." His tongue flicked out and slathered his top lip with saliva.

She held her spine stiff against chills of disgust. "Crap." She let out a breath, pretending annoyance. "I'm fresh out of condoms, and the gift shop doesn't have the textured ones I like. Do you have any in your room?" She hoped he didn't. After all, what man would have a stock of textured condoms while in hiding?

"No." He swallowed hard—his Adam's apple shot up his throat. "But I can get some down the road."

Relief filled her; her insane plan was working. "Sounds good. What's your room number? I can wait outside your door until you get back." He told it to her but, of course, she already knew it.

"Don't you want to know my name?" he asked.

"Honey, I don't need to know your name, just your size." She winked at him and got to her feet. "Don't take long. If I have to wait, I may not be as ready as I am now." She trailed her fingers up his arm as she walked past him.

Donovan glared at her, obviously not liking that she made physical contact with Buck.

She stopped briefly beside him and scooped up peanuts from a dish. "Don't look at him. Don't make a move," she said. "He's going to the garage. I'll hide in the woman's bathroom." She popped the peanuts into her mouth and left.

From behind the bathroom door, she spied on Buck through the crack as he stood in front of the elevators. The ding of an elevator opening met her ears. When he disappeared, she counted to ten before stepping cautiously into the lobby. At that same time, Donovan entered from the bar. She met him at the wall of elevators. Neither of them said a word until they were inside the elevator and the door closed.

Donovan whirled to her. "Why the hell did you touch him?"

"Because he thought I was a hooker. I had to make him want to buy condoms."

Donovan's eyes flashed with anger. "He's leaving to buy what?"

Beth flinched under Donovan's glare. *Perhaps I should've kept that part to myself.*

"Come on, Donovan, it's not like I was really going to have sex with him, but it worked. He's in the garage right now."

Donovan didn't have time to answer because the elevator door opened. He pushed her back a step as he poked his head out, checking to see if the coast was clear. When he stepped back in, he pointed to the left.

Beth nodded and followed him out. Several paces ahead of them Buck was whistling an upbeat tune.

Donovan sent her a withering glare. This time, she did roll her eyes. *Buck may be happy now but he won't be once Donovan zaps him in the ass with that stun gun.*

They followed Buck down to the next level, trying to gain on him while remaining quiet. Beth's heart did a vigorous tap dance against her ribcage. It was so strong she thought it would fracture her ribs. Her palms were sweating, providing enough perspiration to leave a trail along a wall. She wasn't even this nervous when she snuck up on Chewy before she whacked him in the back with a shovel.

Less than six parking spaces away from Buck, he lifted his hand. The ear-piercing beep of a car unlocking made Beth jump. The sound also prompted Donovan to take out his stun gun. Either it was Donovan's sudden movement or Buck's sixth sense, but he peered over his shoulder and looked directly at them. Recognition didn't register on his face immediately. When it did, his eyes widened, and he ripped a gun out from behind his back.

Beth didn't have to wait for him to fire to know it had bullets. She dove between a red SUV and a black truck as the first pops rang out. Keeping her head down, she teetered on her feet like a duck to the front of the SUV and planted her body behind the tire. Donovan crouched across the way beside a small Volkswagen. He still held the stun gun in his hand, although it wouldn't do them any good now.

Buck shot at them with abandon. The pings from bullets hitting metal echoed throughout the garage. Heart beating so hard and fast that it felt like it would explode, Beth peered left and right, searching for a safe route out of the garage. Even if she could make it to the next aisle over, Buck would no doubt follow with his gun blazing. By the sound of it, she figured it was a semi-automatic, and there was no telling how many magazines he had on him.

Glass rained down on her when bullets sliced through the windows. She ducked her head even lower. Pieces of glass slid off her head to the ground where shards circled her feet like a ring of posies. A few of the glass puzzle pieces from the window had collected on her lap. She brushed them off and pressed her hands firmly against the passenger door. More glass fell on her when the truck's window behind her erupted.

After a moment, Buck directed his bullets toward the Volkswagen. Beth turned her head toward Donovan. Bullet holes snaked across the small hood and hit the ground beside him. One bullet hit the hubcap of the car directly behind him and ricocheted. She couldn't see where the bullet went until he flinched to the side and turned his head to the Volkswagen's door where a metal cavity was level to his shoulder.

Shit. The bullet must've slipped right past him with centimeters to spare.

She didn't even have time to gasp before the bullets came back to her side. Instead of puncturing the metal frame, they skidded along the ground. The moment she realized Buck was shooting under the cars to hit her, the tire she hid behind blew. She squeezed her eyes shut as she tried to make herself smaller by pressing her body into the SUV. The Morse code of bullets hitting metal started up again. She could've sworn she felt the SUV shaking with the continuous beat of bullets slamming into it, except the shaking was below her feet. It started gentle, but as soon as she noticed, it became violent.

Earthquake!

She fell backward and struggled to get back up. Her body bounced up and down and rolled from side to side simultaneously. A light came crashing down from the ceiling and slammed into the concrete floor with such power it exploded into a trillion stars. Glass shot out in all directions like the Big Bang. Beth screamed and covered her face with her hands as tiny pieces of glass bit the skin on her arms.

She fought onto her hands and knees and hugged the tire to keep from falling over again. The intensity of the tremors grew. The concrete below her feet didn't feel solid anymore. It felt alive, as if two gigantic gophers burrowed through the earth. The truck behind her slid with the vicious shock waves and bumped into her, pushing her roughly into the tire. She let out a cry of panic.

"Beth, get under the car!"

She heard Donovan yelling over the roar of the quake and shimmied underneath the SUV. When she was under the vehicle, she lifted her head to look for Donovan. The shaking suddenly increased, as if Mother Nature had her hands on the asphalt that smothered her creation and wanted to rip it off the ground. Chunks of concrete tumbled down. Donovan raised his arms to shield himself, and that was the last she saw of him before a wall of rubble came down between them. She screamed his name, but the sound of the garage collapsing swallowed her voice.

A section of the concrete above fell at a slant and slammed into the ground, giving way to a car that slid sideways down its length and rammed into the SUV.

Flattening her body to the floor, she shut her eyes tight while praying for the earthquake to end and for Donovan to be okay.

A moment later, as if a higher power had answered her prayer, the shaking quieted and all was still. She opened her eyes to a cloud of gray dust. It clogged her lungs and settled at the back of her throat with each panicky breath she took.

Pushing aside small rocks, she slithered out and came face to face with a silver Honda pressed against the rear of the SUV. Choosing her footing carefully, she stepped onto the concrete slab, inched past the Honda, and ducked beneath the ramp, hoping it wouldn't fall and crush her. She checked quickly for Buck but didn't see him before facing the dam of concrete in front of her.

"Donovan! Can you hear me? Are you okay?"

Please, God, let him be okay.

"Talk to me, Donovan!" She tried to find a way around the mess, but the concrete blocked off the entire area.

From deep inside the rubble, she heard the muffled sound of movement. Her heart leapt on a trampoline of hope. "Donovan?"

"I'm okay," she heard him call. "But I'm trapped...can't find a way out. Where's Buck?"

"I don't see him anywhere. He must've escaped."

"He doesn't matter right now. You do. You have to get out of here."

The meaning of his words hit her as hard as a brick. "I'm not leaving without you."

The building rumbled as if it had a belly full of acid and was about to be sick to its stomach. More debris came loose. She crouched with her arms over her head. The slab of concrete holding up the Honda groaned. Grains of sand fell, sprinkling her hair and clothing with more gray specks.

"Beth, this structure's not safe anymore. You need to get to safety."

"That's my point exactly. The structure's not safe, so I'm going to help free you. We can get to safety together."

"It could take a long time for us to move these rocks."

"It'll take you even longer to do it by yourself. Damn it, Donovan let me help you." She bent to pick up a rock.

"Beth, listen to me."

She stopped mid-crouch.

"I don't want anything to happen to you."

Her throat tightened, and she fell to her knees. "And I don't want anything to happen to you."

"Please, Beth, go."

"No—"

"Yes," he snapped. "Don't argue with me. Not now. Go to a shelter, and when I get out of here, I'll find you. I promise."

Tears bubbled beneath her eyelids, washing away the grit that irritated her eyes. "I'll hold you to that promise," she said, her voice catching and betraying the fear she felt inside. "I know I haven't said it—we haven't said it—since that first time outside the police department, but it's true...I really do love you."

"I love you, too, baby." After a brief pause, he added, "But you have to leave."

"I know." She swallowed. "But I'm coming back

with help."

Before he could object, she got up and hurried toward the stairs, maneuvering around parked vehicles and debris. She opened the door to the staircase, thankful to find it intact. Taking the steps two at a time to the ground level, she came out into the lobby to find it empty. Paula had abandoned the front desk, and the doorman had left the hotel's entrance unguarded. The hum of conversation and the clatter of utensils no longer came from the restaurant. No guests or employees were in sight.

She stepped through the doors into a chaotic Union Square. Cars had smashed into each other all over the square. People were screaming, running, bleeding. Everywhere was panic.

Chapter Sixteen

Dust particles from the crumbling concrete swirled in the air. The back of Donovan's throat felt as though an inch of crud coated it. Even his eyes felt gritty. He coughed, stirring the dust in his lungs. The wall that kept him from Beth surrounded him on all sides. He was lucky it hadn't buried him.

The single light clinging to the ceiling behind him was dim. He could barely see the numbers on his watch, but it hadn't been long since he listened to Beth's retreating footsteps. Each echo of her shoes beating against the concrete matched the frantic beat of his heart. When the sound of her footsteps faded, his chest felt hollow. He'd sent her away for her safety, but now she was on her own. He hated that. Even though he knew she was more than capable of taking care of herself, many dangers lurked in large cities after natural disasters; he didn't want her to face those dangers alone.

He shifted a lump of concrete the size of a bowling ball. He needed to get out of the garage, and the only way to do that was to create an opening. While he worked, he thought about his luck. He had been a few feet away from his brother's murderer, close enough to capturing him, and an earthquake struck, an earthquake powerful enough to make a parking garage collapse. Now debris trapped him. The odds of finding Buck again were slim, especially since he was aware they were after him.

Donovan carefully climbed on top of a car to remove boulders from the top down. The edges of the concrete slabs cut his palms. Each one he picked up grew heavier, but he didn't stop. He had to get out, had to find Beth. With each breath, more lingering dust passed through his airways. At this rate, they'd have to scrape the grime out of his lungs with a spackle.

Second to finding Beth was taking a breath of fresh air. *As fresh as San Francisco air can be.* At this point, he would take smog over lungs filled with God-only-knows-what.

He pulled out a large chunk, causing an avalanche. Concrete tumbled to the ground and the mound widened as it lost height. When the shifting stopped, he hopped off the roof of the car. With tentative steps, he inched up the pile toward the gap he'd created at the top. Rocks shifted under his weight. At the peak, he had to squeeze through by inching the top half of his body into the opening. He swung his legs up and was about to ease them to the other side to begin his descent when the unstable structure started to shake. A segment of loose concrete detached from the broken level above him and fell onto his ankle.

An explosion of white stars blinded his vision. He yelled in pain.

Chapter Seventeen

Beth went up to a man in jeans and a thick flannel jacket. "Sir, my boyfriend is trapped in this hotel. Can you help me get him out?"

The man shook Beth off as if she were a bug. "I'm trying to get home."

She watched him storm away, leaving a gap in the flood of earthquake survivors. She approached other men, begging them for help. Every one of them dismissed her by lifting their hands to show they couldn't offer help or with a mere shake of the head before rushing away. "Please," she shouted at the current of people flowing past the hotel. "I need help. My boyfriend's trapped behind rubble in here." People glanced at her but didn't so much as give her eye contact.

She took her cell phone out of her back pocket, wanting to call for help, any help, but the screen was cracked in half. Praying it wasn't damaged beyond use, she tried to turn it on, but the screen stayed black. Her heart sank to her feet. She tossed the useless device to the ground and looked left and right, hoping to find a police officer but only saw frightened people.

With the goal of finding a first responder, she walked down Powell Street. Not knowing the area, she didn't know where to look for the closest fire station. She was alone in a city she'd never visited before, a city falling apart at the seams.

Although San Franciscans were used to quakes, it became obvious they weren't used to ones of this magnitude. Women ran in their business suits. Their nude stockings were ripped to their knees. She figured they must've scurried out of their offices or cubicles and into the streets, desperate to get to their loved ones. Their meticulous hair-dos fell down their necks. The panic in their eyes was as visible as a pair of glasses.

Men had abandoned their briefcases and tugged the knots loose on their ties. Sweat poured down their faces. Their shirts had giant wet spots under their arms and between their shoulder blades. Their usually shiny shoes were scuffed and dingy.

Tourists were even more frantic. Tears streamed down their cheeks. Many people wandered around with vacant expressions on their faces. Beth imagined she looked like them. She definitely didn't look any better. Gray dust covered her from head to foot, and blood dotted her arms from the glass shards that had punctured her skin. She didn't know what to do, or how to help anyone, so she kept walking.

Glancing into shop windows, she saw racks of clothing tipped over, mannequins lying on the floor like murder victims at crime scenes, and shelves slanted on the walls, dropping the merchandise they held. On the sidewalk, glass sparkled in the sunlight, and trashcans lay on their sides, spilling newspapers, to-go cups, and food wrappers.

All the skyscrapers in the distance still stood, but some shops she passed weren't so lucky. Ceilings had caved in; walls had collapsed. A few older buildings that weren't earthquake resistant had turned into heaps of two-by-fours, drywall, and roof shingles. She paused next to the damage and told anyone who needed help to call out. When she didn't hear any cries, she continued on her way.

She thought about Donovan. Her chest constricted with fear and love.

Is he okay?

Did he make it out of the garage?

Should I turn back?

She lifted her eyes from the ground to find herself in a deserted area. No cars drove on the road. No pedestrians clogged the sidewalks. All the shop owners had closed, locked, and barred their businesses, and she didn't know how she'd gotten there. Her feet had carried her without her knowledge. She couldn't even guess how long she'd been walking.

A movement to her right caught her attention. She looked in time to see a man race across the street with a length of pipe in his hands. He cut right in front of her and swung the piece of metal into a shop window. She jumped back with a yelp. The glass broke, and he leapt into the shop. He didn't so much as glance at her.

Beth took off at a run. As she ran, she noticed several shop windows had already been smashed. A glance into an electronics store revealed two men destroying display cases to get at the laptops and cell phones. A third stuffed random merchandise from shelves into a black trash bag.

She pushed her legs to take her faster, farther. Her heart ticked frantically, her thoughts tumbled in her head. *Where do I go? How do I get out of here?*

A group of women teetered out of a shop on high heels. Their arms were piled high with designer jeans, tops, purses, and shoes. One of them even had a fist full of thongs.

Across the way, a looter slid a wide screen TV into the trunk of a car and hopped into the passenger seat. The car sped away with loud music blaring from its speakers.

Beth eyed the intersection ahead. She needed to find her way back to Union Square, back to Donovan, but she didn't want to head the way she had come. She was a few feet away when a body blocked her path. Her feet skidded to a stop, and her surprised gaze fell onto the knife pointed at her chest. She raised her hands and gaped at the Hispanic man demanding money.

"I don't have any."

"That's bullshit, lady. Gimme your money!"

"What do you think I have?" she shouted back. "Do you see a purse, a backpack, or a fucking fanny pack? I don't have anything!"

He advanced, plunging the blade toward her stomach. She jumped back in fear. "Empty out your pockets. Now!"

"All right." She slowly dipped her hands into her pockets and pulled them inside out to show she didn't even have a gum wrapper. Lint occupied the deepest recesses of the cotton squares. "See," she said, forcing calm. "I don't have any money. Now let me go."

"Turn around."

"What?"

"I said, turn around. I want to see your back pockets."

Beth glared at him as annoyance washed over her. *I don't have time for this. I have to get back to Donovan.* She grabbed his wrist, stepped around him, and wrenched his arm behind his back, forcing his hand toward his head while twisting his wrist at an awkward angle. He let out a growl and released the blade. It clattered to the asphalt at her feet. She didn't waste a second to peer down at it. She kicked the back of his knee with the side of her foot as hard as she could. He crumbled, and she let him fall. When he was on the ground, she gathered a fistful of his dark hair and slammed his forehead into the ground, knocking him unconscious. Then she launched into an all-out sprint.

She made a right onto Market Street, hoping to find her way back to Union Square so she could dig Donovan out with her bare hands. Running down the middle of the street, she passed even more storefronts, hotels, and restaurants. They must've evacuated the area because no customers or workers stood outside. It was nothing like the hell of Union Square, but if the authorities evacuated this area, it was for a reason. Beth wasn't sure if she wanted to find out what that problem was, but she refused to turn back.

A few blocks later, she saw water shooting into the air. She ran toward it. After a few strides, her sneakers slapped water. The street was flooded. Soon, it covered her feet, soaking her shoes and socks. When she got closer, she made out the length and color of two fire trucks through the thick mist. Near the heart of the geyser, she could see firefighters and other city workers. They looked as if they were standing in the middle of Niagara Falls.

She ran toward them, hope filling her like helium. Surely, one of the trucks could go to Union Square. They could help her dig Donovan out of the rubble and help others who were hurt and trapped.

About a block away, the ground beneath her feet started to shake, causing her to trip. She hit the asphalt hard, and her body rolled through the water. The shaking was nowhere near the velocity of the quake that happened earlier, but it was strong enough she couldn't get to her feet. A crack splintered the road in front of her and snaked toward her, drinking the water flooding the road and severing the asphalt between her hands. She jumped to the side. Even though the shaking stopped, the crack continued to widen, reaching out toward her as if it wanted to swallow her. She crawled away, using her heels to push herself from its jaws.

With wide eyes, she watched the road disappear into the hungry fissure that raced toward the first responders at the water main break.

No!

She cupped her mouth with her hands and screamed with all her might. "The road is breaking!"

One of the city workers turned toward her, not sensing the immediate danger.

"The road," she yelled. "Get out of the way!"

The worker's head lowered. Seeing the expanding crack, he spun around. She couldn't hear him shouting, but she could see him waving his arms above his head.

Her gaze lowered. The rift was the size of the road, plowing forward like a beast devouring everything in its path. When it reached the area the fire trucks had blocked off, a cloud of brown dust erupted into the air, and everything aboveground vanished—the vehicles, the light posts, the people.

Beth reached out as if she had the power to suspend the chunk of road and raise it back up, but she didn't. The sound of rock and metal falling into the earth plunged her heart into her gut. She let out a cry. Her other hand covered her mouth in horror.

After the dust settled, all she could see was an enormous sinkhole and that damned water main feeding it large quantities of water. The city workers, the police officers, and the firefighters were gone. Crushed. Dead.

Tears clogged her eyes and throat as she rose to shaky legs and cautiously inched up the road as far as she could go. With the tips of her sneakers toeing the edge of the crack, and her hands groping the side of a building for balance, she leaned forward to look into the sinkhole. Between slabs of earth and rock, she spotted the back end of a fire truck, but she couldn't see a single person. The water filling the crater mixed with the dirt, creating a thick mud.

Despair filled her. Her chest heaved, and tears streaked down her cheeks. *Why? God, why?* She had been so close to them, and yet too far away to do anything but yell.

A piece of asphalt crumbled at her feet. Not wanting to tumble into the muddy pit, she backed carefully away, placing one foot at a time behind her, her hands never once leaving the side of the building. The moment there was enough room for her to turn, she pressed her back to the wall, shifted her feet, and launched forward, wanting to get as far away as possible.

Chapter Eighteen

Seething, Donovan managed to dislodge the rock pinning his leg. On the other side of the pile, he collapsed onto his hands and knees. He raised his head to look at the last place he had seen Beth. She wasn't there, thank God. But neither was Buck.

That son-of-a-bitch!

He fought to stand, wincing when he put weight onto his left leg. Electric pain rattled his bones from foot to hip. The marrow in his ankle felt fried. He took a couple of tentative steps. He didn't think it was broken, but the bruising would be substantial, and he could have torn ligaments. He dragged his foot up the stairs and limped through the lobby of the hotel. Outside, he squinted against the sunlight.

A quick assessment of the area revealed the destruction a sudden quake could have upon a city. It was worse than a hurricane, because you could see a hurricane coming, you could prepare, but an earthquake struck randomly. No one was ready for it. Everyone was going along with his or her day as usual, but the second catastrophe occurred, the city morphed into mass devastation.

The normally cool facades of San Franciscans dissolved, along with the windows of buildings, during the strongest shockwaves. They were all unraveled like bundles of yarn in a knitting shop. Fear marred their faces. Everyone from surfers to bohemians, tourists to workers, looked the same, because they were all afraid. For themselves. For each other. For their loved ones.

"Beth?" He limped along, scanning the faces of the people clogging the streets.

"Beth?" He caught sight of a brunette in a black T-shirt. His heart skipped a beat. He took a few urgent steps; the pain in his leg distant as he moved toward her. "Beth." He took her arm, but when she turned, it wasn't Beth. "I'm sorry."

He continued on, shouting Beth's name over the din. Each step he took brought him closer to the sound of a child crying. He looked around to see a mother trying to soothe her little girl of about five with blonde pigtails dangling from either side of her head. She had a tiny fairy nose, now red from crying and dripping with snot. Her sapphire eyes were the size of half-dollars and welling with tears. She was cradling her arm to her chest and wailing as if she wanted Zeus on Mount Olympus to hear her.

He smiled at the mother. She held her daughter in an attempt to calm her, but it was obvious she didn't know what to do in this bizarre, post-earthquake situation. Despite his injury, Donovan crouched in front of the little girl.

"Hi, sweetie. Does your arm hurt?"

She nodded, and her lower lip jutted out in a pout.

"We were in a car accident," the mother explained. She pointed to a black car on the road where a truck had plowed into the rear passenger door.

Through the window, Donovan could see a child's seat tilted in the back; the door caved in toward it. He turned to the girl. "Can you move your arm?"

She shook her head, swinging her pigtails from side to side.

"Squeeze my thumb." He put his thumb under her hand.

She whimpered when she lowered her arm a fraction and curled her fingers around his thumb.

"Squeeze as hard as you can," he encouraged. He felt her fingers tighten ever-so-slightly before the pressure quit.

"It hurts," she whined. Her eyes shed fresh tears.

The mother tightened her arms around the little girl's waist. "Does that mean it's broken?"

With a sigh, Donovan nodded. "Do you have a blanket?"

"Yes." The mother hopped to her feet. "Stay here, honey." She hurried to her car, reached in through the back window, and came back with a pink blanket.

He took it. "Is this your favorite blankie?"

The girl gave him a watery smile. "Yeah." Her voice quivered with pain.

"Well, your blankie is going to help you feel better."

"How?"

"It's going to hug you."

The girl giggled.

"Are you ready?" When she nodded, he tied the blanket around her, creating a makeshift sling. "There. Now I have to warn you...a blankie can be very powerful, but it won't help you if you move your arm, so you have to keep it still. Can you do that?"

She nodded once, like a soldier taking an order. "I can."

"Good."

He rose stiffly and lowered his voice to talk to her mother. "If you have any children's Tylenol, I would give her some. It won't be as effective as what a doctor will give, but it'll tide her over until you can get her to the ER."

"Thank you so much."

"It was no problem." He put his hand on the girl's head. She was petting her blanket with her free hand. "Take care, sweetie." She smiled at him, with dry eyes.

Moving on, he called out Beth's name. While searching for her, his sweeping gaze landed on a man with blood streaming in rivers down his face. He held a bloody T-shirt—his own T-shirt as he was shirtless—to his forehead.

"What happened?"

The man squinted up at him and shook his head. "One minute I'm standing, the next minute I'm on my back with a piece of glass sticking out of my face."

"You removed it?" Donovan pounced forward on his feet and snatched away the bloody shirt to inspect the wound. He poked and prodded the man's forehead with his fingers, not even stopping when the man made guttural noises. "Well, it didn't puncture your skull, and I can tell you that confidently because I can see your skull."

He ripped off a strip of fabric from the stained T-shirt and fastened it tightly around the man's head. "It'll need stitches, so keep pressure on it. Don't get up. Wait for an ambulance to arrive." Already sirens stirred the air with their monotonous tones.

"You don't have to worry about me getting up." The man gave Donovan a smile that lifted half his face, the side not coated with blood.

Donovan patted his shoulder before leaving him.

Over the sirens, which grew louder with each passing moment, he heard a woman calling someone's name. Her wails were louder than his call for Beth.

"James. James!" Her voice was high-pitched and frantic. "JAMES!"

He turned in a full circle, trying to locate where the woman was and found her across the way. She was stopping people on the sidewalk, grabbing their arms as she asked them if they had seen James.

He approached her. Up close, he realized she was no older than twenty. "Miss?"

Eyes wide, she spun to him. Beneath her tears, he could see fear and worry collected within her gaze.

"Who are you looking for?"

"My brother. He's fourteen. I was in this shop." She pointed over her shoulder. Her hand shook. "But he didn't want to go in, so he sat on the sidewalk to play games on his cell phone while I shopped. Then the earthquake hit, and now I don't know where he is."

"It's okay. I'll help you find him. What's your name?"

"Lizzie. The last time I saw him, he was right here." She pointed at the curb less than a foot from where she stood. The curb was empty. Not a trace of evidence remained that a boy had sat there, only his sister's memory.

While Lizzie moved down the sidewalk, Donovan stayed exactly where he stood and studied the spot her brother had been last. He glanced along the length of the sidewalk and out across the street. His gaze roved over the asphalt. Several yards away were two long, black tire marks streaking across two lanes. He followed their trajectory, which came directly to the curb at his feet. Shifting, he peered to his right, tracing the invisible path with his vision. A few paces from where he stood—nestled between the wall and the concrete sidewalk—lay a cell phone. With a slight wince, he crouched to pick it up. A spider web of cracks stretched across the wide screen. The back fell off in his hand, exposing the crushed battery.

He stood and peered farther up the sidewalk. A car sat there. The hood was smashed into a wall.

He limped to it while searching for the owner, but he couldn't see one. He lowered onto his hands and knees to check beneath the car. Lying there, with his head under the engine, was a young boy. Blood coated his face and pooled beneath him on the concrete.

Donovan reached toward the boy and probed his neck to check for vitals. When he found a weak pulse, he said a quick prayer. He pulled his hand away to see his fingers were slick with blood. He reared back onto his knees and searched for the boy's sister.

"Lizzie."

She ran over and fell beside him. "Oh God...James?"

Donovan took her arm to keep her from grabbing her brother. "He's alive, but his pulse is faint."

"You have to help him," she sobbed.

"I will. Now stand back, okay?"

She scrambled to her feet, as tears gushed down her cheeks.

Donovan looked toward the crowd behind him. "Hey," he called out. "I've got a kid under here!" Everyone within earshot turned to him. "Does anyone have a car jack?"

"I have one." A man hurried to his truck and opened the toolbox in the back.

"So do I." Another man opened the trunk of a car and yanked out a jack.

"I need this side jacked up," Donovan told them, indicating the driver's side.

The two men worked on pumping the levers to lift the car while Donovan hunted for something he could use in place of a backboard.

"If his spine is broken, I can't pull him out by his arms. I need a sheet of wood or something I can use as a backboard," he said to the crowd. "And duct tape."

Many of them looked at one another, unsure of what to do.

"Wait," a woman shouted. "I have something in my shop." She hurried into the store next door, disappeared a moment, and reappeared with a large, flat cardboard box and a roll of duct tape. "Will this work?"

He took the cardboard and the tape. "Yes. Thank you."

Donovan went back to the car. The two men had jacked it up as high as they could. It didn't offer much space, but it was enough. He lay on the sidewalk and squirmed beneath the underbelly of the car.

He ignored the warmth of the boy's blood against his arm and the smell of gasoline that swirled in his nostrils. Heat seeped from the engine and touched his face. Fighting the limited space, with his nose a few inches from the car's metal organs, he carefully slipped the sheet of cardboard under the boy's head and shoulders. He took hold of the corners of the cardboard and shimmied it down to his hips. Then he tugged off a strip of duct tape, used his teeth to rip it, and fastened it to the cardboard on either side of the boy's head. He wound another strip of tape across the boy's shoulders.

When he was done, he slipped out from under the car, knelt on the concrete, and reached for the edge of the cardboard. With slow and steady movements, he pulled the boy onto the sidewalk. The smog-filtered sunlight settled onto the boy, lighting up what Donovan couldn't see before. A long gash split his cheek, creating a second mouth. It appeared to be trying to swallow a mouthful of blood, but the blood leaked from the corners, streaking down the boy's face. More blood smeared the surface of the cardboard. The side of his head was pink from his scalp being peeled away. His face was puffy, and his lips were swollen from the car's bumper slamming into him.

Donovan couldn't see his chest rising anymore. He laid a finger below the boy's nostrils, searching for a sign of breath, but there wasn't one.

"Is he alive?" Lizzie's high-pitched voice came from behind him.

In answer, Donovan started CPR. "He's not breathing."

"You can't let him die!"

Donovan glanced at her. "I won't."

Two ambulances stopped inside the square. The crowd watching him began waving their arms in the air. He was still doing chest compressions when the paramedics arrived.

"We've got this, sir."

He moved out of the way, letting the male paramedic take over CPR. The female medic removed the strips of tape and fashioned a foam brace around the boy's neck to stabilize his spine. After maneuvering him onto a backboard and strapping him in, they lifted him onto a stretcher.

Donovan watched the female medic insert a breathing tube. She faced him as she squeezed the balloon.

"Did you do that?" She gestured at the soiled cardboard and the coil of tape.

"Yeah."

"Good job."

He blinked, not knowing what to say because nothing felt appropriate.

The paramedics ran to the ambulance with Lizzy following them.

"How did you know how to do that with the duct tape and cardboard?"

Donovan turned to the woman who had provided the items in question. "My mom was a nurse. She taught me a lot growing up.

"Well, thank God for her. And for you."

He didn't respond to that, either.

I don't know if God would be thanking me if he knew how badly I'd wanted to kill Buck a moment ago.

And then he had the unsettling thought that the quake occurred to preserve Buck's life. But he shook that thought from his head. If anything, the quake had saved them from Buck.

The ambulance's sirens screamed as it whisked away Lizzie and her brother, reminding Donovan that not everyone's lives were for the better because of the quake. But he hoped, despite his murderous thoughts earlier, that he had saved a life after all.

He began to make his way out of Union Square, intent on finding Beth.

Chapter Nineteen

Beth turned down a side street she'd passed when she was running toward the first responders, hoping it would bring her back to Union Square and Donovan. She walked with shaky steps, tears flowing freely down her cheeks. In her mind's eyes, she watched them fall into the earth again and again—all those lives gone in the blink of an eye. Each step she took brought her grief.

She soon came upon a neighborhood of apartments and condos. Staring down the road, she could see people rushing in and out of buildings. One man was putting a limping Golden Retriever into the back of his car. A few were cleaning up debris and hauling it to the end of the road.

The sun aimed its rays right at her unprotected eyes. Using her hand to shield them, she stepped up to a woman who was sweeping glass off a stoop. "Excuse me?" The woman paused in her work. "Do you have a working phone I can use?"

The woman scrutinized her before replying. "Yes, come with me." She set aside her broom and led Beth inside the building to a condo. Beth couldn't imagine what it would've looked like before the quake because a bookcase was on its belly, scattering books across the tile. A flat screen TV dangled from wires, and none of the pictures on the walls were able to hold on to their nails.

The kitchen didn't look any better. The cabinet doors were wide open as if an intruder had been hunting for something. Ceramic and glass lay in shards on the kitchen floor.

"There's the phone." The woman pointed to a cordless phone on the kitchen counter.

"Thank you so much." Beth snatched it up, dialed 911. Silence stretched on the other end. "Hello?" She peered down at the phone, disconnected the call, and brought it back to her ear. Dial tone hummed to her. Heart pounding, she dialed 911 again. She stood in the kitchen, anxiously shuffling her feet, but no one came on the line asking her what her emergency was.

"No, no, no." She tried once more in vain. When she heard nothing, she put the phone back on the charger and dropped her head onto the counter. Fear was a strong tonic in her belly. Donovan was trapped in an unstable garage. It could've collapsed again; he could be dead and she didn't know it.

"Miss?"

Beth lifted her head and quickly wiped away her tears. "Yes?" she croaked.

"The emergency call service must be down. Sometimes there are power outages after major quakes, or too many calls coming in shuts it down."

"My boyfriend is trapped underground and I can't get help for him."

"I'm so sorry. Where is he?"

Beth gave her the name of their hotel in Union Square.

"I can keep trying for you."

"If you get through, you need to tell them

something else." With the sound of crumbling earth and bending metal echoing in her ears, Beth told her about the sinkhole that killed first responders on Market Street. The visual of the road falling away, taking the first responders with it, came back to haunt her.

The woman gasped and made the sign of the cross. "I'll tell them," she vowed.

"Thank you, thank you so much," Beth said as she walked back outside with the woman. "Is Union Square that way?" She pointed in the direction she had been heading.

"Yes, it is, but are you sure about going back there? On the radio, they said it's a mess."

"I have to. I need to know if Donovan is okay." The fact she left him and was unsuccessful in finding help, or a shelter, made her feel like a failure.

"If I had a car, I'd drive you."

"That's okay. I appreciate your help."

Beth left the small neighborhood. After navigating her way from street to street, she finally found herself on Powell Street again. *Oh, thank you, thank you, thank you.*

Except she didn't know how far down Powell Street she was or which direction she should go to get to Union Square. She easily could've passed it. Winging it, she went uphill. A car came up behind her, heading in the same direction she was going. From the side of the road, she waved her arms back and forth above her head. As the car approached, she heard the engine roar louder as it sped by her, not slowing even when it passed.

Her arms fell to her sides. She continued to walk. Her leg muscles now burned with exertion. Several minutes went by, and she didn't recognize a single thing she passed. Only a homeless person was available to ask for help, and he was either sound asleep or dead. She didn't care to find out which. Eventually, she came across a shop owner locking his door. She hurried to him.

"Excuse me?"

He jumped, and she put up her hands to let him know she wasn't a threat.

"I'm sorry," she said. "I just want to know where Union Square is."

He finished locking the door and stashed the key before answering. "You're heading in the wrong direction. It's that way." He pointed behind her.

"Thank you." She turned to go downhill, her energy deflated. She was shuffling toward a store when she heard two voices arguing. She paused at the edge of the building and peeked around the window frame. Her eyes widened.

Holy shit. It's Buck!

She crouched by the window. It was a clothing store with mannequins strewn on the floor as if a massacre had occurred. Two men stood in the middle of the carnage of plastic limbs. One of them was David Buckland. She didn't recognize the other man, who had ice-gray hair pulled into a low ponytail and sun-roasted skin. He wore a leather jacket over wide shoulders. Compared to Buck, he was far more menacing.

He crossed his arms. "And why in the hell should I help your sorry ass?"

"Because if Goldwyn's brother finds out about you, he'll come after you and all the others, too. Then your whole fucking operation will be blown to shreds, and we'll all be in prison."

Beth figured Buck fled to California because he knew someone, but she never thought that person would be the man in charge of the drug ring responsible for killing Donovan's brother.

"So what do you want me to do?" the man asked Buck, his voice condescending as if the thought of Buck ordering him to do something was laughable.

"I want you to help me kill Donovan."

Beth's mouth opened in horror. *No!*

"And what about the woman? The one who tricked you?"

"I have a special order of punishment in mind for her," Buck said.

"I'm sure you do."

Beth swallowed. She didn't like the sound of that.

"What's your plan? How do you expect to find them?"

"If it was so easy for them to find me, it'll be a piece of cake to find them. They can't go far in this mess, and I suspect they have a room at my hotel. We can scrounge the streets and set up surveillance at the hotel. If you can get some of your men in the city to help, we'll be able to find them by nightfall."

"They better be found by nightfall. I don't want a dead detective's little brother and some bitch bringing down everything I've created. You and Chewy fucked up again and again. This is your last chance to fix your mess or I'll be using one bullet for Donovan, one for his bitch, and one for you."

Risking a glance over the window's ledge, she saw the man pull out a cell phone. He punched a button and brought it to his ear. "Two people are threatening to bring us down," he said to the person on the other end. "Round up the boys. We have a job to do." He disconnected the call and pointed at Buck. He was about to say something when an explosion sounded.

Beth turned to see a cloud of flames rolling toward the sky a few blocks away. After the flames disappeared, plumes of smoke, as black as charcoal, began to rise. She couldn't explain why, but at that moment, she thought of Donovan and feared for his life.

She backtracked to an alley and used it to slip past the building. Then she ran for all she was worth, praying Donovan was still alive.

Chapter Twenty

The explosion blew out the windows in the top floor of a building Donovan approached. Balls of fire rolled through the windowpanes. He lifted his arms to cover his head as glass fell to the street. Then he looked up to see flames dancing on the windowsills; their yellow and orange bodies shaking.

Screams escaped between the flames and met his ears. He peered over his shoulder. A fire truck was in Union Square, trapped by the collision of cars and hurt people. He didn't think about the consequences or consider the danger; he ran into the building and took the stairs two at a time, wanting to warn the people inside about the fire.

On the top floor, he glanced between the doors on either side of the hall. Smoke curled from beneath the door on the left, telling him the fire was there. He rushed to the other condo, banged on the door, and shouted about the fire before returning to the door leaking smoke.

He touched it with the back of his hand. It wasn't hot. Nor was the doorknob. Bracing a hand on the side of the hallway, he used his right foot to break down the door. On the other side, flames swayed along the floor and climbed up the walls. Fire engulfed the couch and curtains. Patches of the white carpet and the ceiling were also on fire. Shielding his face, he hurried into the living room where a body lay. Flames ate away at its clothes and skin, turning the body to crisp, black ash.

A scream sounded from the back of the condo. He whipped around. "Where are you? Call out!"

"Here," came a woman's voice. "Down here…in the baby's room."

Donovan followed her voice to a hallway lined with fire. The smoke in the air was as thick as water, making it hard to breathe.

"Keep calling out," he shouted over the sound of joyous flames devouring everything they touched.

"Help us! Please. Help!"

He leapt through the fire. The heat was intense. None of the flames touched him, but the heat made it feel as though they caressed every inch of his body. He kept his body crouched low. Holding the collar of his shirt over his mouth and nose, he coughed. The air was so rancid he couldn't catch his breath. He paused outside the room where he could hear the woman's frantic calls. Flames blocked the door. He cupped his hands around his mouth to shout over the roar.

"Is there fire in the room with you?"

"No," she yelled back. "But there's smoke. Too much smoke."

"Move away from the door and get low to the ground."

A few seconds later, he heard her shout, "Okay."

He thrust his boot into the door. The force of the blow knocked the door wide open and splintered off a piece of wood from the frame. He jumped through the flames and into the room. He couldn't even tell it was a baby's room because the dark smoke whirled thickly, stealing the oxygen and obscuring his vision.

Coughing sounds brought him around, and he found a woman cowering on the ground a few feet away. She cradled a baby in her arms. A blanket covered its small form from head to toe. "Don't move."

Coughing, he went to the large, rectangular shape in the corner of the room. He felt the bars of the crib, searched inside it, and pulled out a quilt, which he wrapped around the mother.

"Run. Don't hesitate."

The top of the quilt cocoon bobbed up and down, letting him know she was nodding.

His heart beat double time, and his thoughts were fearful. He couldn't let the baby and mother die, couldn't carry that guilt on top of his brother's death.

Not wanting to spare another millisecond, he pulled her to the flaming doorway. Together, they ran through the fiery condominium as the baby wailed. As soon as they made it out, he ripped the burning quilt off the mother and tossed it to the ground. He checked her for signs of injury.

"We have to get out of the building," he told her.

"Where's my husband?"

Donovan coughed as he attempted to breathe whatever oxygen remained in the air.

"We have to go!" He tried pulling her.

"No! My husband...he's in there. You have to get him."

Donovan held fast to her arm as she tried to wrench free. "Think of the baby. You can't go back in there," he shouted and pulled her to the staircase a second before another explosion shoved them to the ground and sent a rush of flames over their bodies.

Chapter Twenty-One

Beth's energy tanks were running on empty, her leg muscles quivering, when she saw the barricade set up outside of Union Square with city workers standing near the roadblocks. She came upon a flashing sign and put her hands on it to keep herself from crumbling.

"Excuse me?"

The city worker in front of her turned. "Yes, ma'am?"

"I need to get through."

"That's not possible. There's been two explosions. We're not letting anyone into Union Square."

"But my boyfriend is in there. I have to find him."

"The rescue teams will find him. He could even be in one of the shelters. They set one up not far from here." He gave her the name of a hotel.

She nodded. "Okay, but I need to tell someone...on Market Street...there's a water main break—"

"We have a team out there dealing with it."

She shook her head. Her throat tightened. "A massive sink hole opened up...everyone who was there..."

The man's lips cracked open. His eyes reflected the horror she felt inside. "What do you mean?"

"I saw it," she gasped. "The sink hole opened up right under them. They're gone."

The man removed his hard hat and raked his hands

through his hair. He looked around as if suddenly lost. Without another word to her, he ran toward his team. After a moment, they all jumped into action, cramming into their vehicles and picking up their radios. Watching them made a crack form in her heart like the fissure in the road that killed the first responders.

Her watery gaze searched for a police officer. She spotted one farther down the road, too far for her to shout to him. She stood a moment, paralyzed by her mental and physical exhaustion and hypnotized by the rising smoke. A vicious tug in the middle of her chest pointed her to Union Square, telling her what she wanted most was there. Except she couldn't get there. It was within walking distance, and yet, out of reach.

A tiny spark of hope flashed inside her. Donovan had told her to go to a shelter, and the city worker told her there was one nearby. If Donovan had gotten out, he could be there now, waiting for her.

Shuffling her feet, she turned, took one step, and then another in the direction of the shelter. When she found the hotel with a handmade sign with the word "shelter" scrawled in bold, black letters, she pulled her tired legs up the few steps. She walked through the doors and immediately stilled. Her body swayed as she studied the lobby, now an active post-quake shelter.

The small chandelier hanging from the ceiling, and the massive fish tank full of exotic fish, clashed with the despair around her. Several cots were set up, and a few people lay on them, bleeding and shaken. The sound of crying and frantic conversation met her ears. She scanned their faces, but none of them were Donovan.

"He's not here," she whispered. "He's not here."

A woman with curly red hair and glasses came up to her. "Oh, dear, you look like you're about to fall flat on your face." She waved two other women over who took her arms and sat her down in a chair.

"What happened, honey?"

Beth blinked at a woman with butterscotch skin, deep laugh lines, and a braid of black and silver hair reaching down her back. "Didn't you hear? An earthquake hit."

The women laughed.

"I think you're going to be fine." The woman with the braid patted her knee.

"My name is Beth Kennedy. Has a man by the name of Donovan, with brown hair and violet eyes, come here looking for…me?"

All three women shook their heads.

"Not that I can recall," the woman with the glasses said. "Is that what you meant by 'he's not here'?"

Beth nodded. "I left him…I left him in a collapsed parking garage. He was trapped behind rubble and, instead of helping him get out, I left him. When I got out, I couldn't find anyone to help, so I went looking. Someone tried to mug me, then there was a sinkhole…" Her voice caught as that memory crashed into her skull. She couldn't bring herself to explain what happened again. "I got lost. I tried to get back to him, but Union Square is blocked off. I couldn't get through. They sent me here."

"And good thing they did." The third woman, a black woman with dreadlocks and a warm smile, said as she handed her a bottle of water. "If you continued to walk, you would've fallen over dead somewhere."

Beth unscrewed the cap on the bottle and took a

couple of swallows. When she lowered the bottle, a banana with a few brown spots appeared in front of her.

"Eat this."

Hunger prompted her to snatch the banana, peel it in one quick motion, and consume the soft, sweet insides in five bites. Once the banana was gone, the urge to go back out to look for Donovan became overwhelming. If Buck found Donovan before her, he would kill him. But Donovan told her to go to a shelter and that he'd find her. She was torn between staying at the shelter and going back out into the quake-ravaged city.

"Let's clean you up. You look like you've been attacked by a bunch of kittens." The women held her arms hostage as they cleaned the cuts with hydrogen peroxide and cotton balls.

Beth dozed while the women tended to her. Sometime later, a hand patted her knee, rousing her. Her eyelids peeled open. Through the haze of exhaustion, she saw the dark face of Sandra, the woman who had given her water.

"Why don't you lay down on one of those cots?" She pointed across the lobby. "Come on." She helped Beth stand and ushered her over with a hand at her elbow.

Beth drifted down, weightless. Her eyes were already sealed. She vaguely recalled the feel of a blanket settling on top of her.

Chapter Twenty-Two

The flames flowed back into the condominium from the explosion, taking the extreme heat with it and leaving scorch marks on the walls and ceiling. Donovan sprang to his feet, not even noticing the pain in his foot, and swiped at his back to check for flames. Not feeling any, he lifted the mother off the floor and rushed her and the baby out of the building.

A fire truck sat at the curb and firefighters were preparing to storm inside. Uniforms of all kinds surrounded them. A paramedic took the baby from his arms and another whisked away the mother. Seeing the medics fitting oxygen masks over their faces reassured him they were still alive. He rotated in place, searching for the fire chief. When he found him, standing near the building, talking into a radio, Donovan limped over, coughing as he went.

"Chief?"

The fire chief finished giving orders to his men inside the building and turned to Donovan. "Sir, you need to get back."

"I will, but I have to tell you I went inside the building and pulled out a mother and her baby." He pointed to the ambulance. "I think the fire started in the condo to the left on the top floor. I didn't check the other condo."

The chief issued more orders based on what

Donovan told him.

"There's one more thing." Donovan lowered his voice. "When I went in, I saw a man, her husband, on the floor. He was on fire. I'm sure he was dead."

"Thank you for your help. Now please get checked out by the medics. And don't run into any more burning buildings."

"Yes, sir."

Donovan went back to the ambulance. "Excuse me?" He waited for the medics to face him. "I want to know how the baby and mother are doing."

"You're the man who got them out, aren't you?"

He nodded.

"They're alive thanks to you. We're treating them for smoke inhalation and will take them to the hospital for scans and fluids." She hopped out of the ambulance and waved a mask at him. "Have a seat."

With a dramatic groan, he lowered onto the bumper. She fashioned the mask around his head. "There. Now don't you look like a charmer?"

He winked at her.

"You know, you could've killed yourself going into that fire."

"I wasn't thinking about me."

"That's clear enough. Do you have any burns?"

He lifted his hand.

She took it, cleaned it, and wrapped his hand with gauze. "Any other injuries I should know about?"

He shook his head.

"I noticed you were limping."

A fog of oxygen floated in front of his face when he moved the mask. "That didn't happen in there. When the quake hit, a piece of concrete fell on my foot."

"Mask back up." She knelt at his feet and eased off his boot. "I'm going to wrap it. It'll help with the swelling."

After she fastened the end of the wrap into place, he slipped his foot back into his boot. The paramedic shook her head. "The more you walk on it, the worse it's going to get."

He lowered the mask. "I have to find someone first, and then I'll go straight to the hospital for an X-ray. I promise."

"You better."

"I will." He coughed, and she positioned the mask back in place.

"But you're not going anywhere until you stop coughing. If you try to leave, I'll tackle your ass. I may be small, but I didn't become a paramedic because I was a weakling. I can handle six-foot-something men with violet eyes."

Even though the mask covered his face, he grinned at her. "You and my girlfriend have a lot in common."

Chapter Twenty-Three

The ground shook beneath the cot Beth slept on, jostling her awake. She jumped to her feet, afraid the earth would open up beneath her.

"It's okay." Sandra, the woman with the dreads, put a hand on her shoulder. "That was just an aftershock. After a big quake like the one we had, it's normal to feel aftershocks while the plates settle."

Beth sat back down on the cot. "Do you know what the magnitude was?"

"On the radio, they're saying it was a seven-point-four."

Beth's jaw dropped. "That's...that's..." Words failed her.

"The worst quake we've had in decades? Yes, it is, but if the plates moved that much already, they won't be moving that much for a long time."

"I hope you're right."

Sandra left her to rest, but she couldn't. Her nerves were like a bird's nest, jumbled and twisted. She was tired, afraid, and frustrated that she wouldn't find Donovan.

More people were at the shelter now than before she'd fallen asleep. A woman rocked a toddler in her arms, trying to settle him down for a much-needed nap. Two tweens sat on the ground playing a game of Monopoly while their parents looked on.

Several people had backpacks and suitcases stuffed full with whatever they could grab.

The sound of muffled crying drew her attention to a cot a few places away. An elderly woman with a cap of white hair sat there holding a gold-framed photo in her weathered hands. Her stooped shoulders shook with her sobs.

Beth went to her. "Are you okay?"

The woman shook her head. Her bout of tears never ceased. "My h-house. I had to leave my h-house." Her voice reminded Beth of a child.

"Was it damaged?"

She shook her head and pouted. "The police told me to leave, but I don't have a car or anywhere to go, so they brought me here. This is all I could take." She showed Beth the picture she clutched. It was a black and white photo of a young man in a military uniform circa World War II. His slick hairstyle and smile captured the image of a heartthrob. The gold frame had spots of rust on it. "This is my Bobby. He passed away last year."

"He was very handsome."

"This is all I have left of him."

"I'm sure your house is going to be just fine and that you'll be able to go home soon."

Beth sat with her, offering comfort and listening to random memories of "her Bobby."

The woman's stories helped pass the time, for which Beth was grateful. She heard about the day they met, their wedding day, their tough times apart during the war, their reunion after the war, and their struggle to have children.

"And you know, dear, even though we never had

194

children, we went on many adventures together." She peered deep into Beth's eyes. "Make sure you find a man who will take you on many adventures, too, even when you're an old biddy like me. A man like that will make life interesting. He'll make life worth living, because you'll never be disappointed. A man like that is worth finding. But if you have to wait, he's worth the patience."

Beth smiled. "You're absolutely right." Her gaze swayed toward the door as someone entered. She turned away but then froze when she recognized the limping, soot-covered earthquake survivor as Donovan. Her head snapped back, and she drew in a quick breath. "I think I found that man," she mumbled. "Excuse me."

She rose on shaky knees. After the first few stabilizing steps to test her strength, she sprinted to Donovan and threw her arms around him in a desperate embrace.

His arms tightened around her. "You have no idea how happy I am to see you," he whispered in her ear.

"I think I know," she whispered back.

She framed his face with her hands and kissed him. Feeling his soft lips and the warmth of his mouth reassured her he was really there, safe and sound. She leaned her forehead against his and closed her eyes. "I was scared you wouldn't get out of the garage, that I wouldn't see you again."

"No one and nothing, not even a natural disaster, can keep me from you."

Beth eased back from him. "When you came in, you were limping." She swiped at a streak of soot on his neck. "What happened after I left?"

"That's a long story."

"Then it's a good thing we have plenty of time." She led him to her cot and coaxed him down.

He drank half a bottle of water and then told her about the concrete landing on his foot, the boy who had been hit by a car, and the explosion.

"You went into a burning building?"

"I had to, otherwise that mother and baby would've died."

Beth took his bandaged hand. "I know. I don't blame you. If I were you, I would've done the same thing." She told him about watching the firefighters, cops, and city workers vanish right before her eyes and being powerless to stop it.

"I'm sorry, Beth. I wish you hadn't seen that." He kissed her knuckles.

She didn't want to tell him how it haunted her. Whenever she blinked, she could see the cloud of dust swallowing the firetrucks. "I'll think about how you saved a baby and young boy instead. Hearing everything you did makes me proud."

"What? You didn't think I had it in me to be good?"

"No, I definitely knew. I think *you're* the one you had to prove it to." He frowned at her, so she continued, "You needed to know you had good in you, especially considering the fact you were called a murderer, even by me. More than that…the guilt. You weren't able to save your brother, and you felt, to some degree, responsible for his death. But today you helped many people and saved three lives. I think you doubted you were capable of doing that. You proved yourself wrong."

Donovan lifted their clasped hands and kissed the

back of her hand. "You're good for me."

"Your mom said the same thing."

He raised an eyebrow. "When? During Christmas?"

"Before she left after Ryan's funeral she said she saw the difference I'd made in you and that she was happy you found me." She held her breath, waiting for his reply. Now that he knew what his mom felt about the two of them being together, would he shrink from her?

"I'm sorry she realized it before I did," he said.

Beth stared at him. She never expected him to say that. *A joke?* Yes. *But the honest truth?* No. And part of her suspected it was his exhaustion talking. *He could regret this later.*

"Here, babies." Sandra came over with two wrapped sandwiches. "A group of church ladies dropped off a box of peanut butter and jelly sandwiches." She handed one to both of them.

"Thanks, Sandra."

Beth ate half of her sandwich and offered the other triangle to Donovan.

"No," he said. "You eat it."

"They already gave me a banana, so I'm fine. You need it more than I do." She pushed the sandwich at him again.

He accepted it. "I never thought, after eating so many of these following Hurricane Sabrina, that I would be grateful to have another one, but I feel like praying to the peanut butter god."

Beth laughed. "I don't think there is a peanut butter god."

Donovan took another bite. "There is now."

Sandwiches devoured, they lay together on the cot with Beth wedged into Donovan's side. Her eyelids were drifting with the weight of exhaustion when the face of the man she'd seen with Buck invaded her memory like a burglar. She sat up so fast she brought Donovan into a sitting position with her.

"What is it? What's wrong?"

"I almost forgot," she panted. "I saw Buck."

"Where?"

"Umm...inside a store past Union Square. He wasn't alone, though. A man was with him, and I think he's the one who orchestrated the whole drug ring."

Donovan got to his feet and held out his hand to her. "Show me."

"Now?"

His face looked as if it was etched in stone. His violet eyes were several shades darker. "Now."

Beth understood why he needed to go and didn't want to hold him back from getting his closure. Not when they'd been so close before. "Do you have your cell phone? Mine got damaged, but if yours is okay, shouldn't we tell the police? The system might be working again."

"My phone is fine." He patted his front pocket. "But the police have a lot more to worry about after a quake of this magnitude. They're probably stretched thin as it is." He held out his hand to her. "Ready?"

In the light of a dying day, she led him in the direction from which she had come. Walking against her invisible footprints on the asphalt felt different with Donovan beside her. Good different. His presence eclipsed all the anxiety, fear, and pain from earlier that day. She never thought she needed that from another human being—a man. Being the modern-day woman she was, she always rescued herself, preferred it that way, but she found she liked the extra dose of security Donovan offered. He did it so easily, too. But did he know he could give her an extra tank of strength with his presence alone?

Fewer people roamed the streets now. Most had gone home or to the shelters. Police officers with weary faces ushered stragglers on; they didn't want anyone on the streets once the sun went down, because the absence of sunlight always enticed criminals to come out of hiding. A lot of looting had already happened throughout San Francisco, and the police didn't want any more to occur, especially in Union Square, in the expensive stores with thousands of dollars worth of merchandise.

Beth and Donovan slipped past the police officers' barrier and into desolation. The emptiness of the streets was uncharacteristic for San Francisco, making it feel like an abandoned ghost town. They walked through one vacant block after another in silence. Even their shoes seemed to have padding over their soles, quieting their footsteps. Several shops had their gates drawn in front of their glass doors. More had sheets of plywood over the windows to keep out looters.

The sun sank below the horizon. Behind the skyscrapers, the sky was a smear of orange and pink.

Beth scanned the buildings on either side, searching for familiar landmarks to let her know they were getting closer to the place where she'd spied on Buck and his boss. She wasn't paying attention to the road ahead of them when Donovan grabbed her arm, yanked her into an alley, and pushed her into the side of a building. She opened her mouth to demand an explanation but couldn't get a peep out before his hand clamped over her mouth. He put his mouth next to her ear and whispered one word, "Buck."

Shifting back, he laid a finger over her lips. She nodded, and he released her, but not completely. He kept a hand on her hip as he flattened his back to the wall beside her.

She waited with him, with her gaze pinned to the road near the entrance of the alley.

Adrenaline pulsed through her body like a star flaring brighter, bigger, and hotter. A matter of seconds went by before Buck came into view and walked past them, but to her, it felt like sixty minutes weighed down each millisecond. In the space of one of those milliseconds, Donovan's hand vanished from her side. Beth watched him launch out of the alley and tackle Buck to the ground. Her heart vaulted into her throat. She ran out of the alley as Donovan rolled, pinning Buck beneath him.

He pounded his fist into Buck's face again and again. Drops of blood floated into the air, splattered onto the asphalt, and coated Donovan's hand. His teeth gritted together in a fierce snarl. His face twisted with rage.

Buck managed to throw Donovan off him. The two men scrambled to their knees at the same time and pounced at each other like bloodthirsty lions fighting over a carcass.

They twisted into knots on the ground; each one trying to gain power over the other and get in a hit at the same time. Buck's fist plowed into the side of Donovan's head, giving Buck the opportunity to take control of the fight. He straddled Donovan and hammered his right fist into Donovan's ribs, one blow after another in the same spot, as if he wanted to turn those ribs into a pile of splinters.

Beth searched frantically for something to hit Buck with, but she couldn't find a shovel, pipe, or anything else that was hefty enough and long enough to make an impact. She eyed the fast food to-go cup at her feet. Throwing it at Buck's head wouldn't faze him in the least. In his state, it would resemble a fly bopping him in the forehead. And she knew jumping into the fray would make matters worse. Despite all of her self-defense skills, she didn't know what to do to stop two grown men from beating the shit out of each other without getting pummeled herself.

Donovan thrust a fist into Buck's gut, effectively ending the assault on his ribs. When Buck bent forward, Donovan squirmed until his upper body was out from beneath him. Then maneuvering his body, he wrapped his legs around Buck's hips and tossed him backward, switching their positions. Donovan brought his fists down like hammers, one connecting with Buck on either side of his face. It was clear to Beth he wanted to beat Buck into a mound of flesh.

She rushed forward. "Donovan."

He didn't so much as tilt his head in her direction.

"Stop!"

He continued to rain punches down on Buck's face.

"Shit." If she waited for him to get tired, Buck would be dead, and she couldn't allow Donovan to do something he'd regret.

Buck's fingers curled around a rock. He lifted his arm and slammed the rock into Donovan's head. The blow knocked Donovan to the ground a couple of feet from where they fought. Buck pulled his body along the road as blood drizzled from his face. When Buck reached Donovan, he lifted the rock for another hit.

Fear spiked in Beth. The jagged edge of the rock could penetrate Donovan's skull. The blow could kill him. She had to intervene. She rocked back on her heels, crouched into a ready stance, and shot forward. She made the few strides quickly and rammed into Buck when the rock was an eyelash's width away from cracking Donovan's forehead. Her hit caught Buck off guard and knocked the breath from her lungs. She plowed into Buck so hard they flew together through the air.

After a handful of seconds, gravity spat them back down. Their bodies crashed into each other before splitting apart. Beth bumped against the road. Her shoulders, elbows, knees, and head rapped violently against the hard, rough road. She was lying on her back with her stare pointed to the sky when Buck's face hovered over her.

"You should've stayed out of it, you stupid bitch."

His fist came down on her. Her brain functioned too slowly for her to do anything about it. Her eyelids lowered to blink and that was when his fist crashed into her left eye socket. A cry escaped her lips. Then his fist hit her two more times. The punches were so strong it felt as though her eye would explode in her skull.

"I'll finish you off later," Buck snarled and disappeared.

Darkness crept around the edge of her vision. She was descending into the black world of unconsciousness but fought against it while she focused on breathing. If she let the pain circling her head take over, she would slip further away. She moved her fingers and felt the grainy surface of the road. Her legs twitched, and she pushed her thoughts to them. *Recognize what they are and what they do. Now raise them, bend the knee.* She pulled her legs up so the soles of her sneakers were flat on the ground and her knees pointed to the sky. *Move your arms.* Her arms floated from her sides and draped over her middle. Her stomach growled. *That's good. Pay attention to your hunger. You're dying for food, for a loaded cheeseburger and salty fries.*

The darkness stopped closing in on her and started to retreat. Her other senses also returned. She could smell a hint of smoke in the air, taste the metallic flavor of blood in her mouth, and hear the sound of flesh pounding flesh.

Donovan!

Her thought was so explosive that her whole body flinched. *Turn over!* Her body obeyed, and she rolled onto her side to see Buck on top of Donovan. Even though he had the advantage, they took turns hitting each other. When Buck socked Donovan, Donovan would return the favor, and vice versa.

Beth pushed herself onto her elbow. Her head spun dizzily. She closed her eyes and sucked in a breath. When she opened her eyes again, she noticed the back of Buck's shirt was lifted, revealing a gun tucked into the band of his jeans. Her body turned to ice. Mustering the dregs of her remaining strength, she yelled Donovan's name. She could only manage a few words after that and narrowed her warning to, "Gun. His back."

Both men heard her and fought to get the gun first. It disappeared from its hiding spot, but she couldn't tell who had it because four hands were knotted together. They became a twisted mess of limbs while they struggled to gain control. In one moment, Buck would be on top of Donovan, and in the next moment, it would be the other way around.

Grappling for a gun was dangerous, and she couldn't tell in which direction it was pointed. She looked around, hoping to find someone who could help. Her gaze fell to the ground in front of her where she found Buck's rock. She grabbed it and looked toward the wrestling men.

Donovan resumed his place on top. The gun was somewhere below him, locked between their hands when it went off. The shot echoed throughout the quietness. Neither man moved. Beth stared at them. Her breath was trapped in her lungs. After several excruciating seconds, Donovan fell to the ground.

"Donovan!"

Oh, God, no. Please, don't let him be shot.

Still clutching the rock in her hand, she crawled along the ground. She made it to Donovan's side and latched onto him. "Donovan?" Blood streaked his face. His gaze shifted toward her, and something tapped her thigh. She looked to see his hand, which held the gun. Beside Donovan, Buck lay on his back with blood flowing from his shoulder. His eyes were closed, but his chest rose and fell. He was still alive. For the moment.

Relief swept over her. She lowered her forehead to Donovan's chest. *Thank you, God, thank you.*

Lifting her head, she dropped the rock in her hand

to tenderly cup Donovan's face.

She touched his forehead with feather-light kisses as tears burned her eyes. "I love you," she whispered. "I love you so much." Her tears dropped onto his face, mixing with his blood. "Don't do that again. Okay?" His head flinched, and she took that for a nod.

"We need...police," he said, his voice breathless.

"Ssh." She kissed his lips to silence him. "It's okay. I'll take care of it." She slipped his phone from his pocket and held her breath as she waited for it to turn on. When the screen lit up, she saw the battery was almost dead. With shaky fingers, she dialed 911. *Please let the system be back up. Please, please, please.*

"911, what's your emergency?"

The sound of the dispatcher's voice sent relief crashing over her. "Need help," she said breathlessly. "Someone's shot. My boyfriend is badly injured, and I'm hurt. We're on Powell Street, in the middle of the road, past Union Square."

"I'm sending help to you right now. Please stay on the line."

Pain pulled her to the ground next to Donovan and threatened to take her. She kept the phone pressed to her ear, but her eyelids drooped. The dispatcher said something, but she could no longer comprehend words.

Her arm shook. She tried to speak, but her lips wouldn't move. A feeling of weightlessness overcame her, and her hand fell to her side. She was spiraling into unconsciousness when she heard sirens pierce the air.

Chapter Twenty-Four

Donovan woke to the blare of sirens. One of his eyes fully opened, but his other eye opened partway. His teeth ached, his head throbbed, and he couldn't take a deep breath without searing pain ripping across his middle. He tried to sit up but only succeeded in lifting his head.

"Easy," a woman told him. "I should've known you were trouble and wouldn't go to the hospital as I advised."

He turned his head to look at the woman who spoke and managed a smile when he noticed the female paramedic who treated him after the fire.

"Lucky for you, you won't have a choice about it now. I'm going to personally strap you to the stretcher." She winked at him.

Donovan realized he was still in the middle of the road. "Alive?"

"Yeah, you're still alive. Even the man with the GSW is still alive. He's been patched up and is getting ready to be taken to the hospital."

"Police. Where are the police?" The paramedic waved her hand in the air.

A police officer's face appeared above him. "Sir?"

"That man's name is David Buckland. If you call the Orlando Police Department in Florida, Chief Cormac, Officer Burnett, and Detective Thorn will all tell you he's a wanted criminal charged with murder and numerous drug charges. The gun is his."

"Don't worry, sir, we'll call. We'll get this all straightened out. The other man will have police with him at all times. You don't have to worry about him getting away."

Donovan turned back to the medic. "Girl?"

She smiled. "Your body is so numb you can't feel her? She's right next to you. She's okay."

Despite the excruciating pain, he turned on his side.

"Easy. We don't know the extent of your injuries. You could have fractured vertebrae," the medic said, but he stopped paying attention to her the instant he saw Beth.

He pressed his hand to the side of her face and kissed her eyelid. It was red and swollen. He put his mouth next to her ear. "Come back, baby."

Beth let out a whimper, and he kissed her cheek. When she turned her head to him, her left eye was barely open. If it swelled anymore, it would be sealed shut.

"Do you remember what you said when you were kissing me?" he asked.

Beth gave a slight nod and winced. "I said I love you."

He tapped his lips to hers. "I love you, too."

She lifted her hand and swiped away the trail of blood that tickled his brow. "I also asked you to never do this again."

"I won't."

Beth sighed. "I don't think you'll be able to make that promise. Not until this is over."

207

"But I do promise to love you. Forever."

Her lips stretched into a slow smile. "That's a nice promise."

Two stretchers arrived next to them. "All right, lovebirds. Time to break it up." The female medic crouched next to him with a backboard in her hands.

"I can get up on my own," Donovan said.

"Like hell. Your ass is being rolled onto this backboard whether you like it or not."

Donovan started to chuckle but the pain in his ribs stopped him. "Lucky for you, I don't feel like arguing."

A male medic fitted a neck brace around Beth's neck. Two of them shifted her and placed a backboard beneath her. As they secured her to the board, her gaze ticked over to Donovan. "Well," she said. "I guess I'll be seeing you around."

"Count on it."

The medics lifted her off the ground, forcing him to let go of her hand. They set her onto a stretcher and rolled her out of sight.

The female medic and her partner put a brace around Donovan's neck and strapped him to the backboard. During the ride to the hospital, the female medic started an IV, placed oxygen tubes in his nostrils, hooking them behind his ears, and cleaned the blood from his face.

"This is the second time we've come across each other," Donovan said. "I think I should call you something other than 'the female medic,' and you should call me something other than 'that-idiot-who-doesn't-listen,' don't you think?"

She laughed. "Kimberly."

"Donovan. There. I feel so much better now."

Kimberly dabbed at the cut above his eyebrow. "I think it's time for you to answer a question. How do you know the other man is a murderer?"

"Because I've been hunting him."

"Are you a bounty hunter?"

Donovan snorted. "No, but that's not a bad idea."

"So, how did you know?"

He thought about lying but decided it would be better to tell the truth. "He killed my brother."

"Oh." Kimberly's hand stilled. "Shit. I'm sorry." She started to clean the blood from his hands. "And the woman you were with is your girlfriend, right?"

"Yeah."

"She's a tough one. The dispatcher said she gave detailed information about where you guys were and the situation you were involved in before she went unconscious."

Donovan had no idea. He had slipped into blackness when Beth told him it was okay, because he believed her, trusted her the way she had always wanted him to trust her.

When he arrived at the hospital, he searched for Beth but couldn't find her. Nurses, doctors, sick people, and worried family members choked the halls. Apparently, everyone flocked to the hospital after the earthquake struck, whether they were injured or not. They probably felt safer there, or maybe they were there for loved ones.

"Well, this is where I leave you," Kimberly said.

"Wait. Can you ask about Beth? Beth Kennedy."

"Sure." Kimberly left to talk to the nurse at the desk and came back a moment later. "She's getting a CT scan to see if she has head trauma. After your marathon of X-rays and scans, you'll be reunited with her. I made sure of that."

"Thank you, Kimberly. You're my favorite medic in the whole world."

"I appreciate that but, no offense, I don't want to see you again. You need to get better, go home, and stay out of trouble."

"If you knew me, you'd know that's not possible."

She sighed. "Just not in Cali, okay?"

"Okay."

Donovan endured dozens of X-rays on top of a CT scan of his body. He used his time inside the CT gantry to think about Beth. He thought of the fear he felt when Beth sailed over him to take out Buck and how he was unable to help her. He recalled the relief when he saw her face again, and how she professed her love with tears in her eyes and her lips on his bloodied face. Not being with her now was difficult after what they had been through together. His one desire now was to take her in his arms and hold her.

After the imaging tests were complete, a nurse wheeled him through a maze of hallways to the emergency room that was divided by curtained cubbies. She deposited him in a shielded corner.

"Another nurse will be coming to check on that cut on your forehead," she said.

"Thanks."

"Take care." The nurse tugged the curtain around his bed before leaving.

"Donovan?"

The curtain to his left swished to the side, revealing Beth. She stood there holding onto an IV pole with a tube leading to her right arm. She wore blue scrub pants under a large gown. In the time they were apart, her left eye had swelled to the size of a halved orange and had turned several shades of purple, from plum to fuchsia.

"You're late for our date," she teased.

"I was delayed." He reached out his hand to her.

She took it. "Since you look so cute with a busted brow and lip, I guess I forgive you."

She bent over the bed and planted a gentle kiss on his forehead, above his brow, and at the corner of his mouth.

"How are you doing?" he asked. "Are you okay?"

"I'm fine. A little dehydrated and anemic, so they gave me this…" She waved her hand at the half-empty IV bag. "And a tray of rather bland food. The custard was good, though."

"What about your head? Did you get the CT scan results yet?"

"My head is fine, but my eye socket has a hairline fracture."

"Are you kidding me?" Donovan fought to get out of bed, but the searing pain that clawed its talons along his chest and abdomen forced him to still. He grabbed his ribs. "I'm going to find a way to kill that bastard," he hissed.

Beth put a hand on his shoulder. "It's okay."

"No, it's not."

"Donovan…" She took his battered hand. "The doctor said I don't need surgery because the facture is so small. He said it's mostly bruised and swollen and will heal on its own. I've been given a nice dose of oral pain medication, so I hardly feel it. I do feel a tad bit loopy, but I'm fine. The most important question is if you are okay."

"Oh, I'm great. My girlfriend has a fractured eye socket, but I'm great."

"You don't look great."

"You should see the other guy."

"I did."

His head whipped to her. "What?"

"I saw him," she repeated. "When a nurse took me to get my scan done, a group of officers and doctors were escorting Buck to the OR to remove the bullet. It apparently clipped his collarbone and lodged in his shoulder."

"Did he see you?"

She nodded. "He said he should've shot us when he had the chance. And, honestly, I've been wondering why he didn't. He had the gun on him the whole time, but he didn't use it. Why?"

Donovan lifted her hand and kissed it. "Don't wonder about that."

"Why not?"

"Because if he had used it, we'd be dead."

Beth brushed her fingers through his hair. "I don't know the extent of Buck's injuries, but he looked like a rainbow puffer fish. I'd be surprised if he didn't have a broken nose and fractured cheekbones."

"Good. The son-of-a-bitch deserves it."

"I agree."

A nurse pushed aside the curtain and stepped up to his bed. "Hello, Mr. Goldwyn. I'm going to administer some pain meds into your IV. Then I'm going to clean your cuts."

"Sounds good, but don't skimp on those pain meds."

"I won't." The nurse did what she said she would

and told him he would need stitches to close the gash on his forehead. "A doctor will be in to do that."

Dr. Cohen, who looked like he should've had Scooby Doo bandages and a plastic stethoscope, poked the gash in his forehead, causing a lot more pain while administering the drug that would numb it. As soon as his flesh was numb, Donovan could feel the sutures pulling his skin as the boy-doctor stitched the gash closed. It took four stitches to get the job done.

"That'll do it," Dr. Cohen said. "I'll be back when I get the results from your imaging tests."

He pulled the curtain back around the track to give them privacy.

Beth got up from the edge of her hospital bed and trailed a fingertip down Donovan's temple. "Sexy," she said.

"I'm glad you approve."

She sat in the chair next to his hospital bed and laid her head on the mattress. "I'm glad this is finally over," she said, her voice muffled by the blanket.

Donovan stroked her hair. "Me, too." He closed his eyes. The realization Buck was finally in police custody slowly registered. He took a cautious breath. Even though it hurt, it felt good.

"Damn! The two of you look like you've been through hell."

Donovan opened his eyes. It took a moment for him to recognize the man's face. "Thorn?"

Detective Thorn stood there in a black T-shirt and dark jeans, with his hands on his hips and his shield visible on his belt. "It's not the painkillers, Goldwyn, I'm really here. Apparently, too late to stop you from doing something stupid, though."

Beth picked up her head, forcing Donovan's hand to drop to his side. "Thorn? What are you doing here?"

Thorn turned to her. The grin he had aimed at Donovan vanished. "Holy shit." He stepped up to Beth and cupped her face in his hands. "Did Buck do this?"

"Yeah, but it's fine."

"Fine, my ass!" He angled her head with his fingers.

Even though he knew Thorn was concerned for Beth, Donovan didn't like the tenderness in his eyes. "Get your damn hands off my girlfriend."

Thorn looked at him and arched a brow. "Or what?" He turned to Beth, pulled her face to his, and laid his mouth over hers in an elaborate kiss that ended with a loud smacking sound. When he stepped back, he dipped his hands in his pockets and gave Donovan a devilish grin.

Seeing Thorn's mouth on Beth's sent Donovan's blood roaring through his veins like a volcanic eruption. "You're lucky I can't get out of this bed, or you'd be on the floor with your own black eye."

Beth shoved Thorn's shoulder. "Don't tempt him. He already tried to get up to avenge my honor."

"I don't blame him."

Donovan shifted in bed and winced when a flash of pain ricocheted through his body. "You never said why you're here," Donovan pointed out, unable to mask his annoyance.

"Other than kissing your girlfriend?" He winked at Beth, making Donovan see red. "When I couldn't get a hold of you, I didn't have a good feeling about it. I checked your computer, Donovan, and found the search for plane tickets to San Fran. I knew the two of you were here, up to no good, and I was right."

Donovan tilted his head. "And how did you get access to my computer?"

"I broke into your place, found it, and turned it on."

"Really? So, you're not above breaking-and-entering? And what about the password?"

Thorn shrugged. "I hacked it."

Donovan glared at him for a moment. The anger he felt over Thorn kissing Beth gradually faded, and a slow grin took over his face. He may not like the detective at times, but he had to admire Thorn's balls. "I would've done the same thing. When did you arrive?"

"My flight landed just before the quake hit. I've spent most of the day at the San Francisco Police Department. I was there when a call came in about a man and a woman having taken down a wanted criminal. I've already talked to the chief. He knows all about Buck. I also told him the two of you were here to help me find him, and since the quake delayed me, the two of you did what you had to do to keep Buck from getting away again."

Donovan nodded. "Thanks for that."

"They think the two of you are nuts for trying to take him down without at least a stun gun and handcuffs, though."

"Oh, Donovan had both," Beth announced.

The two of them looked at him—Thorn with his arms crossed, and Beth with a disapproving look on her face. *She still hasn't forgiven me for sneaking those into the hotel room without telling her first.* He made a vow not to keep another secret from her, if only to avoid that look.

"I lost the stun gun and cuffs during the quake," he explained. "They're somewhere in the rubble of the collapsed parking garage."

"So, you figured your fists were good enough to get the job done?" Thorn asked.

Donovan thought about that. "Yeah. They've been my best weapons in other fights."

Thorn shook his head. "You're lucky we have Buck in custody right now, and that the two of you are still alive."

Donovan glanced at Beth and her bruised eye. "Believe me, I know that."

Silence stretched between the three of them. Donovan thought about what he would've done if Buck had taken Beth's life. A hundred ways for how he could've tortured and killed him flashed through his mind, followed by images of a life devoid of happiness, love, and everything good. He would've been a hollow man without Beth.

"Excuse me." Two police officers stepped around the curtain. One of them was pushing a wheelchair. "We need to take your statements now. Come with me, ma'am."

Beth glanced at Donovan, with worry etched on her face. She got to her feet, sat in the wheelchair, and the officers took her away.

"Where are they taking her?" Donovan asked Thorn.

"To another room. They need to question the two of you separately."

"Go with her."

Unspoken words passed between them. Thorn nodded, spun on his heel, and followed the police

216

officers who led Beth away.

Although there was no evidence anyone in the San Francisco Police Department was part of the drug ring, Buck had come to the city because he knew someone. It wasn't a far-fetched idea that he might also be in league with a few of the officers here, even one of the officers questioning Beth. Donovan would never trust her to be alone with a single one of them, and he was glad Thorn understood. He felt much better knowing a man he trusted was keeping an eye out for her when he couldn't do it himself.

Beth had been gone for an hour when the same two officers came to get his statement. He used Thorn's lie about expecting to meet up with him this morning, but the earthquake ruined their plans. He told them about following Buck into the underground parking garage because they didn't want to lose him, and how Buck shot up two cars when he realized they were following. He skimmed over the events that happened between Beth leaving and reuniting with her again.

"When Beth told me she saw Buckland, I had her take me to where she saw him. We were walking that way when I spotted him. I pulled Beth into an alley. He walked past us, and that's when I tackled him to the ground. I forgot I didn't have my handcuffs on me. A fight ensued."

"Can you tell us about the gun?" one of the cops asked.

"Buckland hit me with a rock. I was half conscious from the hit when he climbed on top of me to slam the rock into my face. That was when Beth attacked him. I'm unaware of what happened after that, but you can clearly see what he did to her eye.

"He came back to me, I guess to end what he started. We were hitting each other when Beth shouted he had a gun behind his back. I reached for it and so did he. I wanted to get it before he could use it to kill us. I got my hand on it, but he fought with me. At the time, I didn't know my finger went onto the trigger. All I remember is wrestling with Buck and wanting to get the gun away from him. The sound of it going off startled me. I didn't move for a moment, not sure if I was shot or if he was. I collapsed before I could even figure it out. Beth came to me, and it was after I saw her face that I went unconscious. The next thing I heard was the sirens."

The officers finished jotting their notes and nodded to each other. "Thank you, Mr. Goldwyn. That's all for now."

Donovan leaned his head against the hospital bed. He was tired of cops. He was tired of the hospital. He was just plain tired. He wanted to be home, lounging on his couch with a cold beer in one hand and his arm around Beth. The image of that made half his mouth tilt up in a smile. Beth had become a permanent fixture in his thoughts and in his life. He couldn't imagine being in his apartment without her, which was odd because he never fantasized about another woman living with him before. *Only Beth. Always Beth.*

A whisper touched his ear. "Are you asleep?"

He shook his head. "I'm fantasizing about taking you home."

"Careful, she's not alone."

Donovan opened his eyes. Thorn had his arm around Beth's shoulders. "And you're still touching my girlfriend."

"That's because I'm trying to steal her away from you."

Beth laughed. "Where were the two of you when I was a single girl?"

Donovan cocked his head to the side. "Which one of us would you have picked?"

Beth looked from him to Thorn as if debating the possibilities, weighing the pros and cons of their looks and personalities. "Gee, I think it would've been a tie," she teased. She slipped out from under Thorn's arm and sat in the chair beside his bed, obviously making her choice.

"You may be a pain in my ass," Thorn told Donovan, "but the two of you are my friends. If Buck had done worse and gotten away, I would've hunted him down and emptied my clip in him the second I saw him."

Donovan and Thorn locked gazes. They understood each other very well.

"I'm going back to the station to do what I have to do to make sure this gets put behind you."

"I appreciate that," Donovan said.

"Bye, Thorn," Beth said. "Thanks for the kiss."

He winked at her. "I'll be in touch."

The doctor returned soon after Thorn left. "I have your test results, Mr. Goldwyn. You have four fractured ribs and a broken knuckle in your right hand."

"What about my ankle?"

"Severely bruised and swollen from what I could tell. You're going to have to stay off it, though. In a few minutes, a nurse will be in to wrap your ribs and splint your finger."

"Okay, but can I get some custard first?"

"I'll see what I can do."

A tray with a turkey sub, vanilla pudding, and a carton of apple juice arrived. He ate every bite but still wanted more. When he was done, a nurse wrapped his ribs and strapped an aluminum splint around his finger. Then she took them to a private room.

"I think Thorn might've pulled some strings for us," Beth said when they were alone. Being careful not to disturb his injuries, she joined him on his bed and put her head on his shoulder. "Night, Donovan."

He turned his head to kiss her forehead. "Night, baby."

****

"You know you're supposed to sleep in your own beds, right?"

Donovan opened his eyes to see a stern-faced nurse with her arms crossed over her starched uniform.

"The night nurse didn't mind."

"Well, I'm the morning nurse, and I do mind."

"Give us a minute, please."

The nurse huffed out of the room, clearly not happy.

Donovan caressed Beth's arm with his good hand. She had stayed stitched to his side the entire night, and she had more of an effect on him than the pain medication the nurses had given him.

"Beth, it's time to wake up."

"No," she grumbled.

"I'm sorry, but if the nurse comes back, she may hose us apart."

Beth mumbled something incoherent into his shirt. Whatever she said, it ended with, "hose her." She sat up with an exaggerated yawn and shifted on the bed, giving him a full view of her eye a day later. It looked like a ball was trying to push out of her face. Her eyelid was thick and plum-purple.

He sucked in a sharp breath. "Damn."

"You just confirmed what I think my eye looks like," she said and climbed off the bed. "I imagine your ankle and ribs look just as bad." Her right eye scanned him from head to foot. "How are you feeling?"

Looking up at the ceiling, he took a slow breath. He could barely move because of the crippling pain in his side. His ankle throbbed with lightning powerful enough to rival Zeus's trident. The burn on his hand still seared as if an invisible flame continued to lap at his skin, and his head felt like a quilt of pain.

"I feel okay."

Beth shook her head. "You don't always have to be tough. You can bitch and moan if you want."

He closed his eyes. "I internalize my pain."

"I've noticed." She kissed his cheek. "I'll be right back." She left the room and returned with the grumpy nurse.

"How is your pain today, Mr. Goldwyn?"

"As good as can be expected."

The nurse pursed her lips, picked up the patient-controlled pain medication pump connected to Donovan's intravenous line, and jabbed the button with her thumb. She held it in front of him. "Use this when you need it. That's what it's there for." Before marching back out, she gave Beth more oral pain meds and stood with her hands on her hips until she swallowed them. Then she turned on her heel and left.

"She's delightful," Beth muttered.

Donovan's gaze swept over to her. "You told her I

was in pain, didn't you?"

She nodded. "That's because you are. And it's fine that you are. It's understandable. Right now, I feel as though my head is going to explode. And you have far more injuries than I do. I can't even imagine the pain you're in."

"When I was six, I fractured my arm by falling out of a tree my mom told me not to climb. I didn't tell her what happened until she noticed it was red and swollen. That was two days later." He shrugged. "I don't like to show my pain. I've been that way for as long as I can remember."

"I don't think you like people worrying about you."

"That's probably true, so don't tell my mom about this. She'd worry."

"Your secret is safe with me," she vowed. A smile started to form on her face but only got halfway before she flinched and cupped her eye with her hand. She lowered onto her bed with a groan.

Although Donovan was in pain, he hated seeing Beth in pain even more.

Their breakfast arrived, which consisted of oatmeal, eggs, triangles of toast, and orange juice. They were watching the morning news when Thorn sauntered into the room.

"The two of you are being released, and I'm your ride out of here."

"Already? That seems fast," Beth said.

"Donovan's injuries aren't that serious. They've done what they can for him. They could also use your beds, since they're swamped."

"So where are you going to take us?" Beth asked. "We're not exactly fit for travel, and our belongings are in our old hotel room."

"I booked you a room in the hotel where I'm staying."

"Sounds good to me," Donovan said. "What are we waiting for?"

"We're waiting for a wheelchair for your sorry ass."

"I don't need a wheelchair," he protested.

"Even tough guys get wheeled out of the hospital," a middle-aged nurse said as she pushed a wheelchair into the room. A second nurse followed her in with a wheelchair for Beth. After their IVs were removed, one of the nurses helped Donovan into a sitting position, a task that wasn't easy when his ribs felt like dried spaghetti noodles that could snap with the slightest touch. The red-hot pain that raked across his side made it impossible to breathe. Using a crutch, he got to his feet, hopped on his good foot, and made a faint growling sound when the movement vibrated his fractured ribs.

Offering him a hand, the nurse eased him into the chair, lowered the footrests, and pushed him all the way out of the hospital, making him feel like an invalid. The fact he wasn't capable of doing much under his own power irritated him to no end.

From the back seat of Thorn's rental, Donovan looked out the window at the aftermath of the earthquake. Several shops were closed off with yellow caution tape. City workers blocked the entrances to roads with dump trucks as they used jackhammers to break-up damaged asphalt. Large excavators scooped up the broken asphalt. Groups of volunteers helped shop owners sweep sidewalks and board up windows.

Donovan had a hard time finding a position that didn't bother his ribs or ankle. Giving up, he asked Thorn the one question that was on his mind, "Is Buck still at the hospital?"

"For now. When he's released, he'll be booked into the San Francisco Police Department."

"What about the man Beth saw with Buck?"

Out of the corner of his eye, he saw Beth lower her head. "I didn't get a good look at his face," she said softly.

He reached out to touch her knee. "It's okay. It's not your fault."

During the rest of the ride, Donovan closed his eyes and dozed to the lullaby of a running engine. Every bump in the road jarred him from his light slumber, though, and sent electricity zigzagging along his ribcage.

The hotel where they were staying wasn't as elegant as their last hotel, but Donovan didn't care. All he wanted was a private room where nurses wouldn't be barging in every thirty minutes and that had a bed big enough to fit him and Beth comfortably.

Thorn retrieved the key card at the front desk and led them to their room on the third floor. "Here you are," he announced as he pushed open the door.

Donovan's gaze swayed from one side of the room to the other. The bed had an ugly comforter on top of it, and a TV was positioned on the dresser in front of the bed. An air conditioner took up the space beneath the window, and there was a small kitchen complete with a coffee pot, mini-fridge, and microwave.

"The little old lady who lived in a shoe wouldn't even live here," Beth commented.

"The department is paying for your room, so this is what you get," Thorn said.

"What about the things we left at the other hotel?"

"I called the owners. They had to close the hotel until the city can come out to stabilize the underground parking lot. They'll notify all the guests when it's safe to retrieve their possessions."

"Thanks for making the call."

"It's the least I could do."

Donovan teetered into the room on his crutch, too tired to engage in small talk. With a hand clutching his ribs, he eased himself onto the bed and managed to lay on his back. He knew he wouldn't be getting up for a long time, so he let himself sink into sleep like an anchor dropping into the depths of the ocean.

Chapter Twenty-Five

Beth tiptoed the first day they were in their new hotel room, careful not to make noise. She wanted Donovan to rest and his body to heal quickly, and sleep was the best way to do both. She took a nap beside him for a few hours. When she woke, she took a long, hot bath. The water turned her achy muscles to liquid. It felt so good that she would've fallen asleep if it wasn't for the pain enveloping her left eye. Using a white washcloth and clumps of ice from the mini fridge, she created an icepack and held it to her eye while sitting on the balcony in a lounge chair. Despite her bruised face and the cold air, relaxing felt wonderful.

Glancing at Donovan through the sliding glass door, she noticed he hadn't moved an inch since lying down. *I had it easy.* She couldn't even fathom what it felt like to have his injuries. One alone would be painful enough, but all at once would be misery.

She dropped the icepack on the armrest and got to her feet. Standing at the rail, she leaned against it and peered down. If she were in better condition, she'd float on a pink raft in the indoor swimming pool. Heck, she would float on a raft and scare all the children with her bulging, bruised eye if she had her bikini, but it was in her suitcase at the condemned hotel.

Her stomach growled, reminding her it was time for dinner, and she hadn't had a bit of food for lunch.

Leaving Donovan safe in bed, she went to the room across the hall and knocked on the door.

Thorn answered it. "What can I do for you, Beth?"

"I was hoping you knew of a good place around here where I can get a decent meal."

"As a matter of fact, I do. Where's Donovan?"

"Sleeping. I didn't want to wake him."

"That's probably for the best." He held out his arm to her. "I'll buy."

At a small café, they each ordered a sandwich and bowl of soup and sat outside at an umbrella table. Beth took a bite out of her chicken salad sandwich. The taste and texture of the toasted bread, grilled chicken, creamy mayo, and crisp celery tangled with her taste buds. She ladled yellow-squash soup into her mouth with a satisfied moan. The iced green tea topped off the parade of flavors.

"Wow. I have to say that since I've been in San Francisco I've had the best meals."

"They certainly do know their food here," Thorn agreed and bit into his BLT.

Beth could hear the crunch of the bacon and lettuce from across the table. The smell of his potato soup overpowered the aroma of the soup right under her nose.

When Thorn finished eating, he leaned back in his chair and folded his arms across his stomach. "So, what exactly were your plans after you found Buck?"

Beth lowered her spoon. "My plans? What makes you think I had anything to do with it?"

"Did you?"

She shook her head. "Not really. I came because I couldn't let Donovan come here alone. I found out about his plan to make a citizen's arrest with a stun gun after we checked into the hotel."

"And how were the two of you going to accomplish that? It would've been hard to get close to Buck."

"Well…I was the bait."

Face stern, Thorn sat upright. "You were the *what*?"

"Easy." She raised her hand to calm him. "It was my idea, not Donovan's. As a matter of fact, he was against the whole thing, but I convinced him to let me do it."

"Do what exactly?"

Casting her gaze down, she told him about how she had lured Buck to the garage with the promise of sex. Thorn rubbed his eyes with a groan, as if he couldn't believe what he was hearing.

"Hey, it worked," she reminded him.

He dropped his hands to the table, rattling the silverware. "You're lucky the quake happened when it did or he could've riddled the two of you with bullets. I think Mother Earth had your back."

"Yeah, I owe her big time." While sipping the last of her green tea, Beth realized Mother Earth had introduced her to Donovan, too. Without Hurricane Sabrina, they never would've met. Now Mother Earth had saved their asses with a seven-point-four earthquake. If Mother Earth were in human form, she would be the Maid of Honor at their wedding.

Wedding? Beth shook her head to dislodge that thought from her brain. She was positive Donovan wasn't ready to talk about Holy Matrimony. She wasn't even sure if she was ready.

"Are you finished?"

She perked up at the sound of Thorn's voice. "Oh, yeah, I'm ready to go."

Before they left, Beth ordered Donovan a roast beef sub on Italian bread. Back at the hotel, she thanked Thorn for the dinner and the company.

"It was my pleasure, and you can tell Donovan I said so, which reminds me, I have something for the two of you." He retreated into his room and returned with two bags of clothing. "I picked these up for you. They're handing out clothes and other essentials at shelters for people who need them. I was able to guess Donovan's size, but a woman is…different."

She laughed. "It's okay. I appreciate the thought. Thanks."

He gave her a parting wink and closed the door to his room.

Inside her own room, Beth found Donovan lying on his side. Touching his shoulder, she whispered in his ear, "Are you hungry?"

A faint "no" escaped his lips, but she doubted he was fully out of the Sandman's influence when he answered.

He'll wake when he's hungry. Or when he has to empty his bladder.

She stashed his sub in the mini fridge and climbed into bed with him.

****

The next morning, Beth ordered room service for breakfast—two plates of eggs, sausage, and biscuits— but Donovan didn't even stir at the smell of the fresh coffee leaking through the room. She ended up eating his toast and drinking his coffee, the two items that wouldn't be good reheated. She put his plate of eggs and sausage in the microwave for later.

A groan pulled her from the bathroom, where she was inspecting her eye, to see Donovan fighting to get into a sitting position. She rushed to his side, supported him with her arm, and helped him to his feet. Seeing how vulnerable he was twisted her heart into a knot. He took small steps toward the bathroom.

"I'm okay," he muttered. She checked to see if the toilet seat lid was up before releasing him and shutting the door. Sitting on the bed, she wrung her hands. When the toilet flushed, she shot to her feet again, ready to meet him at the door. She helped him back into bed and even stretched out beside him. Her fingers stroked his temple and combed through his hair. It wasn't long before his breathing became deep with sleep.

Mid-day, she peeled the gauze off his burn to clean it and reapply salve. Removing tape from skin and hair—not to mention from an irritated wound—always hurt, so she bared her teeth and lifted the strips centimeter-by-centimeter. Donovan's eyelids fluttered open when she was half-way through the task. Her fingers stilled.

"I'm sorry," she whispered. "Your burn needs to be cleaned."

He made a soft humming sound from deep in his throat before his lids lowered, curtaining his worn-out eyes. Stroking his brow, she murmured endearments to him even though she figured her words wouldn't have enough power to penetrate his subconscious. Regardless, she hoped he would hear them in his dreams.

After she followed the doctor's instructions to take care of his burn properly and applied a clean sheet of gauze, she took turns icing either side of his ankle, which she had propped up on an extra pillow. She wanted to do more for him but didn't know what else she could do, so she spent the remainder of the day watching shows on the small TV with the volume turned down low. Every few minutes, she'd glance at Donovan as if he was a sleeping newborn and she was a nervous mother who wanted to make sure her baby still breathed.

The day crawled by at a glacial pace. She ordered a cob salad for lunch and ate it cross-legged on the floor. For exercise, she roamed the halls of the hotel, venturing from one floor to the next. Finding ways to keep herself occupied wasn't easy with a swollen eye. Not to mention the fact Donovan was her guide to San Francisco. When walking the halls grew old, she did yoga on the balcony until a group of men in the parking lot noticed her and started to whistle and shout at her whenever she twisted her body into a new pose.

"Oh, yeah, baby."

"I bet you're bendy in bed."

"Come down here and let me get to know your downward dog."

With a parting middle finger in the air, she went back into the hotel room. Their harassing requests for her to come back quieted when she closed the sliding glass door. What would Donovan have done if he had been awake to hear them? She decided it was for the best that he was unconscious.

Dinner—an avocado burger and sweet potato fries—was a lonely meal at the small table next to the kitchen. Even though he was a few feet away, Beth missed Donovan. She longed to hear his voice, to see his violet eyes.

The next several hours before she decided to go to bed were longer yet. She watched a black and white silent film and then read a few chapters in the Bible and the Koran she found tucked inside the nightstand drawer. At ten o'clock, she took her pain meds and turned in early.

The golden light of a new day filtering through the blinds woke her. She gasped when she opened her eye and saw Donavan staring at her.

"You're awake?"

"Good morning," he said in way of answering her question.

She kissed him in the middle of his forehead. "I thought you'd never wake. You had me worried."

"I'm sorry. I should've told you that when I'm hurt or sick I tend to sleep for forty-eight hours while I recuperate. I've been that way ever since I was a kid. When I fractured my arm, I slept for two days straight. After I woke up and ate two cheeseburgers, I was a rowdy little boy again, climbing that tree."

He gave her a wicked grin.

"I don't think you'll be able to bounce back as quickly this time."

"Is that a challenge?"

She shook her head at his quirked brow. It was sure good to see that look on his face again. "For once, it's not." Smoothing back a lock of his hair, she added, "I'm just happy to see you're okay. I don't want you to push it."

"Well, I'm going to get out of this bed to take a

shower."

"You've been lying in this bed for two days," she pointed out. "Your muscles are going to be extremely stiff."

"That's why it's going to be a hot shower."

"Stay here. I'll start the water and then help you up." She hurried into the bathroom, whisked aside the tacky, flowered shower curtain, spun the knob, and yanked up the lever. The water burst from the showerhead in beaded streams. As a thin haze of steam formed at the bottom of the tub, she went back into the bedroom. At the threshold, she came to a halt. Donovan leaned against the bed, with his arm braced across his middle.

"What are you doing? I said I was going to help you."

"I'm not an invalid, Beth." He limped toward her like a robot with a bad leg and every joint in need of oil.

"Says the man who can barely walk."

"Criticizes the woman with a black eye."

Crossing her arms, she glared at him with her one good eye.

"Your scowl power is not as strong as it used to be." Stepping in front of her, he planted a kiss between her furrowed brows.

He was about to teeter around her when she put her hand on his shoulder. "Does your rejection for help mean you don't want me to help you in the shower? Because I planned on lathering your back..." Her fingers moved over his chest. "...and your front." She hoped the look she gave him was seductive, not psychotic, but with a battered face, it was hard to be sexy. "If you don't want any help, then I guess I'll leave you to it." She started to shift away, but he caught her arm.

"I think I can make an exception."

"I thought you might." Taking his hand, she led him into the bathroom. On the bath mat, her fingers curled around the hem of his shirt to pull it up his body, but he stopped her with a shake of his head.

"I won't be able to lift my arms over my head. You can cut it off. I don't care."

"Okay." She checked under the sink but couldn't find so much as a first-aid kit. In the kitchenette, she scrounged through the drawers and cabinets. No scissors, so she returned with the next best thing...a knife.

"This is all I could find," she said while brandishing the small steak knife. She lifted his shirt and brought the tip of the blade to it. Donovan cuffed her wrist with his thumb and index finger. "What? You don't trust me to cut your shirt without gutting you like a fish?"

The corner of his mouth lifted, and he released her wrist. "Go ahead."

With the blade under his shirt, she poked the tip through the cotton then pulled the knife toward herself, cutting a clean slit down the middle. She set the knife in the sink, took the sides of his shirt in her hands, and ripped it the rest of the way. Then she unwound the wrap holding his ribs, revealing a pattern of bruises like red and purple fireworks in the night sky.

"Damn," she breathed. "I'm sorry."

"Why are you sorry? It's not your fault."

But she felt responsible regardless. After all, she was the one who led him straight to Buck without backup, without a stun gun and handcuffs, and knowing how badly he wanted to kill the man. If she had been smarter, she would've done everything in her power to keep him away from Buck until the situation was in their favor.

Donovan lifted her chin with his thumb. "I don't care that I'm injured. I'm just glad I have the worst injuries this time...instead of you." His finger trailed along the scar on her chest.

"I guess it's always hard to see the person you love hurt," she said and eased his torn shirt from his shoulders. After unclasping the button to his jeans, she took the zipper in her fingers and lowered the slider one link at a time. She slipped his pants down his muscular legs, followed by his boxer briefs.

"Get underneath the hot water before it turns cold. I'll join you in a minute."

She undressed, wishing she had a razor to shave the two-day-old stubble on her legs. And her underarms. She climbed into the shower, and steam swooped around her, but it wasn't nearly as hot as Donovan's stare. He was under the spray. His dark hair dripped, and streams of water glided down his chest.

"Is it too hot?" Her voice came out breathier than she intended.

"No." He took her by the elbows and pulled her to him so the water also hit her. "Is it too hot for you?"

She shook her head; it was all she could manage with his eyes intent on her. She couldn't help but recall the first time they shared a shower together. Picking up the hotel bar of soap, she cupped it in her palms and created a thick lather. Inching behind him, her breasts brushing against him, she laid her hands on his shoulders and soaped his back. The muscles under her fingers shifted at her touch. She marveled at the strength in those muscles as she spread suds along the length of his arms and down his spine. Her hands massaged his shoulders, unraveling the kinks buried deep within his flesh. When a cast of sweet bubbles covered his back, she used a wet cloth to exfoliate his skin and then directed him to the pulsing drops of water.

Standing in front of him, she stroked his chest with her soapy hands. She made sure not to apply pressure to his ribs, only letting her fingers flutter over his side with the gentlest of touches. The whiteness of the suds couldn't mask the hideous bruises, though. She reached for the soap again and caressed bubbles into circles over his abs. When she finished soaping his body, he cupped her face with his wet hands and sighed. "I haven't brushed my teeth. Otherwise, I would kiss you."

She smiled. "First, I need to get some food in you before you drop. Then you can brush your teeth and kiss me as you should." She gave him a wink and picked up the bottle of shampoo to wash his hair. She hated seeing him in pain, but she enjoyed this part of taking care of him.

Chapter Twenty-Six

Donovan ate the cold roast beef sandwich and a stack of Belgium waffles Beth ordered for breakfast. He couldn't get his hands on enough food to fill the bottomless pit that was his stomach.

"Here." Beth held out her hand to him. Two white pills sat in the center of her palm.

He groaned.

"Take them or I'll strap you down and force you."

"Bondage with you would be fun," he said. "I think I might enjoy being your submissive."

She shook her head as if she disapproved of his thoughts, but the corner of her mouth twitched.

"We'll pick up this conversation again when my body can handle your foreplay," he added and plucked the pills from her hand. Knocking them back, he swallowed them with the rest of his coffee. When he set down his cup, he noticed Beth's cringe. "What?"

"I don't know how you can take pills with coffee. I can only swallow medication with water at room temperature."

He chuckled. "I'll remember that for when you're sick and I have to take care of you."

Beth's head jerked to him, and he sensed he said something wrong. "What now?"

"Nothing."

"That look doesn't mean *nothing*. You can tell me.

What did I say that was so wrong?"

"No, it wasn't wrong. It was right." Sighing, Beth sat across from him at the small table. "You're the first man to willingly want to take care of me when I'm sick. When I was engaged to—"

"The asshole whose name you won't tell me?"

"My ex," she continued. "I couldn't even get him to heat me a bowl of soup when I had a cold."

"Because, and I repeat, he was an asshole. He didn't deserve you. And you don't have to worry...I'm nothing like him. I'll make you soup and tea and do whatever else that'll make you feel better when you're sick or hurt." He took her hand. "I promise."

"And I'd do the same for you," she said.

"I already know that."

She frowned, making him want to kiss the lines between her brows. If he could get up and stretch across to her without seething in pain, he would do just that.

"When I woke up, you were cleaning my burn," he explained. "And I know you kept my foot elevated while I was asleep. I also felt you frequently touching my forehead."

Beth shrugged as if it didn't mean anything. He knew differently.

"I was checking for a fever," she said. "The doctor mentioned the possibility that one could develop."

Donovan lifted her hand to his lips. "Since a wall of rubble isn't blocking us from each other, and we're not suffering from concussions..." He gazed into her eyes. "I love you, Beth Kennedy."

Beth leaned across the table and kissed him in the same way he had wanted to do a moment ago. "I love you, too, Donovan Goldwyn. Now go brush your teeth."

****

Two weeks after the quake, Beth's swollen eye had deflated, much to Donovan's relief. Only yellow and green bruising in the shape of a cauliflower surrounded her eye socket now, and he was finally able to walk without limping too badly.

The days had gone by with little excitement while they waited for the hotel to give them a green light to retrieve their possessions, and for news on Buck. He could tell Beth was bored out of her mind, and he figured they were overdue for a little fun. "Let's go to the beach," he announced.

Beth's eyes lit up, and then faded as if a gust of wind had blown them out in a single puff. "Please don't toy with me. My salt, sand, and sun deprived heart wouldn't be able to handle the heartbreak."

"I'm not toying with you. Thorn is busy helping out at the San Fran PD, and we're healed enough. Soon we'll be able to travel, and we deserve to enjoy ourselves outside of this damn hotel room before we have to leave."

Beth bounced off the bed in her excitement. "No need to say anymore. I'm sold." She dug through the pile of clothing on the floor and came up with a teal tank top and yellow shorts. "It'll do," she decided.

The sand at the beach was soft, and the waves were big enough to surf. From the top of a sand dune, Donovan watched a surfer wipeout and longed for his board. Surfing was his favorite thing to do second to racing monster trucks, and it had been a long time since he'd used pineapple sex wax, stuck Velcro around his ankle, and dove beneath waves as he paddled out to catch the biggest wave in a set.

Although it was a chilly January day, the sun warmed his back, and he hoped the vitamin D from the sun's rays would help heal the bruises along his ribs. The salt in the air did make breathing easier and more pleasurable. While taking another breath, he watched Beth wade through rolling waves and kick globs of white foam in the air like a gleeful three-year-old.

She came back with her shorts dripping wet and carrying a handful of shells. "Don't make fun of me, but I've collected shells ever since I was a kid, except the shells I have at home are all from the East Coast, so these are special."

He picked up a swirly shell. "If you think about it, these shells could've come from all over the world and ended up here for you to find."

Beth beamed at him. "I never thought of that." She kissed him, and he tasted the salt on her lips. "I wish you could join me in the water. It's cold, but it feels great."

He dropped his head and kissed her pink shoulder. "When we're back in Florida, we'll have plenty of time together at the beach. I'll even teach you how to surf."

"I'd love that."

She shifted so her body was between his legs and her back against his chest. He hooked his arms around her and held her to him. Cheek to cheek, they looked out at the ocean, enjoying the beauty and tranquility that could still exist after a disaster.

****

Donovan opened the hotel room door for Beth. His gaze lowered as she walked in, and he noticed a piece of paper on the floor. He picked it up and read the message scrawled in black ink.

You're lucky you weren't home when I came knocking. Donovan slipped the note into his pocket before Beth could see it.

Closing the door, he said, "So did you have a good time at the beach?"

She kicked off her cheap, charity flip-flops. "Are you kidding? I had a blast." She rinsed off the shells and laid out her loot on the kitchen counter. "I wish we could come back here for a real vacation sometime. But, you know, ask a psychic if there's going to be an earthquake first."

"You believe in psychics?"

"Absolutely. A psychic warned me that if I accepted my boyfriend's proposal, he would cheat on me during our engagement."

"So, she was right?"

"Of course, she was right. She was the bitch I found in bed with him."

Donovan's jaw dropped. "The psychic?" Beth nodded, and he could see the anger roaring through her veins as if she was finding out the truth of the affair for the first time. "How did he even know the psychic?"

"When we first started dating, we went to her shop after a movie to get our palms read for fun. I ignored her flirtations toward him, and thought the prediction she gave him about *great passion* in his future was about us. I went back to her, not even thinking she remembered Craig or me, and asked her if we'd be happy together if we got married. She told me there was no chance for happiness in our future, and he'd have a secret affair with a blonde woman.

"It wasn't until I threw the bitch out by a fist full of

her blonde hair that I realized the great passion she told him about was between her legs. She planned the whole thing from the time she met him. Before I broke his balls, he admitted she had slipped him her phone number when we were leaving. The whole time we dated, he was unfaithful, and he honestly thought he could get away with having sex with her and a relationship with me for the rest of his pathetic life." Beth's brown eyes had darkened with anger while she told the story. They were as black as coal.

No wonder she was cautious when it came to relationships. *What would it take to make her comfortable with the thought of marriage after what that asshole did to her?*

A moment passed before he realized her slip. He smirked. "Craig, huh?"

Beth blinked at him. "Did…did I say Craig?"

"Yes, you did."

"Well, at least you won't be able to hunt him down with just a first name."

His smirk grew.

"Right?"

He didn't agree or disagree.

"Donovan, you can't find someone with just a first name. There are a lot of Craigs out there. You're not going to hunt down every single one of them."

He tilted his head slightly. "Oh, but I could," he joked.

She laughed. "Fine, but don't kill him. I helped you prove your innocence once already, but if you kill him, my streak will end." She dropped onto the edge of the bed. "If you beat his ass, though, promise me one thing."

"What?"

"Make it hurt." Her face twisted into a grin, and he chuckled. She picked up the room service menu. "Are you hungry?"

"Always. Order me whatever you want. I'm going to talk to Thorn."

Lowering the menu, she peered at him. Even though she didn't open her mouth, he heard her unspoken question.

"I want to ask him if he heard from the hotel and if he has an update on Buck."

Beth squinted her eyes at him, using her inner lie detector to tell if he was lying. He must've passed her test because she lifted the menu again. "Do you want coffee?"

"Sounds good. I'll be back in a few. Lock the door when I leave."

"You're going across the hall."

"Lock. The. Door."

"All right, all right. I will."

Donovan stood in the hall until he heard the click of the lock. Then he knocked on Thorn's door.

"Hey, Goldwyn." Donovan pushed past Thorn when he opened the door. "Sure, come right on in. Make yourself at home."

"I don't need a friend right now, Thorn. I need a detective." Donovan pulled out the note and gave it to him.

Thorn read it. His eyes flashed once with venom before they cleared, turning into the unreadable cop-stare. "You think the man Beth saw with Buck left this?"

"Don't you?"

"Yes."

Thorn went into his tiny kitchen, came back with a Ziploc bag, and slipped the note inside. "I'll get the San Francisco crime lab to dust this. Hopefully, there's a good friction print we can use to nail this asshole."

"You'll let me know what they find?"

Thorn snorted. "As if I'd be able to keep it from you, Goldwyn."

Donovan nodded, satisfied. "Any news on Buck?"

"Yeah. He's in a cell in Florida."

Anger rushed through Donovan, scoring the inside of his veins with fire. "What?"

"He didn't do any crimes here, Donovan. You technically attacked him. And shot him. At point-blank range. And there's no proof he shot up the garage because no one has been able to go down there to investigate yet. All they have on him are the threats the officers heard him say to Beth, and that's not enough to hold him here, but he's wanted in Florida for the murder of a law enforcement officer. He was transported last week with U.S. Marshals. I'm still here to bring the two of you back home safely. Chief Cormac thinks there could still be a threat on you and doesn't want either of you unprotected."

"Why didn't you tell me Buck was transported? I had a fucking right to know!"

"You were in bed most of the time recovering from a serious beat down. Or do you not remember?"

"He killed my brother, Thorn. I want to know everything that happens with him, and all the rest of them, the second you know something. And I don't care if I'm in a hospital bed with a fucking tube down my throat."

"Understood." Thorn held up the Ziploc bag. "Does Beth know about this note?"

"No."

"Good. She shouldn't be afraid right now." He picked up the keys to his rental. "I'll take this to the department and have it tested. Top priority."

In the hallway, Donovan thanked him.

"No problem, and, for the record, what I've been doing for you and Beth is because I'm a friend first and a detective second."

Donovan could accept that. Having a friend on the inside was a good thing. *Could come in handy. You never know when you could use a cop-friend's help.*

Thorn started down the hall.

"One more thing," Donovan said.

Thorn stopped. "Name it."

"Can you look into Beth's history for a man named Craig? I'd like some information on him."

"Ex-boyfriend?"

"Ex-fiancé."

Thorn nodded once. "Consider it done."

Donovan entered the hotel room he shared with Beth to find her sitting cross-legged on the bed eating an ice cream sundae. "I thought you were ordering food."

"Oh, I did." She waved her hand at the cart with coffee and two covered plates. "But I wanted to start with dessert."

Donovan lifted the covers. Heaps of steaming spaghetti sat in the center of two plates with a basket of freshly made breadsticks on the side.

"Do you want some?" Beth held up the ice cream spoon she'd licked clean.

"Sure."

"Sit down." She stood in front of him when he lowered onto the edge of the bed and removed his button-up shirt from his shoulders. With the bowl in her hands, she straddled him. "Am I hurting you?"

Curiosity rippled through him. "No, you're fine."

She lifted the spoon from the bowl and fed him ice cream, chocolate syrup, and whipped cream. The ice cream melted on his tongue. "Mm. That's good."

"It gets better," she promised and smeared melted ice cream onto his lips with the back of the spoon. She kissed him hungrily. When she finished sucking away the coldness from his lips, she set the bowl aside, framed his face with her hands, and gazed into his eyes. "I love how protective you are of me," she admitted. Heat radiated off her body and slammed into him like a solar flare. "It turns me on."

"Oh, yeah?"

"Yeah."

She drizzled ice cream and chocolate syrup onto his shoulder. As it slithered down his skin, it felt like cold fire that made him burn from the inside. His breathing quickened, and his heart rate rose. When the tip of Beth's tongue touched his heated skin, he sucked in a breath between his teeth.

She licked up the sweet streams with her tongue and poured more down his chest. Her mouth followed the creamy pathways, causing his stomach muscles to clench. What she was doing, using her tongue and mouth on him, was driving his libido into overdrive.

"Do I get to eat ice cream? Or are you going to hog it all?"

Picking up her head from the waistband of his

shorts, where the last bit of ice cream had collected, she licked her lips. "Of course." She started to reach toward the bowl.

"No. I want the spoon." He took it from her. "I hate I can't do this myself, but I'm going to enjoy watching you do it...take off your shirt."

Beth slowly lifted the teal tank top up her body. Her hair dropped to her shoulders when she pulled it off her head. "How's this?"

Donovan shook his head. "Bra, too." Reaching behind her, she unhooked her bra and dropped it to the floor with a flutter of lace.

Using the spoon, Donovan created a pattern of swirls on her tan chest. Her shivers made him smile. He brought his mouth to her, tasted vanilla and the indescribable flavor of Beth's sun-warmed skin. A hint of salt from the beach still clung to her, and the combination of it with the sugar made his mouth water for more.

His tongue curled around one of her taut nipples that a river of cold ice cream painted white. He licked it clean as she moaned in pleasure. Her back arched, and he took her other nipple in his mouth, this one tainted with chocolate.

"Donovan..."

His name was a gasp that told him she wanted exactly what he craved. He worked open the button of her yellow shorts and eased the zipper down its track. "Take them off," he whispered in her ear.

Leaning back, she peered down at his lap where he knew a bulge greeted her. "Are you sure?"

"If I could manage to bend that far, I'd lay you down, pour a spoonful of ice cream between your legs, and lick you clean. Unfortunately, I can't, but I sure as hell can manage sitting. Although, you're going to have to do all the work."

She smiled. "I'll be happy to." Getting to her feet, she took his hands and led him to the couch where she inched down his shorts. When he eased down, with his gaze on her, she stripped out of her shorts and panties then positioned herself over him.

While looking into his eyes, she locked her arms around his neck and lowered herself onto him. A groan released from the pit of his stomach. Feeling her tight, hot, wet flesh around him—accepting him—after so long was wonderful. She moved slowly at first with her forehead pressed to his, and then her pace quickened with the sound of her breath.

Hands on her hips, Donovan kissed, nibbled, and sucked every bit of her flesh he could reach. He couldn't wait to make love to her from head to toe when he could move, lift, and stretch without being reminded of his fractured ribs. But what Beth did, riding him with the energy to match a bull rider, felt amazing. It pushed him over the edge faster than he anticipated.

"Baby, I can't hold on much longer." Her movements became faster, deeper. His body tensed as hers turned fluid, and he let go with her.

Beth rested her head on his shoulder. Her breath warmed the inside of his neck. "Did I hurt you?" she whispered. "I think I got a little carried away."

Donovan smiled. "No."

"Am I hurting you now? Because if I am, I don't think I'll be able to move for another few minutes."

His arms looped around her waist. "Stay as long as

you want."

After a moment, she lifted her head, combed her fingers through his hair, and touched her lips to his. He stared into her eyes and wondered when he'd stop being amazed at the love he saw there. Maybe he'd get used to it, but he never wanted to become blind to it.

The ice cream had completely melted, so they moved on to the spaghetti and devoured it in bed. The rest of the day, Donovan was more than happy to spend with Beth in the crappy hotel room.

****

The next day, Thorn told them he got a call from the owners of the hotel in Union Square letting him know they were open.

"Finally," Beth said. "Now I can get my bikini."

"A bikini?"

Donovan rounded on Thorn, ready to hit him. "Why the hell are you so excited about that?"

"I'm just happy Beth will have her bikini."

"Watch it," Donovan warned.

"That's good advice. I will watch *it*." Thorn's grin was wolfish. "Let's go."

"Is this the reason you're still here," Beth asked Thorn as they left their room. "You were waiting for us to get our stuff back?"

"Why? Do you not like my company?" He tugged her ponytail in a way Donovan couldn't feel jealous or angry over, because he recognized it as something a brother would do to his kid sister. That bikini business, though, was an entirely different matter.

Beth tightened her ponytail. "No, it's not that. I thought for sure you would've gone back home with Buck."

"I would've, but I have orders to escort the two of you back to Florida as soon as you're able to travel."

Donovan cocked his head, considering Thorn's words. "Are you escorting us back home or to jail?"

Thorn's eyebrows lowered. "You really think after all this, all I've risked my ass for and done for the two of you, that I'd lead you into a trap? You should know me better than that, Goldwyn." He jabbed the button to summon the elevator, obviously pissed by Donovan's accusation. "Once we land in Orlando, I'll go my way and you'll go yours."

Paula, the front desk manager, gleamed behind the front desk, mannequin perfect with a plastic smile on her Botox-injected face as if the earthquake had never occurred. She still smelled as if she bathed in perfume.

"It's nice to see the two of you again. I'm glad our quake didn't scare you off." She said "our quake" as though it was a pet everyone in California co-owned.

"Oh, no, that sweet little quake didn't scare us off," Beth said, her voice dripping with acidic sarcasm. "It nearly killed us though." She snatched the key card from Paula's hand and marched off.

Following her, Thorn muttered under his breath so only Donovan could hear, "Fifty bucks says Beth would have the front desk manager flat on her back in five seconds or less with a broken nose."

"Broken nose *and* a black eye," Donovan added.

Up in their old hotel room, Donovan helped Beth pack their things while Thorn examined the flat screen television, full kitchen, and sunk-in-bathtub.

"No wonder you grumbled about the other room. Shit, Goldwyn, how much money do you have?"

"Enough," he said and zipped up his suitcase. He

set it on the floor. "Are you done with yours, Beth?"

"Yeah, I just need to get my makeup and jewelry from the bathroom, and I want to double check the room before we go."

"Okay. Thorn and I will take these down."

She nodded and headed into the bathroom with her small carry-on bag.

Donovan closed the door and led Thorn through the lobby. "Have you uncovered any information on Craig yet?"

"Not yet, but I do have news on the note you found under your hotel door."

Donovan slammed the trunk to Thorn's rental and spun around. "They got prints off it?"

"No."

"Then what?"

"Forensics was able to match the handwriting to their database. We know who wrote the note."

"Who?"

"Jackson Storm."

Donovan's hands clenched into fists. Jackson Storm was a criminal ten times worse than Viper. He killed without a thought, and he had committed every crime in the book, multiple times over. For fun. The leader of countless lesser criminals, he was responsible for the deaths of many innocent people and law enforcement officers alike. He even had ties to a police-killing Mob in Cleveland, Ohio. Having Jackson Storm after you was not a good thing, because that meant an unknowable number of criminals were after you, too. The fact that he wrote the note and delivered it himself showed he was serious. Serious and cocky.

"Jackson Storm is the orchestrator of the drug

ring?"

Thorn nodded once. "It looks that way."

"Fuck."

"My thoughts exactly, which is why I'm getting you and Beth out of here tonight."

Chapter Twenty-Seven

Beth's makeup was all over the bathroom floor because of the earthquake. Behind the toilet, she found her favorite tube of lipstick. In the trashcan, she had to dig through used Q-tips and wads of tissues for her mascara and blush brush. All the shampoo, conditioner, and body wash bottles lay at the bottom of the tub. She collected them, lining each bottle in her arms, and dumped them into the trashcan. When she double-checked the tub, she spotted her shaver sticking out of the shower drain.

"Hallelujah!" She grabbed it and held it up as if it were the Holy Grail. The cheap, plastic razor she had acquired for her shaving needs didn't cut it, always leaving behind unattractive stubble. She hoped she would have a chance to tackle her legs soon before she had to throw out the razor for the flight home.

The sound of the room's door clicking shut met her ears in the bathroom. "Donovan, I think I finished in the bathroom. I still want to make sure we didn't lose one of my bras under the bed though." She expected to hear a sexual innuendo, but Donovan didn't say a word.

She grimaced, having forgotten Thorn was with them. He was probably stunned silent or on his hands and knees searching under the bed himself.

On her way out of the bathroom with her carry-on, she picked up a hotel pen she spotted against the wall.

Her fingers curled around it as she stepped into the bedroom.

A figure sat on the bed. Out of the corner of her eye, she noticed a black shirt.

But Donovan is wearing a blue shirt. And Thorn is wearing white.

She whirled around. Sitting on the bed was the man she'd spied talking to Buck. He pointed a semi-automatic gun complete with a silencer at her chest. In his other hand, he held a roll of duct tape.

"Donovan isn't here, but I can help you look for that bra." He sneered at her. "I'm Jackson Storm and you would be..." He tilted his head to the side. "The sweet-piece-of-ass I saw running down the alley after the explosion."

Beth calculated possible plans of action to disarm him and get away, but none of them would prevent her from getting shot, which was her number one objective. Fear swamped her, making her palms sweat. "What do you want?"

"Isn't that obvious?" He waved the gun at her. "You."

Beth never thought a monosyllable could cause such terror, but she was ready to pee her pants. "If you wanted to kill me, you could have done that the second I walked out of the bathroom."

"I don't want to kill you here. I have somewhere special picked out for your murder. And I plan on having fun with you first. When I do kill you, though, I'll make sure to have plenty of body parts left over so I can send Donovan pieces of you...one by one. Then I'll kill him in a way he won't ever see coming."

Beth felt her stomach roll with the thought of

Donovan opening a package and finding one of her fingers in a bed of foam peanuts. *I have to get out of here. I have to do something. I can't just let him take me.* Her thoughts were so urgent that her arm muscles flinched.

Jackson jabbed his gun toward her. "Drop your bag. Now."

Hiding the pen in her hand—the length of it up her arm—she released her carry-on from her fingers. It hit the floor at her feet with a rattling thud as the contents jumped.

"That's a good girl." Jackson got to his feet. "You're going to come with me."

Her heart beat furiously. "Where?" she asked, wanting to stall him.

Donovan and Thorn will be here any minute.

The gun in Jackson's hand grew larger when he took a step toward her.

When the gun was a foot away from her, she decided she had to do something. Even if she got shot, at least she could say she tried to get away. Or whoever found her dead could say she did.

Her left arm shot forward, and she knocked the gun to the side with her forearm. Then she reached out with her other hand and stabbed Jackson in the bicep with the pen. He let out a roar of pain. The pen was about an inch deep in his flesh. She made a move to run past him, but he caught her and threw her into the wall with enough force that her body bounced off it. She let out a cry when he shoved her temple into the wall as if he wanted to crush her skull.

He rammed the muzzle of the gun into her forehead. "If you try something like that again, I'll shoot your brains out all over this room. Do you understand me?" He applied pressure against her head, making her wince and whimper.

"Yes," she hissed. Tears bit her eyes from the pain and from her failure.

"I'm going to put my gun down, but I've killed men twice your size with my bare hands, so don't think I won't do the same to you."

Considering how hard he had crushed her head into the wall, she didn't doubt his word.

He set the gun on the bedside table, yanked the pen from his arm, and tossed it to the ground.

Then he picked up the duct tape. Chills shook Beth's spine at the unmistakable sound of duct tape ripping off the roll. Jackson grabbed her and wrapped her arms in front of her from elbows to fingers. With her wrists pressed together, she couldn't move her arms a single centimeter.

She eyed her kidnapper with a blend of hatred and fright. Blood streamed down his arm. "Why are you doing this?" She despised how small her voice sounded. "I didn't even know your name until you told it to me. You could've let me go. You could've let this whole thing go."

"But Donovan wouldn't have let it go. I'm beating him to the punch. So to speak." He ripped off another strip of tape. When he brought it to her face, she sucked in her lips before he slapped it over her mouth. She breathed through her nose, each inhalation and exhalation becoming more ragged as her panic grew.

This is it. I'm screwed.

Without another word, Jackson yanked her to the door and out into the hall. His right hand cuffed her arm, holding her to his side, and he pressed his gun painfully to her stomach, right into her kidney. She looked left and right, hoping someone was around to assist her, but all she saw were closed doors. As Jackson dragged her down the hall, she wondered how he would manage leaving with her, a woman covered in tape. Someone would see and, hopefully, intervene.

"Stop, Jackson!"

The order came from behind them.

Beth's pulse jumped and relief overpowered her fear. *Oh, thank you, thank you, God!*

Jackson spun around. His arm banded across Beth's shoulders to use her as a shield. The muzzle of the gun came to her temple, not as a warning but as a statement. He'd shoot her if it meant getting away.

Thorn stood a few yards from them, with his gaze pinned to Jackson and his gun pointed at his head. Beth was never happier to see him. "Let her go, Jackson."

"Sorry, I can't do that Officer—"

"Detective Thorn."

Jackson laughed in her ear, a sound full of mockery. "Aren't you out of your league here, Detective?"

Thorn didn't bat an eyelash at the insult. "I take down men like you all the time."

"Not today."

The two men glared at each other as sweat beaded on her brow. *Shit! What do I do? If I try to pull free, he'll put a bullet in my head. I could sweep his feet out from under him, but he'll most likely take me down with him. That's a risk I'll take.*

She lifted her right foot marginally, preparing to perform the sweep, but Thorn's gaze shifted to her. His eyes fell to slits a millisecond before his stare moved back to Jackson. The order he gave her, though silent, was loud and clear. He didn't want her to do a thing.

"Jackson, you don't need her. I have Donovan Goldwyn downstairs in my car. He's handcuffed and waiting. We can trade. You can give me the girl, and you can take him. Isn't he the one you want? The brother of the IA investigator your men killed?"

Beth stared at Thorn in horror. He couldn't be serious. Fear had sweat dampening her underarms. Her chest constricted.

"You're just going to let me, a wanted criminal, leave with him?"

"I would for her." Thorn's stare never once flinched from Jackson. Not even when Jackson laughed.

"You're good, Detective, but I'd rather shoot you and take them both." He pointed the gun at Thorn.

Beth's mind screamed. *No!* Thorn was like a protective brother to her. Well, when he wasn't flirting with her or pushing Donovan's buttons. She didn't want him to die at the hands of the man responsible for Ryan's death. She didn't want him to die for her.

Her heart rate was so erratic it was painful. *You can't shoot him!* She would've screamed that thought at Jackson if she could.

Thorn moved his arms out to the side, exposing his chest. "Go ahead," he taunted. "Shoot me."

Beth's eyes widened. *What is he doing?* She shook her head, silently pleading with him not to do this. *Don't sacrifice yourself for me. Please!*

Jackson's hold on her loosened a fraction. He took a step toward Thorn while thrusting his gun forward.

"Do you think I'm kidding, pig?"

A whisper of a smile appeared on Thorn's lips, confusing Beth. "Frankly? Yeah, I do."

Beth's gaze flickered to the gun in Jackson's hand. His finger shook on the trigger, about to set the gun off at any second. She wanted to throw up. She wanted to—

Before she knew what she was doing, she rammed Jackson with her shoulder, shoving him. His arm hit the wall, and the gun discharged. The bullet sailed past Thorn.

"Hey!"

The shout came from behind Beth. She was about to spin around when Thorn snatched her and tugged her free. Using his body to cover her, he backed her against the wall. Her heart galloped, and questions swirled in her head as if her mind was a whirlpool. Thorn removed a knife from his boot and used it to slice through the tape trapping her arms. While she fought to tear off the sticky strips from her long-sleeves, Thorn peeled the tape from her mouth.

"Who?" It was the first word she could say. The rest of the words in the English language were lost in a void between her brain and mouth.

A gunshot sounded. Beth looked around Thorn to see Donovan and Jackson locked in a struggle. Donovan forced Jackson's outstretched arm into the wall repeatedly until Jackson's fingers released the gun. It fell to the floor a few feet away.

Beth's gaze followed the gun's descent. She was considering how fast she could get to it when she heard a man's scream. Looking up, she saw Donovan pushing his thumb into the bleeding hole in Jackson's arm.

Blood dripped from Jackson's fingertips. His other hand lifted, and he hit Donovan in the side, rattling his healing ribs. *Donovan!* After Jackson gave Donovan two more quick jabs, she took a step forward, wanting to come to Donovan's aid.

Thorn stopped her and pushed her into a doorway. "Don't move!" Thorn launched into the mix as Donovan fell to the floor, cradling his ribs. Thorn tackled Jackson into the wall as he tried to flee.

Peeking past the wall, Beth watched Thorn stab Jackson with the blade he used to cut away the duct tape, but Jackson swiveled his body at the last second, so instead of sticking the blade into his abdomen, it sliced along his side, cutting him open. Blood spurted from the cut and flowed heavily down his side.

Somehow, Jackson still found the strength to pound his fist into the side of Thorn's head. Thorn staggered back with a hand cupping his ear, and Jackson made a break for it.

"You two, stay here!" Thorn ripped his gun from his holster and took off after Jackson.

Beth rushed to Donovan as he fought to get to his feet. His arm across his ribs. Heart in her throat, her hands ran over him. "Are you okay?"

"Fine." He gripped her elbow. "I need to make sure he's caught. Stay here." Then he ran down the hall, following Thorn.

Mouth open, Beth stood there a moment. *You've got to be kidding me!* Without another thought, her feet launched her into a sprint. She zipped around the corner. Donovan was ahead of her by several paces. He wouldn't be happy to know she was following him, but she couldn't just sit back while he put himself in further danger. What was she supposed to do? Knit? Screw that! She was going to help.

Donovan threw his body into the stairwell door and shoved it open with the force of his impact. Beth launched into the stairwell after him. The pounding of their shoes beating against the steps echoed throughout the enclosed space. Donovan surged a few steps ahead of Beth but she held on, urging her feet to be swifter, her legs faster.

They wound their way down to the first floor. At the bottom of the stairwell, the door was closing. Donovan angled his body and plowed into it with his shoulder. The door banged open. Beth followed in his wake. Her shoes slapped against the tile. While running through the lobby, she finally caught up to Donovan and matched his stride. He glanced at her, and his eyelids lowered into a hard glare.

"Damn it, Beth, I told you to stay put," he said between labored breaths.

"Thorn told us both to stay," she shot back.

Paula stood behind the spotless front desk with her mouth open in shock at the scene unfolding in front of her. Donovan pointed at her. "Call 911. Tell them Detective Thorn needs back up. Give this address. Now!"

As Beth breezed past, she saw Paula snatch up the phone. A few strides brought them into the parking lot. Beth paused, blinking in the sunlight, and spotted Jackson running into the road. A few paces ahead, Thorn was diving into the car he had parked near the entrance. Donovan ran to the passenger's side. Beth threw open the door to the backseat and jumped in as Thorn started the engine.

Thorn paused briefly to look at Donovan then turned to peer into the backseat. Beth watched his jaw clench. He rotated around and jerked the stick shift into drive. "Damn it, Beth." He stomped on the gas pedal.

She gritted her teeth. "Will you guys stop saying that! I wasn't going to wait in that hotel, not knowing whether or not the two of you are okay." Through the windshield she saw Jackson weaving his way in and out of traffic. "Where is he going?"

"He probably parked somewhere his car wouldn't be noticed," Donovan said.

Jackson shot across the street, stopping traffic, and disappeared into an alley.

"Hold on," Thorn shouted.

Beth gripped the door when Thorn whipped the steering wheel. Her knuckles whitened as the car took a hard turn.

Jackson was halfway down the alley, heading toward a parked car. "You're not getting away this time," Thorn growled.

Beth felt the car pick up speed.

"Donovan, when I tell you to open your door, do it."

Beth's eyebrows lifted when Donovan prepared to follow Thorn's order. He clutched the handle with one hand and braced the other on the frame. "Ready."

When the car shot past Jackson, Thorn slammed on the brake. "Now!"

Donovan threw open his door. Jackson ran right into it, cracking the thick plastic shell on the inside, and breaking the window into several large shards. He fell straight back on the road like a two-by-four.

Beth opened her door. She walked around the car

to see Jackson's arms and legs splayed out and his eyes sealed. "Damn!"

Thorn rolled Jackson onto his back, cuffed him, and hauled him to his feet. Right then, Donovan shoved out of the passenger's seat and plowed his fist into Jackson's face. The blow sent him into the side of the car.

Thorn opened the back door, pushed Jackson inside, and flipped the child lock. Then he faced Donovan. "Seriously? You did not just hit him after I had him in custody."

"He tried to kidnap the woman I love. I think that gives me leave."

Thorn seemed to think about that. He nodded. "I think you're right."

Beth's heart melted. "And thanks to both of you, I'm safe." She snaked her arms around Donovan. "Fact is I've never felt safer than when I'm with you." She kissed him deeply, wanting him to feel her love for him beyond her words, with her touch.

After a moment, Thorn coughed, prompting Beth to pull back as if she were a teenager and her father had caught her smooching her boyfriend on the front porch.

"Sorry to interrupt," he said, "but I have a wanted fugitive I need to get to the PD. Donovan, you drive. Beth, front seat." He held his gun in his hands. "I'll sit in the back and make sure the bastard doesn't escape again."

Chapter Twenty-Eight

Jackson Storm had been stabbed with a pen, filleted with a knife, hit with a car, and punched in the face, and he could still smirk as police officers escorted him into the San Francisco Police Department.

Donovan knew exactly why the bastard was smiling. Jackson had been arrested a long time ago but was "accidentally" released due to a technical error. And he managed to not get caught for years because corrupt cops would look the other way. Jackson was notorious for doing his own dirty work because he knew he'd get away with it. He probably thought that now, but he never had to deal with Donovan or Thorn before and they wouldn't look the other way. Neither would Chief Cormac.

"That guy creeps me out," Beth muttered. "He's indestructible."

"Yeah, but he's bleeding," Donovan said, and that gave him a great deal of satisfaction.

With a sigh, Beth folded her hands on the counter at the police department's front desk and dropped her head onto her forearms. Donovan put his hands on her shoulders and applied pressure to her tense muscles. "When we're alone, I'll give you a full-body massage," he whispered in her ear.

"You promise?"

"I more than promise, Beth."

She picked up her head. "What do you mean?"

"I mean..." He lowered stiffly to one knee.

Beth's mouth cracked open, and her eyes widened. He took that as a good sign; she hadn't seen this coming.

Taking her hand, Donovan peered up at her. "When we were separated after the quake, I realized how I never want to be apart from you again. Since we met, we've been through a hurricane and an earthquake together, and if there are other disasters in my future, I don't want to face them without you. Beth Kennedy, will you marry me?"

The police department was uncharacteristically quiet. Donovan wasn't the only one waiting for an answer. The female police officer behind the counter with a front row seat to his proposal waited for Beth's answer. The hooker chained to a chair, the mix of uniforms and plain-clothes police officers, and several civilians waited for her answer, too, but he was the only one who was afraid she'd say no.

He hadn't considered a rejection before he got down on one knee, and now he knew how foolish that was. Beth loved him. He had no doubt about that, but whether she was ready for marriage was another matter. With his heart lodged painfully in his throat, he gazed into her brown eyes, remembering the first time he stared into them. He had thought she was an angel sitting beside him in his car, with his head feeling as though it was split in two. And he had been right. She was *his* angel.

Beth blinked at him. Her gaping mouth transformed into a smile. "Yes," she said, her voice a whisper and then again, louder. "Yes."

Relief as he'd never felt before washed over him. His heart became light after shedding the weight of possible denial. He jumped to his feet, not even feeling his aching ribs, and lifted Beth off her feet. The department erupted with applause and cheers as he kissed her.

Beth pulled away with a laugh, and Donovan picked up her left hand to stroke her ring finger. "I'm sorry I don't have a ring to give you."

"Wait. Yes, you do," a woman announced.

Donovan turned to the female officer behind the counter as she removed a ring from one of her own fingers.

"Oh, no," Beth said. "I couldn't take that."

"It's okay," the officer said. "I got it at China Town. I can easily get another one. Besides, you need something to make it official." She held out the ring to Donovan. "I insist."

He accepted it. "Thank you."

Facing Beth, he asked her, "Is this okay?"

She nodded. "It's perfect."

With the ring in place, he admired the silver infinity knot encrusted with diamonds. The silver might not have been worth anything and the diamonds might not have been real, but Beth was right. The ring was perfect for her, for them, for their love.

"This will make a great story," Beth said. "We'll be able to tell our kids you proposed to me in a police department after we took down a wanted criminal."

Donovan drew her to his body. "You're thinking about kids?"

She smiled. "Aren't you? I think our genes would make some attractive, smart kids."

"How many do you want?"

"Um...you say first."

Donovan considered a moment, picturing how he wanted his life with Beth in the future to look. He imagined a house where their children could grow up and return to after college. For a year, max. A golden retriever roamed in the backyard complete with a screened-in pool and grass he'd have to cut every weekend in the summer. When he thought about their future children, he saw three. At least one of them a boy.

"Three." He tried to gauge her reaction. "Too many?"

"No, three is good. You've got yourself a deal, Goldwyn."

Cupping her face, he kissed her in the middle of the hustle and bustle of the police department. He kissed her with his newly realized desires. He kissed her with his heart.

A throat cleared behind him. Donovan released Beth and turned to Thorn.

"Sorry to interrupt again, but I thought you'd like to know Jackson has been booked with pages worth of charges. He probably won't stay here in San Fran long, though. He'll have to be transported to Florida to get charged for the multiple crimes he did there, one of which is being an accomplice to Ryan's murder. That case isn't closed yet, but there's no chance he's going to get off the hook."

"That's a relief," Beth said. "The last thing I wanted to worry about was him getting released and coming after us again. All of us."

"You don't have to worry about that." Thorn

jiggled his ear with his finger as he spoke. "Oh, and congratulations on your engagement."

"Thanks," Beth said with a jaw-cracking smile.

Despite Thorn's grin, Donovan could see he was in pain. "How's your ear?"

"I think the bastard burst my eardrum."

"Sorry about that."

"The important thing is we got him." Thorn shrugged. "I have another piece of news for the two of you...we have a flight home tomorrow morning."

"Just as long as there aren't any out-of-season hurricanes headed to Florida," Beth said. "I don't think I'd be able to handle another disaster so soon."

****

With his brother laid to rest, Buck in custody, and the threat of Jackson Storm eliminated, the plane ride back to Florida was light-years more peaceful than the other two plane rides Donovan had taken with Beth. He felt as if he was going home a winner. The nightmare that started with Hurricane Sabrina's arrival was finally over. For the first time since he'd run from Chewy and Buck, Donovan could relax mind and body.

The plane touched down and all the passengers filed off with places to go in a hurry.

Donovan let Beth out into the aisle first. He was about to follow her through the door when Thorn pulled him to a stop.

"About that other thing you wanted me to look into..."

Donovan straightened. "You have information on him?"

"I do. I emailed you everything. When you get home, check it out."

Once he and Beth were home, Donovan waited two hours before booting up his laptop and opening his email. Among the junk and emails from distant family members, he found the one from Thorn with a blank subject line. He read the information within it twice and then grabbed his keys.

"Beth, I'm going to stop at my garage, check on my truck."

"Okay," she called from the bedroom. "Do you want me to order dinner?"

"Chinese," he said. "I'll call you when I'm on my way home."

He drove to a house near Beth's old town. The mailbox out front was a giant stone manatee with a plastic box in its flippers. A sports car the color of sunburst orange sat in the driveway.

Donovan marched up to the door with one part of Thorn's investigative research circling in his head, *Friends and colleagues have all said the psychic left Craig months ago, and he's recently been saying he's planning to win back his ex-fiancé. One of his friends says he sounds obsessed with the idea. He even stated, in confidence, that he wouldn't be surprised if Craig was stalking Beth.*

Donovan's jaw tightened. *He better not be!* He pounded on the door. It opened to a man wearing a navy-blue suit. His dark blond hair was slicked back.

"Are you Craig Mitchell?"

"Yes, I am."

Craig's beady eyes looked Donovan up and down in scrutiny, openly judging the man on his doorstep. Donovan resisted the urge to punch him right at that moment.

"Do you know a woman by the name of Beth Kennedy?"

Craig's eyes brightened at the mention of Beth's name. "Oh, I know her all right." He smiled smugly. "What about her?"

Donovan took a step forward. Although Craig was a step higher than he was, they were at eyelevel. "She's *my* fiancé." Craig's face turned ashen-white at his claim. "Soon, she's going to be my wife. If you come anywhere near her, you'll regret it. And that's a promise. Don't bring up her name again to your friends and colleagues, and don't ever fantasize about getting her back. She's happy, as she deserves to be, so stay the fuck away from her."

Donovan backed off the front step and drove away feeling satisfied he'd killed Craig's obsession with Beth, once and for all.

Chapter Twenty-Nine

Beth hung up the phone. Donovan was on his way home, and she needed to order dinner. She pulled the pamphlet for the local Chinese restaurant off the refrigerator to examine the options. Her mouth was watering when the phone beside her started ringing again. She blindly reached for it, expecting Donovan to be on the other end requesting sweet-and-sour chicken.

"Hello?"

With the phone wedged between her shoulder and neck, she flipped open the pamphlet to search for lo mein noodles.

"You've pissed off a lot of people, Beth." The voice in her ear was deep, angry, and did not belong to Donovan. "The wrong people."

Her gaze lifted as if she expected to see the face of the man threatening her on the surface of the cabinet door. The pamphlet fell from her numb fingers. Her heart clanged against her chest with such force, she was surprised it didn't explode from fear.

"Who is this?"

The man laughed. No way would he reveal his name to her, but asking was instinct.

"Jackson and Buck aren't the only ones you have to worry about, sweetheart. There are a lot of us, and we all know about you and Donovan. I'd watch your back, because we're coming."

Chrys Fey

The threat echoed in Beth's head even when the line went dead.

We're coming. We're coming...

Her hand shook as she lowered the phone to the counter. One thought came to her mind. One.

It's not over.

A word about the author...

Chrys Fey is the author of the *Disaster Crimes* series, a unique concept blending romance, crimes, and disasters. She's partnered with the Insecure Writer's Support Group and runs their Goodreads book club. She's also an editor for Dancing Lemur Press.

Fey realized she wanted to write by watching her mother pursue publication. At the age of twelve, she started her first novel, which flourished into a series she later rewrote at seventeen.

Fey lives in Florida and is always on the lookout for hurricanes. She has four cats and three nephews; both keep her entertained with their antics.

Get your free copy of LIGHTNING CRIMES on Amazon!

www.ingramcontent.com/pod-product-compliance
Lightning Source LLC
Chambersburg PA
CBHW060527260626
47161CB00003B/795

* 9 7 8 1 5 0 9 2 0 7 2 5 1 *